T0083275

Praise for

THEIR HOUSES

"Full of surprising twists and turns, this sharp, tough-minded, compelling novel takes us deeply into its high-low milieus and conflicted characters. A cross between noir and redemption, it's a terrific read."

—Phillip Lopate, author of *Portrait Inside My Head*

"Every move in this jolt-filled tale—told in the sweet, slyly humorous cadences of West Virginia—is perfect. Willis has the stuff from beginning to end."

—Diane Simmons, author of *The Courtship of Eva Eldridge*

"With deep sympathy for her characters, Willis writes in lucid and compelling prose about one of the dark undersides of American life. *Their Houses* reads fast, as a compelling series of mysteries, and reminds us of how much legacy we all carry, not only in our bodies and our genes but in our stories."

—Jane Lazarre, author of *The Communist and the Communist's Daughter* and *Beyond the Whiteness of Whiteness: Memoir of a White Mother of Black Sons*

THEIR

MEREDITH SUE WILLIS

HOUSES

WEST VIRGINIA UNIVERSITY PRESS · MORGANTOWN 2018

First edition published 2018 by West Virginia University Press

Printed in the United States of America

ISBN:

Paper 978-1-946684-34-9

Ebook 978-1-946684-35-6

Library of Congress Cataloging-in-Publication Data

Names: Willis, Meredith Sue, author.

Title: Their houses / Meredith S. Willis.

Description: First edition. | Morgantown : West Virginia University Press, 2018.

Identifiers: LCCN 2018010254| ISBN 9781946684349 (softcover) | ISBN
9781946684356 (epub)

Subjects: | BISAC: FICTION / General.

Classification: LCC PS3573.I45655 T48 2018 | DDC 813/.54--dc23

LC record available at https://lccn.loc.gov/2018010254

Book and cover design by Than Saffel / WVU Press

"Raymond and the Mountain Militia" was previously published in *Unbroken Circle:
Stories of Cultural Diversity in the South* (Huron, OH: Bottom Dog Press, 2017), and is
reprinted with permission.

To Andy, Joel, Sarah, and Shira

———

I'd like to thank my writers' group for deep and abiding support and sharp, creative critiques for over thirty-five years.

The brilliant, deeply insightful women from the group who gave me specific feedback on *Their Houses* include Carole Rosenthal, Suzanne McConnell, Joan Leibovitz, NancyKay Shapiro, Shelley Ettinger, Edith Konecky, and Carol Emshwiller.

CHAPTER 1

When they were children, Richie had adored the sisters. They made the air electric with their shining hair and calmed him with their lavender and rose tee shirts. Colors a boy could love only from afar. Even now that the bullies worked for him, he would never wear pink. Now he had a helicopter pad and a safe room, an organic vegetable garden, a team of ex-militia patrolling the boundaries of his property, and a security system created by former Mossad operatives.

He had all this, but there were still rules. One rule was that he must never appear weak. He must avoid using his cane. When he did use it, he intimated to his employees that his lameness was from a youthful brawl or sometimes an adventure in the tribal areas of Pakistan. Whatever. Poke and Bobby Mack didn't fact-check.

He picked up Poke and Bobby Mack after the collapse of the ramshackle Mountain Militia plot to blow up the FBI fingerprint headquarters. He bought property from the National Alliance just as it was disintegrating. Had he time enough, he might have done something with all the inchoate energy and melodramatic plotting of those right-wing hangers-on, not that he ever believed any of their racist nonsense. There was no evidence he had ever observed that white men were smarter, stronger, or in any way superior to other kinds of men. All men, as Richie saw it, were venal, and most were stupid.

What interested him about all these little groups was how they needed someone to follow. He had wanted to be that one. The one who scanned the horizon with cool objectivity and made what he wanted to happen happen. He was good at strategy. He had some money, what his father left and what he had invested. He might have been a power. He might have used the Mountain Militia and even leftovers from the National Alliance. But there wasn't enough time, at least not enough time when he would be physically strong enough to manage them.

He was good at managing people, he believed, although he did better with people he hired than with people he married. He had not been heartbroken or particularly surprised when his third wife left, reminding him that Thai wives were no more loyal than Americans, but it was clear that he should buy what he wanted. So he paid for and managed his sex workers just as he paid for and managed his doctors and his majordomo/cook Enrique, who had the bottomless supply of putative cousins in Mexico.

His only faith was that there was no such thing as altruism, with a handful of exceptions, outliers in the universe, particularly Dinah.

When he was small, Richie carried quarters and candy bars for the big boys. They would stop shoving him long enough to stare in wonderment, take the candy and coins, and then go back to pushing him or maybe pulling his pants down to see if he was a boy, or, equally likely, ignoring him. Being ignored was the worst. As a child, he always preferred battery to loneliness.

His mother bought him expensive clothes, not appreciated by the other kids. When his glasses got broken and his knees bruised, she sent him to private boarding schools as if there were no bullies there.

His mother never learned the money lesson, that it has limits. She married his father when he was already sick, and Richie had been born in the first year of their marriage. They all knew that she was waiting for his father to die so they could live with his money but without him. Richie felt that he and his mother had both been pathetic in their dependence on money. She used money to buy friends, and he used it to placate the neighborhood boys.

Thus, when he was treated kindly by Dinah and Grace for absolutely no reason, it was a great widening of the mysteries of the universe. Thirty-five years later, he still didn't believe in altruism, but he did believe in Dinah and how she had refused his quarters and only accepted one candy bar for herself and one for Grace.

Once he had been inside Dinah's warmth, when they were in their teens, at a time when she was welcoming everyone, without checking the cost, out of generosity and, he thought, because none of them could really touch her. All he ever wanted, all he wanted now, was to feel Dinah's warmth.

The way it worked when they were small was that Richie played with Grace while Dinah gave instructions. Usually they started with action figures and dolls, sometimes board games, sometimes building forts or digging holes in the garden. The garden was at Lockwood, which was Richie's father's property. Sometimes they played in the Lockwood carriage house where the girls lived. From time to time, quietly, they played in the big house.

In the big house, they always went to the train rooms, which were next door to his father's bedroom and dressing room. The trains were the only pleasant thing he ever associated with his father. Richie understood better now how being ill can make you resentful, irritable, and full of rage, but it didn't mitigate his hatred for his father.

His father had loved trains as a boy and insisted that Richie love them too. What Richie liked was turning on the power and the spotlights, and the engines whirring and running through two whole rooms, everything in Richie's power, the villages with lights, the train bridges, the signal arms that went up and down, the hooting engines.

After his father died, he had parties and his mother had parties, and she redecorated, and he liquidated the trains for capital to invest in pills and marijuana that he sold at school. But back when he was seven and eight and nine, the best thing in his life was to have Dinah and Grace in the train rooms. Dinah liked saving the toy people from disasters. Grace and Richie liked making the disasters: train wrecks and volcanos and tornados and tidal waves.

Dinah would say, "Okay, the volcano finished erupting. Now it's time to save the people."

Grace would lay out the wounded in rows. "This one is burnt to a crisp," she would say, "but this one is only half-burnt. This one is dead and this one is alive."

Richie ran around the train tables moving things and making explosion noises. He could still feel that incredible freedom, the explosions low in his throat, rumbling through his body. Every once in a while he would stop and stare at the sisters for a long time: he remembered every detail of them. Grace had a small white face and a lot of thick brown hair. Dinah had dark honey hair just a little darker than her skin.

"Okay Richie," Dinah would say. "Your job is to set up the hospital train that has to bring all the wounded people over the mountains for me to fix up."

"Can we have a funeral for the dead ones?" said Grace.

"No," said Dinah. "None of them died."

"Yes they did!" cried Grace. "They really did die!"

"My father is going to be dead soon," Richie said. "We're going to have the biggest funeral in the world and limousines for everyone and you're invited."

"No," said Dinah. "No funerals. Some of them are hurt very very badly, but no one is going to die."

Sometimes, though, she did let them have a funeral, a dump car full of plastic bodies and a burial in one of the train tunnels, and then, miraculously, just as they were thrusting them deep into the mountain, Dinah would declare them alive again. Grace struggled to keep them dead, and Dinah brought them back to life. When all the dead were alive again, Grace would burst into tears and laughter because she was actually glad that Dinah could do this, and really only wanted to be sure that Dinah was powerful enough to make it happen. Then Dinah would hug her, and if Richie was lucky, him too.

Once he smacked Grace when she was being particularly stubborn. He immediately started to run away for fear of Dinah's anger. "I'll fix it! I'll fix it!" he remembered yelling as Grace cried and Dinah moved toward him. "Hit me back! I'll do anything!"

What he meant was, he'd do anything just so they didn't leave.

"No more hitting!" said Dinah, hugging Grace. "No more hitting allowed."

"Okay okay!" cried Richie.

"Say you're sorry, Richie."

"Okay okay! I'm sorry Grace! I'm totally sorry! I'll kill myself!"

"Stop that, Richie," said Dinah. "We don't talk like that," and he felt so much better. Grace rolled her eyes at him and snuggled against Dinah so he would know who Dinah loved best and who she took care of first.

"We need bandages for the hurt people," said Dinah. "Do you think there are bandages?"

Richie knew exactly what to do. He sneaked out into the hall, to the back entrance to his father's bathroom and from there to the dressing room where his father had special thin drawers in the bureau for the monogrammed handkerchiefs he never used. Richie opened a drawer and stole two handkerchiefs, watching the door to the bedroom all the time, expecting his father to rise there huge and vengeful.

Dinah approved, and sent him after the scissors to finish the job— oh, that was a feeling that ran from his collarbone to his toes, stirring all the way through him. He remembered that above all, the feeling of her approval, down his spine deep into his butt crack, starting back along the center line of his balls and up his penis.

He wanted that feeling so much, he had wanted it for his whole life. He wanted it now.

He understood very well that he was trying to recapture something that he never really had. He understood that it was a long shot, to get her back, but he was making his plans carefully. He would give the long shot his best shot. He prepared a house for her and her family, a Craftsman-style cottage with a stone foundation. There was a space for an herb garden already turned over and ready for planting. Bedrooms for the whole family, a schoolroom with a miniature laboratory for teaching her children science, high-speed internet, beautiful blue and green globes with interior lighting.

It was the one thing, he believed, that would save him. To have Dinah.

CHAPTER 2

Dinah didn't remember exactly when she invented the game for Grace, but it was long before they moved to Lockwood, so long ago that their mother had still been living at home. Even in my darkness, she thought, I was given the power to do good, praise Jesus! At first it had been little empty matchboxes with tissue beds for a plastic fairy and a rubber pig. Then she made safe houses for some shells and acorns and refrigerator magnets. Soon Grace, who was always good at crafts, started making her own. They put the smaller matchboxes into larger matchboxes. Sometimes they used shoeboxes to store the larger matchboxes with the smaller matchboxes. Dinah would construct fortresses of cans and blocks around the shoeboxes, and sometimes a cave of blankets over the kitchen table. Diligently, for hours at a time, they struggled to protect the safe houses from all danger.

It was harder, as grown-ups, because there were more points of vulnerability, and they were separated from each other. Dinah was in Pennsylvania with her husband and five children, and Grace and David and their two girls had moved to West Virginia, where he had bought a medical practice. They met halfway now because their husbands didn't get along. Really, it was Grace's husband David who avoided Raymond, but Dinah didn't want to cast blame. Most often, they met at a rest stop on Interstate 81 between their homes.

One sunny, dry, bitterly cold day in February, when Dinah was oppressed with worries about her teenage daughter and about Raymond being out of work again, the two sisters huddled against the cold at one of the picnic tables, hating to sit in their vehicles. Jacob seemed happy to run around picking up things off the ground and baby Benjamin was inside Dinah's coat, napping after nursing.

It was Grace who had brought up safe houses. Grace said, "Do you think it was our magic against her?"

Jacob came and leaned his chubby face against Dinah's knee.

Dinah hoped Grace wasn't going to start in about their mother. She said, "Do you know what my earliest memory is? It's of holding you on my lap. I must have been Jacob's age or even younger."

"Me?" said Jacob.

"I felt like there was a huge spotlight beam on my head. And a voice. It was Jesus, although I didn't know it then. It said, 'This is Dinah. She is a very good girl and a big girl and she is holding her beloved baby sister Grace on her lap.'"

"Maybe it was Daddy talking," said Grace "Or her."

"Maybe." But Dinah was sure it was Jesus: This is my beloved child in whom I am well pleased.

"It's a good thing you were there to take care of me," said Grace. "With what *she* tried to do."

Dinah never wanted to talk about their mother at all, but sometimes Grace got determined.

Dinah said, "Do you remember the dresses she made for our dolls? Do you remember how she smocked those dresses, the doll dresses and ours too? And how she loved to wrap presents. You were good at those things too, you always decorated your safe houses with Christmas wrapping paper."

Grace made a sour face. "You're saying I'm good with my hands. Like her."

"I'm saying she had a healthy, creative part."

"Did you know I still have the trunk?"

Dinah couldn't remember if she knew or not. They used to put everything in the trunk, in case they had to make a quick getaway. "I remember we got the trunk before we moved to Lockwood."

"We got it after she tried to kill us. Tried to kill me the second time."

Dinah focused on the trunk. One of the great advantages of being born again was that the past was truly, truly over. That's what it meant to be born again. "That trunk. It's funny how you've always kept it."

"What I'm afraid of is that I'm like her. Sometimes I can't go out of the house. I get stuck inside the house. The trunk reminds me, I guess, that we can get away."

Dinah felt her heart beating faster, as if Grace were in danger. She said, "We did get away. We got away safely. I think it's time for you to do something, one of the things you talk about, Gracie: go back to teaching or run for school board."

"No," said Grace. "I'm stuck."

It always felt urgent to Dinah that Grace should be happy. "Oh Gracie. You'd be good at it. Your girls are both in school. You can do it now. Do either one of them."

Grace said, "I know you have problems too, Dinah, but yours are real. Mine are all in my head. The new house is almost done, and it just feels like too much to have to pack and then set up the new house and also apply for a job, let alone run for board of ed. It was easier to make a getaway when everything was in the trunk."

"We were all we had to think about then," Dinah said, remembering now when they bought it. They already had a plastic pocketbook for emergencies with clean underpants for each of them, a wax tube of Ritz crackers, and a travel-pack of Kleenexes. But the trunk allowed them to have those things plus their best safe houses and toys and stuffed animals. Much later, when they were teenagers, they kept tapes and CDs and emergency money in it.

And, Dinah reminded herself, for a while, she used to put ill-gotten drug money there too.

Thank you Jesus! Thank you Jesus for saving me!

They had been brave when they were small. They had been out for a walk, where were they living then? Dinah wasn't sure. They moved so much. Their dad's jobs, their mother. They had been two little girls alone on the street, probably seven and five or maybe only six and four. They had seen the footlocker, prominently placed, in front of old bicycles and racks of clothes and ski boots: it was made of green fiberboard with gouges and black electrical-tape patches.

Dinah asked the woman on the lawn chair how much it cost, and the lady said something, two dollars or five dollars, but even one dollar was more than they had. Dinah said she would go home to get the money, and the woman shrugged. Dinah made Grace sit on the trunk with her dress spread out to hide it, so no one else would buy it, and she ran back and got all the change she could find on the bureaus and beside the phone where their father dumped his pockets. She got some out of a pair of his pants too.

Where was he that time? she wondered. It must have been a Saturday. On a date? In a bar? Their mother had already gone to the hospital, she thought.

"That's not enough," the tag-sale woman said when she got back.

Dinah remembered another light shining on her, another smile of Jesus that she didn't recognize at the time. She held very still in the light, feeling absolutely certain that she would get what she needed "That's all we have," she said. "We have to move soon, and we need to pack."

Grace had sucked her thumb and looked up trustingly.

"And my little sister has nowhere to put her clothes."

"Oh for chrissake," said the woman, "I'll take what you have. Go ahead, the lining's all loose anyhow."

Dinah remembered a rich sensation of power. She had kept her hands extended toward the woman. "This is all the money we have," she said.

The woman threw up her hands. "Okay! Keep the money! Take the trunk! Take it for free! I'm glad to get rid of the smelly old thing." And they dragged it away, bump-scrape down the sidewalk, and the change Dinah had found was the first thing they hid in the trunk.

Dinah would have talked about the trunk for hours, but Grace insisted on discussing their mother. She said, "There are a lot of similarities between me and her. I married a man with the same name as Daddy. I have two daughters, just like she did. I get low. Depressed, like she did."

"Stop it, Grace. You get a little low sometimes. She was psychotic."

"It's just—it's just that. Sometimes I feel like I'm tending in that direction. Or might under certain circumstances. I worry all the time. There are so many opportunities for things to go wrong."

"That's just being an adult," said Dinah. "I think about my kids every day, what awful things could be happening right now. A fire, a broken arm. Disease. Focus on the happy things, Grace. You're going to love having that new house with everything brand new."

"I have dreams that I'm on this long shaley hillside with everything lost in fog."

"You have to let the old things go. You have to cut off the parts that are unhealthy. Everything in my life, the good in my life, everything except you, Gracie, everything dates from when I was born again in Jesus Christ. I strung my carabiners along the rope and pitons of Jesus Christ!"

"That sounds like one of Ray's sermons."

"There was a TV show on mountain climbing. Ray gets his ideas from whatever's around him. He says you can start anywhere because it all leads to Jesus."

Grace said, "You don't like to talk about her."

"No," said Dinah, "that's not true. We should say her name and lift her up for how hard she tried and how she suffered. It's the details that don't matter. There were lots of good things."

"Tell me a good thing. Besides the smocking on the dresses."

"Oatmeal cookies. She sang to us when we were little."

"I don't remember," said Grace, then, "Maybe I do. Did she sing songs from West Virginia?"

"I remember folk-revival stuff. Judy Collins and Joni Mitchell."

"Wasn't there a song that made us cry about two people who die and lie side by side in their graves forever?"

"Barbry Allen. That one may be from West Virginia."

"I remember that one. It's one of my earliest memories, her in bed with us singing and you sobbing and me sobbing and I thought it was about her and Daddy being dead."

Dinah said, "She told us stories about West Virginia. When she was a girl. Blackberries and a field up behind her house and animals and fairies made out of leaves and sticks. Milkweed ladies. We had a good time when her weather was good. She did the best she could, Gracie. You don't want to keep thinking about the sickness."

Grace said, "I'm glad you remember the good things, because I need to balance out the times she tried to kill us."

"Shh," said Dinah.

Grace said, "She tried to drown us."

"No," said Dinah.

"I know you remember the bath," said Grace.

Of course Dinah remembered the bath. She jerked her chin toward Jacob who had begun to tug at her skirt to get her to take him back to the van. She knew what he wanted. Grace had brought donuts.

"And before that, the lake," said Grace.

"I don't remember any lake. I definitely don't remember any lake. And, anyhow, I think I'd better get on the road."

"You don't want to remember."

"*Please* let it be, Grace. She was a sad, damaged woman, and she died in the hospital and we are doing just fine and we're not at all like her."

"The bath was the second time for me," said Grace. "She tried to kill just me the first time, when I was still a baby. At the lake."

"What lake?" said Dinah. "We never went to any lake." She gathered up the diaper bag. She stood up. "Come on, Jakey, we have to go now."

Grace refused to stop talking. "Yes we did. I remember it. Yellow flowers on her bathing suit, flowers floating in the water, probably it was really beach toys. I was floating with her, I had a little pink tube, and you had a blue tube, and all the sounds got softer."

Dinah did remember the tubes. She walked faster. They were almost to the van.

Grace's voice getting stronger. "She was swimming me out into the open lake. The reason I'm so sure she meant to kill me was how quiet it was, no other children or mommies or daddies, just me and her and she was nudging my tube out toward the open water."

Dinah stopped at the van. She pressed Jacob against her thigh.

"And then she said, 'No! I won't! I won't!' and then she turned the tube back toward shore. And then the noises came back, and you were standing in the shallow wearing your tube and jumping up and down yelling for us."

Dinah let her breath out. "If it really happened, Gracie, don't you see, that's a happy story. If really happened, she won a round over her voices that time. That's a good thing."

"It did really happen. And she didn't win the other time. The other time was water too. In the bath."

"We won that one," Dinah said, and started strapping Jacob into his car seat and the sleeping baby into his.

She embraced Grace because she loved her. She said she'd call soon. Her breath didn't get regular till she was on the road, away from Grace and their mother.

CHAPTER 3

Grace told herself the story about the bath over and over. It was the immediate cause of their mother leaving permanently. They had been renting a second-floor apartment on a commercial street of some town in New Jersey. It had a living room, a kitchen, and an archway that led to a short hall with the bedrooms and the bath. Grace was old enough by this time to recognize the good weather and bad weather. That evening started out with iffy weather. She and Dinah were playing safe houses in the living room, and their father wasn't home yet, and their mother was in the bathroom with the door closed for a long time, and they could hear her running a bath, and then they could hear her voices, talking to her other self, and when she came out, the weather was very bad, and she was muttering with her eyes huge in the center of their bony circles. "Bath time!" she called in a breathy, almost musical voice, "Bath time my chickies my ducks!"

She stood in the archway. Behind her the door to the bathroom was open, and they could see the bath was full of water to the very brim, and the tap was still running.

Dinah kept playing and said, "We didn't have dinner yet."

"Bath time!" sang their mother. "Bath time!" She was wearing her nightgown. She had been wearing it all day. That was one sign of bad weather.

Grace remembered saying, "I'm not dirty, Mommy."

"Oh yes! Oh yes you are! You are very dirty. We are all so dirty. You are young and you don't know yet how dirty you are we all are. I am very dirty, and you my little ducks my chickies my tiny baby birdies you are very very dirty."

"Well," said Dinah, "we can't take a bath until Daddy comes and we have dinner."

"Oh but you have to. Take a bath when you're dirty. When you are. You are. Dirty. You need a bath." And then there was a change, and one of the voices started tumbling out: "You have to be sanitized and baptized. Bathtized, you need your bath piss baptist bat piss—"

Grace remembered that Dinah stood up and took her hand. They didn't have time to get the trunk. They left their safe houses on the living-room floor. "We're going outside to play now, Mommy," Dinah said.

It had been long past dark. She remembered that their mother gripped the wooden archway between the living room and the bathroom, braced her body as if she were maybe trying to give the girls a head start, but her face leaned toward them and she screamed, "You have to go under! You have to go under the water for your bathtism!"

By the time their mother broke free of the archway, they were out in the hall. She didn't follow them, but she threw things at the door. Later when they came back they saw pillows, dolls, toys, magazines, safe houses.

They went downstairs and sat in the hall near the front door. After a few minutes, the woman who lived below them came out and said, "There's a flood! There's a—" and looked at the girls sitting there. Then she went up and knocked on the door and listened. The yelling inside continued, and the neighbor told Dinah and Grace to come into her apartment. Then she called the police and their father.

That was when their mother went to the hospital and stayed, and they and their father moved to a motel for a while. While they were staying in the motel, their father met Sharon Lock, and she offered to let them live in the carriage house at Lockwood.

When they moved to the carriage house their father still had hopes that their mother might be cured. Even the doctors, or so he told the girls, thought it was possible, that their mother might get well. He stopped selling insurance and took a job in the men's department at a

14

department store in the mall and told people he met in bars that he was sacrificing his career in order to make sure his daughters got the care they needed. Whenever Dinah and Grace spoke of their father in later life, they always agreed that his affection for them was unimpeachable, but he had been an alcoholic very early on.

They always used the proper words, to remind themselves that they were speaking of illnesses: their father was an alcoholic; their mother was psychotic. Grace used the words early in her relationship with her husband David. He was a medical resident when she met him, someone who would know about genetics. She told him the first time they slept together. She had very limited experience with sex, and this experience, with someone she really liked, in David's neat apartment near the hospital, made her cry.

"What? What?" said David, kneeling in the bed, grabbing her face. "What's the matter, Grace?"

She said, "My father was an alcoholic, and my mother was psychotic. I would understand completely if you walked out and never came back. I mean I know it's your apartment, but you know what I mean."

David lowered his face and kissed her. "These things are not determining factors," he said. "They're genetic tendencies."

She had felt her whole body fill with hope: not determining factors. Just tendencies. Other possibilities. He told her his own genetics weren't so great: his mother died of breast cancer in her early forties and his father of an early heart attack. They were both double orphans.

When the sisters moved to the carriage house at Lockwood, they didn't have the precise words yet. They didn't know that other fathers didn't drink themselves into a stupor every night. They lived, as all children do, believing that the world they knew was the only world. If their father called them from one of his afternoon bar stops to tell them he loved them and he'd bring a pizza home later, they knew to go ahead and have soup and crackers because he probably wouldn't be home till after bedtime, and he'd certainly forget the pizza. If he did remember it, they would eat it for breakfast. They weren't unhappy. They liked the carriage house, and home was much safer with Dinah in charge than it had been during their mother's last months or even when their father came home early enough to cook a steak and start a grease fire.

Grace believed that they never paid rent for the carriage house, and the reason was that women loved their father. They used to be proud of him when he'd take them out to restaurants. He would have them dress up and go to a place with a nice family atmosphere and a full bar. He would order steaks even if they preferred BLTs, and he would insist on pie à la mode. He would drink cocktails and smile at them and tell them how their hair shone. Strange women would strike up a conversation, apologizing for intruding but they just had to mention how beautiful the girls were. Women glowed under his gentle attention and sad eyes, and he would say, "Yes, they are beautiful, aren't they? My poor motherless daughters."

Grace assumed that he had met Sharon Lock in such a place. That he had told her his tragedies, what a beautiful woman his wife had been, how lonely he was, the responsibility of the girls. Sharon Lock had a multitude of faults, but she was generous to the bone. She would have insisted they come and live in the carriage house on her husband's property as soon as she heard the story. She would probably have said that they could work out the details later.

The big question was whether Sharon and their father were sleeping together before they moved in or after, but Grace and Dinah agreed that it wouldn't have mattered to Sharon, that she would have offered the carriage house either way. She was a full-breasted woman with a lot of money to spend on clothes, nails, hair color. She loved to celebrate and she loved to give. She probably liked the convenience of having a lover on the premises so she could get back easily to Mr. Lock.

To Grace, the main thing was living in a place where nothing bad had happened yet, that was near enough their school that they didn't have to depend on their father to get there on time. You approached the carriage house between brick columns with concrete balls on top and a small, dry fountain with a statue of a little boy with a real stone wee-wee. To the right of the carriage house as you faced it was an unkempt garden and one amazing rose bush that bloomed blowzy and pink into November.

The day after they moved in, Dinah made Grace give one of the roses to Sharon, and Sharon got tears in her eyes and hugged both girls deep into her powerfully sweet décolletage and said Dinah and Grace should consider themselves her girls, and then she went shopping and brought them sweaters and knit skirts, and they were amazed that she was able with a glance to guess their right sizes and that Dinah would like blue and Grace lavender.

They each had a bedroom at the carriage house, although Grace was happiest when Dinah slept with her. They were largely content during their first stint there. They sometimes said in later years that their father and Sharon were meant for each other. They both had disabled spouses, and they both liked to drink. Sharon was also addicted to shopping and probably sex. Later, after they moved away and then moved back, after Mr. Lock died, they noticed that the roof of the carriage house leaked rain, the windows leaked wind, and the toilet ran so often that you had to tie up the handle. They noticed that Sharon and David brought out some of the worst in each other.

But in the beginning they loved the carriage house with its empty first floor for races on rainy days. They planned to turn it into an indoor jungle and breed parakeets. They met Richie Lock when he was home from boarding school and stayed a while because of a cold that just hung on. It was amazing to them that someone their age could be sent away to school, and perhaps amazing to Richie too, because he threw a fit and got to stay home for the rest of that year and go to public school with Dinah and Grace. He went back to boarding school a year later, mostly to get him away from the boys on the street.

Richie had nicknames, and the first one he told them was Rocky. He was a small round boy, not quite fat, but soft enough to be funny looking, especially in the polyester running suits Sharon dressed him in. He had, according to Dinah, two speeds: Stop and Go. In Stop, he stared and was silent. This was how they first saw him, standing stolidly behind his mother as she chatted with their father in the driveway next to the wee-wee fountain. Sharon had just picked him up from boarding school and was worried about his health. He stood stock-still and stared at the girls.

The next day, they saw him watching them from the back hall of the big house, and the day after that, he came out into the garden where they were playing and stood catatonic until Dinah made him a robot in their game. When he was in Stop, he would stand wherever you put him.

They first saw Go a couple of days later when Dinah saved him from the gang.

Lockwood wasn't an estate, just a rambling brick and clapboard house with a stone foundation and a brick wall in an old suburban town in New Jersey. It was a town where rich people had at one time come out from New York City by train to what they called summer cottages with endless porches and sprawling grounds. When Dinah and Grace moved there, it was a neighborhood in decline. Houses had been turned into floor-through apartments and even a couple of single-room occupancies and group homes for people released from the mental-health system. There was an abandoned house on their street that was used by drug dealers and burned down while they lived there. Eventually, the town would become chic and expensive again, but—with their father's usual bad luck—they moved to the neighborhood at its low point.

To Dinah and Grace, big houses with trees and gardens were fairyland. Also, there were a lot of children to play with, mostly boys. The day they saved Richie, or rather, Dinah saved Richie, they were out walking and saw some of the neighborhood boys in a circle around him. The little gang was a racial rainbow of apprentice bullies. Eric and James Williams were thin and dark skinned, from a family where the adults all worked at least two jobs, so they had lots of time to hang out. The leader was a big white boy called Wolf who was thick limbed and dirty with a lot of roughly cut dark hair. He was in Dinah's class at school. The fourth boy was thin and graceful with the remarkable characteristic of having hair, skin, and eyes all the same amber color. That was Dylan.

Wolf, big jawed, already approaching puberty, was directing the torture. "Poke him some more! Make him talk!"

"Say something, Rocky!" said Eric Williams.

"That's no Rocky," said James Williams. "That's Jockey!"

To which Eric rejoined, "Jockey-hockey-pucky-cocky!"

This made them all giggle and dance around, and wispy Dylan with the flag of fuzzy hair waved his arms and turned around and around.

They didn't see Dinah and Grace on the other side of the street.

Richie had reacted to the pokes and sneers by going into Stop. His chin was tucked into his neck, and he held perfectly still with his arms not quite touching his sides.

"Yeah, hockey-cock!" said Wolf. "I name you Hockey-cock Butthead Dickface."

Dylan kept on with his supple dance, scooping a twig off the street and sweeping it over Richie's shoulders, over his neck and cheeks. "Dickface," he sang, "dick dick Dickface!"

The Williamses poked Richie's belly and ribs. "Fat boy Dickface," they said.

Dinah, who was used to dealing with much bigger problems than ten-year-old bad boys, looked both ways, then marched across the street shouting, "Okay! You can stop that now!"

Grace stayed close, adding volume, even though her heart was racing: "Stop that right now!"

The boys turned, and Dinah went to stand beside Richie. Grace stayed off to the side, leery of the rusty boy smell. Dinah said, "Look, if you stupid boys ever want to play Star Wars in the carriage house, you had better be nice to Rocky, because he owns it!"

Wolf glowered under his ragged bangs. "Who are you? What are you talking about? Play where?"

"The carriage house of course!" said Dinah. "We live upstairs, but the downstairs is a whole room for playing. It's big enough to play Star Wars or anything."

"Whose carriage house? What's a carriage house?"

"He owns it," she said. "Rocky. The house with the dead flower garden behind the big house at Lockwood."

Wolf glanced at his crew. It was a crucial moment for his leadership. The Williamses appeared to be interested. Dylan was in his own world, making little feints in the air with his stick.

"When?" said Wolf.

"When what?"

"When can we play there?"

"Whenever my sister and I say so, because we live in the carriage house part, but it all belongs to Rocky, so we won't say yes till you're nice to him. He has to give permission too because he owns it."

"Nobody calls him Rocky," said James Williams in a disgusted tone of voice.

Eric Williams said, "We call him Butthead!"

"Dickface!" said James.

"Not Dickface," said Dinah, reasonably. "His nickname doesn't have to be Rocky, but it can't be Butthead or Dickface."

So they all stared at Richie and started arguing if it should be Jock or Pock or Block, and finally James said, "I name him Doc!"

"No, I get to name him," said Wolf.

James sucked his teeth.

Wolf said, "*I* name him Doc."

Dinah glanced at the object of this naming session. "Is Doc okay?" she said, and when Richie didn't so much as blink, she shrugged. "Okay. Doc is a good nickname."

He became Doc to the neighborhood boys, but Dinah and Grace usually called him Richie. Richie followed Dinah and Grace home.

When they got back, he told them to wait, he was going in the house to get something, and he ran full speed inside and then came running back out with a shopping bag full of Star Wars action figures and a battery-operated laser light stick and announced that he was Obi-Wan Rocky, but they could call him Rocky or Richie or Doc, it didn't matter. When Dinah, who liked to get her facts straight, asked him for his real name, he shouted "Richard Rockford Lock! Richard Rockford Lock!! Known as Obi-Wan Rocky and sometimes Doc!"

Shouting and jumping up and down like Rumpelstiltskin. This was Richie in Go.

"I'll save you!" he cried, "I'll save you from the Empire!"

Grace said, "Dinah saved you!"

Richie slashed wildly at invisible enemies, "I'll kill myself for you!"

"That's crazy," said Grace. "Isn't that crazy, Dinah?"

Dinah shook her head and crossed her arms over her chest. "Richie," she said, "Just sit down and shut up, and we'll play with your action figures."

Richie slashed the air once more, then sat down.

So Richie became part of the gang, and so did Dinah and Grace. The boys started playing with the girls in the garden and in the empty first floor of the carriage house. Richie was apparently immensely grateful to Dinah and Grace, although he didn't have the words to say it. Instead, like his mother, he gave gifts.

Two evenings after Dinah saved him, he came to the carriage house with a shopping bag full of jewelry. He had bangles and necklaces, as much as he could sweep off his mother's vanity table. "You can have whatever you want," he said, "you can have it all I thought this one for

Dinah and this one for Grace but you can switch or you can have it all I don't care there's more where that came from *I really don't care!*" He made Dinah try on a wide gold band in the form of a twisted snake and a pearl necklace for Grace. He was in Go. "I'm going to marry you and you and you," he said. "I'm going to be a pharaoh and marry all of you and bury you in a mountain with jewelry!"

"Oh shut up, Richie," said Dinah, lifting the snake on her arm to the light, "don't be a fruitcake. Where did you get all this stuff?"

"I'm the pharaoh," he cried, "and you're going to be my harem. I'm going to marry you!" He whirled around and waved his laser stick and blinked it on and on. "I obtain my objectives!"

Dinah tolerated him, and Grace rather admired his vocabulary. His mother thought he was a genius and said he would only be in public school until she found the perfect private school for his kind of genius.

Dinah and Grace wore the snake and the pearls every day that week, although Dinah made Richie take the rest of the things back, except for a single pearl earring that Grace found on the floor under her bed and hid in the trunk and never did give back.

At the end of the week, their father was sitting at dusk in his chair smoking and having a drink, watching the girls play safe houses on the floor in front of him. He was dressed in a sports jacket because he was going out to a party later with Sharon, and the light from the kitchen behind them fell on Grace's pearls and Dinah's gold.

"What's that?" he said, reaching out and touching the pearls. The string was so long she wore them doubled, but they still looped down over her tee shirt.

Dinah answered for both of them. "Richie Lock gave it to her. He gave me this," and she showed him the snake bracelet.

"Bring it closer," he said, and they both obediently got up and came close to show off. He put down his cigarette and looked most closely at the bracelet.

Dinah said, "Richie tried to give us a whole bag of stuff, but we only took these."

"Well," said David, "I think—Dinah, sweetheart, I don't think you can keep these. I think these are valuable. I think they belong to Sharon, and Richie shouldn't have taken them. Sharon was mentioning something, she was talking about what she was going to wear tonight, and something was missing."

He stubbed out his cigarette, got up, and carried his drink to the phone that hung on the wall in the kitchen.

They stood near and listened to him talk to Sharon, who was very nice about the whole thing and insisted on bringing over replacement jewelry, a big rhinestone armband for each of them that Grace liked better anyhow. Then she and their father went out, and she left Richie with them, along with a twenty-dollar bill so they could order a pizza. As far as Dinah and Grace could tell, Richie was never even scolded for giving away the jewelry.

After that, Dinah didn't let Richie give them anything except food. Richie came over every day and sometimes twice a day, until Dinah told him to go home. One day he invited them to lunch, so they put on dresses, and the housekeeper at the big house served them chicken-salad sandwiches and purple soda and huge slices of chocolate cake with white icing in a yellow breakfast nook. Sharon came by dressed for shopping and gave the girls kisses, and afterward they played with the trains, and Grace was terrified of waking Mr. Lock, who was just one room away.

The next time Richie wanted them to come over and play trains, Grace was still afraid.

"What if your father wakes up?" she said.

"He's going to be dead before Christmas," said Richie. "He never gets out of the bed. He just lies in the bed and I have to go in every night and kiss him and he stinks. Pee-ew!"

Grace said, "What if he turns dead while we're playing trains?"

Dinah said, "We just have to be quiet, that's all."

Richie said, "If he's dead, I'm going to shoot him with my real gun."

"First of all," said Dinah, "you don't have a real gun. And second of all, if you do, we won't come over ever again."

"Okay okay!" said Richie. "No shooting with real guns!"

Dinah added, "And if he's dead, we won't come over either. We're only going to come over if he's alive. So you have to go check." And she made him do it too. "If he's dead," said Dinah, "We'll leave."

Grace felt much, much better.

Richie said his father was asleep and there was a nurse in there keeping him alive for now. They played that day and after that, often in the train rooms, always quietly. One afternoon Sharon clattered in on high heels, pushing before her the cloud of her exotic perfume. They admired her style, which was heavy on animal-skin prints and deep V-neck sweaters with big shoulder pads. That day, she was also wearing Grace's pearls.

They were deep into the world of trains and train wrecks and earthquakes, and Sharon cried out how nice to see them. She gave big hugs to everyone, and then, to the amazement of the girls, slid open the door to the bedroom, left it partly open, and strode in to see Richie's father. Grace held very still, trying to see Richie's father between the sliding door panels. Richie just kept running a train through the tunnel and hurrying along beside it talking to himself.

They could hear Sharon, and then another woman's voice, and they saw a white uniform and white stockings and shoes through the crack, and some bedclothes. Sharon kept talking, and then there was a scratchy man's voice. Richie followed his train right into the second train room, out of the girls' sight. Sharon stopped laughing and the man's voice picked up volume, still muffled but louder and louder, and then Sharon's voice got shrill, but gradually said less and less, and then they heard very clearly: "*You go out drinking in the afternoon and sleeping around I'll make you sorry you fat whore.*"

To Grace, the idea of sleeping around made sense because who would want to sleep in a house where a man was dying, but she wasn't sure what a whore was. She thought maybe he was mad because he wanted company at night like Grace needed Dinah before she could go to sleep.

"*You were a whore when I found you and you're still a whore.*" At that point Richie came back in, came and stood beside the girls. "*And if I didn't believe that boy was mine you would have been out in the street a long time ago you dirty bitch whore piece of shit.*"

It went on for a while, and all three of the children were in Stop, and finally the man's voice seemed to crack and there was an awful coughing and Sharon was calling for the nurse, and they saw the uniform again, and then more coughing and some gasping, and Grace thought he had died, but instead he went back to rumbling and grumbling, and then Sharon came out and pulled the doors together tightly behind her. She stood there for an instant staring at the children but maybe not really seeing them, and then she left without a word.

Dinah said, "We'll go play outside," and they went out, Richie quiet, Grace no longer frightened, but very interested, and after they'd played for a while in the dry fountain, she said, "Dinah, what is that thing he called her?"

Richie went into Go. "Whore!" he shouted. "Not H-O-R-E but W-H-O-R-E whore! It's a bad woman a dirty woman it's a bad name to call someone and my mother is not one he calls her that but it's not true!"

Dinah said, "Of course it's not true. Richie, he was just mad."

Richie leaped up on the rim of the fountain. "And *never, never* let me hear you call her that!" he cried.

"It's the worst name," said Dinah. "We like your mother."

"She looks clean to me," said Grace.

"She is!" cried Richie. "My mother takes a bath every day and I do too!"

Grace sometimes thought that if they had just stayed straight through at Lockwood, if they hadn't left and come back, a lot of things might not have happened. She thought that if they had all stayed as they were, if Richie hadn't gone back to boarding school and if their father and Sharon hadn't had a fight, if they had just continued to live in the carriage house, then maybe there would have been no drugs and Dinah sleeping with boys. But then their mother passed away and there was no reason to stay when their father and Sharon had a fight. He said he could no longer live on her bounty, that there was a new life waiting for them in California.

CHAPTER 4

The two greatest gifts Jesus gave Raymond Savage were what happened to him in prison and Dinah. He got saved in prison, and Dinah was a woman in a million. Loving and hardworking, and she lifted him up in everything. Sometimes her faith was not as clear as his, and she worried about a thousand things that Jesus had assured Ray would be taken care of, but she was the mainstay of his life. He felt sorrow for her concerns and doubts, but didn't criticize. He trusted that one day she too would see more clearly, no longer through a glass darkly.

She had accepted Raymond without asking the details. When he said, "You know I was in prison, but I haven't told you the whole story," she said, "You did your time, Ray, and you came out a new man. That's enough for me."

He prayed over that, and in the end Jesus agreed with Dinah. She had the basic outline, that he'd got mixed up with some bad actors back home in West Virginia. She didn't ask for more. Jesus told him to reveal the details on a need-to-know basis.

Ray said, "I need you to know I can have a foul temper, but I never took a man's life, and I never struck a woman."

Dinah smiled that smile of hers that was just one watt short of a revelation. "Well, Raymond, I already knew you had a temper, and I already knew you were a good man."

Dinah took him the way Jesus took him, failings and all. Dinah and Jesus said, We're here for you, Ray Savage. He felt their love like a trampoline letting him sink down and then sending him back up high. That's what Jesus can do for you! He ran the image through his mind, preparing a sermon. Or a good woman, if you can find yourself a good woman. Or vice versa.

Raymond was pretty sure Dinah assumed he'd gone to prison for assault and battery. And he had spent a couple of nights in jail after drinking and fighting, but he didn't regret his past. Jesus told him that it was all material for reaching out to those hardheaded men who hadn't learned yet.

What got him into prison—not some local lockup but the federal penitentiary—hadn't been alcohol and hadn't been anger, but stupidity. He had been in the dark, which means—he tried it out in his mind—that you don't care enough about yourself to take care of yourself. It takes Jesus to learn to love yourself.

The thing he hadn't told Dinah in detail was about the Mountain Militia plot to blow up the FBI fingerprinting center in Harrison County. It had been in the mid-1990s, and Ray had been chronically short of money, and Poke Riley had told him about it: driving trucks, hauling boxes. Poke also did time for stupidity.

So when Poke showed up now at the service station where Ray was working part-time, all these years later, with a business proposition, Ray knew it was time to tell Dinah the whole story. He was going to have to say, I need you to know how I know this man Poke Riley. He figured Dinah was going to say, Skip the story and stay away from the man.

But he and Poke went way back long before the Mountain Militia. From back home in Cooper County. He and Poke had been in high school together till Poke dropped out, and then, later, they used to hang out around Kingfield. Poke always had plans. Once he was going to tie flies for fishermen and sell them mail order, and he had an idea to make high quality moonshine and sell it to college students who thought it was a cool to buy illegal liquor. Old Poke was a special fan of the plots of caper movies and TV shows, and he liked to analyze what went wrong, and what would have made them go right. He had a job as a night watchman for a while and dealt pills and marijuana, and then he ran a gambling scheme using West Virginia University team point spreads.

Raymond liked Poke okay, personally, in spite of all the nonsense and even the Mountain Militia. He was fine when Poke showed up at the service station and started talking about the old days. He still had the big laugh, big belly, and that ponytail like a rockabilly guitarist which he never was. They agreed that they'd both been young and stupid for getting involved with the Mountain Militia.

"I've got a real good job now," Poke said. "Salary and all expenses paid. And the proposition for you, Ray, is totally legitimate." He told him he worked for a rich businessman. The man had dabbled in growing marijuana at one time, Poke said, but now it was all legitimate investments. "I'm not going to lie to you," said Poke. "He's an oddball, but nothing illegal. And this man is looking to hire a preacher." Poke said he'd been visiting back home and heard Ray was a preacher now. "You know me, Ray, why put an ad in the paper when I know a man from Cooper County, West Virginia? It's all about relationships, you know?" The rich man, according to Poke, was thinking of starting a media center. He had a lot of ideas, but he wanted a religious program for his radio station or his podcasts or whatever it was. Poke said, "So I thought of you, Ray. Come down to Mountain Dome, and get interviewed. It's a real opportunity."

Nothing illegal, Ray would tell Dinah. And could hear her saying, And how do you know that, Ray?

Bobby Mack was working for the businessman too, Poke admitted, and that made Ray a little uneasy, and he said so. Ray wasn't prejudiced against small men, but Bobby Mack had a beaten-down ratty look that always made him think of Judas Iscariot.

The marijuana made him uneasy too.

Poke said, "Look here, Ray, I only mentioned the weed so you wouldn't hear about it elsewhere. I want all the cards on the table. The businessman has been out of that a long time, and even when he was in it, he was diversified. He's always been diversified. And it's all going to be legal soon, anyhow. My boss, he understands people have done things they maybe wish they hadn't in the past. He plans for the long haul, you see? He understands about being young and stupid. He likes people who've made their mistakes and learned from 'em. That's why he took on Bobby Mack and me."

Ray believed in second chances too. We all deserve a second chance.

What is born again but a second chance? He prayed about it, of course, and Jesus didn't say much, but He didn't say no.

Ray and Poke and Bobby Mack had been on the periphery of the Mountain Militia patriot thing. Ray had certainly never meant any harm to his country, that was one thing he was sure of. They never had much to do with the gung-ho ones. Ray went to a couple of meetings, but that was all. They said they were acting to stop the New World Order, and later on, he had found out that meant not only getting the government off people's backs—which he favored, of course—but also chasing out what they called the Jews and the jigs and the ragheads. That part made him uneasy to the point he decided he was going to collect his pay and get out, but he was too slow.

I was in darkness then, Ray said to himself, working on either the sermon or how he was going to explain this to Dinah. That's what I was then. When I needed money for my pleasures, I took it from wherever. I don't think I would have put a gun to the back of a man's head and fired, but I thank Jesus I was never tested. I did take money from people whose lives were about hate, not love. He was looking to enjoy life, and he thought all he needed was a little money, and here came Poke who knew someone who needed men to drive trucks, just carry a few things here and there. And they were paying fifty dollars a pop, sometimes a hundred, for an hour or two's work.

Raymond never doubted for a minute that they were hauling contraband because the pay was too good and got better as time went on. Also the loading and driving was usually at night from garages to deserted barns and vice versa. Sometimes he was pretty sure they were stealing, but mostly they just seemed to be just relocating material that already belonged to the colonel of the Patriots, a man named Floyd Looker, a fellow in real estate, and somewhat of a preacher too. The colonel wore fatigues and a beret, and Ray saw him maybe three times but never had a conversation.

Their meetings drew in all kinds of people, sometimes big meetings, especially after certain things happened in the news, especially after the federal building in Oklahoma. Up until then, Ray had figured it was all about drugs like the semisecret marijuana fields all through West Virginia, but then he realized Floyd Looker and the others had more on their minds. Oklahoma City got them real enthused. They killed little children, he remembered thinking one night. What the hell is good about that? Ray had complained with the best of them about taxes and people taking away your squirrel rifle. All the Savages, his whole family, were independent to their toenails, believed in taking care of their own and devil take the hindmost. But when Bobby Mack started going on about how there was something to it, you had to be ready to fight the government, Ray had said, Wait a minute here, my brother Duke was one of the very last to die over in Vietnam, I'm not interested in going against America.

Poke said, Hey Bobby Mack supports our troops, don't you Bobby Mack?

That was when Ray started thinking about getting out of it, but he was too slow. He never even knew if Bobby's last name was Mack or if that was part of his first name. That was how careless he had been in those days. Straight into the devil's work, for fifty or a hundred bucks.

It was one hundred when it was explosives they were hauling, and that was when he was pretty sure they were stealing, although he was also pretty sure that someone had paid off the guard at the quarry to be off in the woods pissing at 2 a.m. It was very precise, that they had to drive in at 2 a.m. and break into a shed where they found about five hundred pounds of blasting caps and old-fashioned dynamite. By that night if not before, Ray knew these so-called Patriots were planning to blow up something, and he was sick of their meetings and he decided this was it, he was finished.

At that time, Ray hadn't met Jesus. He liked to say, I was wasting my substance and endangering my body and my soul. The next time there was a dead-of-the-night job, he opted out, although he still did some day-time hauling for them.

Then the whole thing broke loose: it turned out Looker and the Mountain Militia Patriots were going to blow up the new FBI fingerprinting facility before it even opened. This fingerprint center was a gift from a West Virginia senator, Robert C. Byrd, who always took care of his own and got the facility moved from DC to West Virginia so people would have jobs, or vote for him, or whatever. Colonel Looker was convinced the fingerprint center was really the command center for the New World Order, the headquarters for sending out gangs of black men to rape white women, after, of course, taking away the white men's guns. So the idea was to blow it up before it opened.

Most of what Ray knew, he got from the newspaper and TV like everybody else. Old Colonel Looker had talked a fireman into giving him blueprints for the new facility, and he was collecting the explosives to do the job. Then the Colonel made a deal with an Arab terrorist (what was *he* doing in West Virginia anyhow? Didn't anyone have the sense to ask?) and the Arab terrorist turned out to be a federal agent, and what's more, there had been agents following the whole thing all along.

Floyd Looker was at least as stupid as I was, Raymond thought. More stupid, because Floyd got eighteen years. Some of the inner circle got ten, and the rest of them, the drivers like Ray and Poke and Bobby Mack, got eighteen months or two years. He had read the whole thing in the paper and congratulated himself on being out of it, never even realized he was about to get arrested himself till they picked him up, back working again at Junior's Auto Repair.

That was the part Dinah didn't know.

What she did know was how prison was the beginning of God's part of his story. In prison Ray met the old man who aimed him straight at Jesus up close and personal. Like the old man was a gun and I was a bullet, and he shot me into the heart of Jesus, and I have lodged there ever since! Ray used that whenever he had an opportunity to preach, which wasn't as often as he'd like. Another reason he wanted to check out the opportunity Poke Riley told him about. More preaching and less shit jobs.

He wasn't quite sure how to present it to her, how to stop Dinah from saying, Oh that sounds real good, another bright idea from the man who got you into prison.

The fact was, Ray thought, probably nothing was going to come of it. The idea of a rich businessman wanting to start a little digital broadcast church up on some mountain someplace. He decided he was going to pray on it for a while longer before he stirred up the whole mess by telling Dinah.

He had always wanted his own ministry. In his imagination he called it the Church of the Cross and the Lighthouse. He imagined a tower like a lighthouse with a huge neon cross fixed on it. To save those poor dumbheaded drunk sailors, which is all of us.

CHAPTER 5

Aleda wanted to know about her real father. It was nothing against Ray, and it wasn't even against Dinah, who watched her like a hawk. Her real father and Dinah had been childhood friends, she knew that much, and she also knew that her amber eyes and dense hair came from him. She knew he was named for a singer who was named for a poet, but that was about all she knew. Once Dinah told her, "Dylan was the only one of that pack of boys who had a good heart. Wolf was stupid and mean, and Richie was smart enough, but never thought of anyone but himself."

"So my father was the good one?" asked Aleda.

"I didn't say that," said Dinah. "I said he had a good heart. He was weak. He went wherever the people around him went. He floated like a piece of milkweed silk on the wind. And, Aleda, that's all I'm going to say. Stop asking."

Aleda always remembered the milkweed part, and when she found some dried milkweed pods behind where they lived, she blew it and pretended she could follow it to her father.

When she was around twelve, she said, "Mom, I'm old enough to know about my father. I want to know the whole story about Dylan."

"You don't give up, do you?" said Dinah. "You're as bad as Grace, asking questions. Just do what you know is right. Pray to Jesus and keep your sights high. That's all you need to do. I've told what I'm going to tell you about Dylan. He's gone."

She said, "Gone like milkweed silk?" even though she wanted to say, Gone like went away or gone like dead?

Dinah gave what books called a mirthless laugh. "Right. Gone like milkweed silk. You're right about that. The past is gone, praise Jesus. Make Jesus your now and forevermore!"

"But, Mom—"

Dinah said, "Stop. I'm really, really through with this topic."

So what Aleda knew was that Dylan had been one of the kids who hung out with her mother and her aunt Grace. And that all those kids, except Aunt Grace, had been in trouble when they were teenagers.

Aleda tried again, from time to time, and once Dinah said, "What do you want with Dylan anyhow? Ray loves you like you his own daughter. You have his name."

"Not on my birth certificate."

"We'll change it one day when we get a little bit ahead on money."

"I may not want to."

"You should be thanking Jesus for giving you such a loving stepfather!"

This was totally beside the point. Aleda knew that Ray was a good stepfather. He was a big softy except when he was preaching, and every so often when he got into a fight with someone, usually a boss, unfortunately. At home, he liked to have the little kids sit on his lap, and sometimes if they begged, he would lift them up and toss them, and he used to do that to Aleda too. But that was beside the point, too, because Aleda wanted to know whose genes she was carrying in her blood and bone and amber eyes.

Dinah was the boss of the family. She told everyone what to do and decided what they should and shouldn't know. She told them the man is the head of his household, but as far as Aleda could tell, that meant that Ray got to talk to God, and Dinah took care of everything else.

Including that Aleda should know nothing about her own birth father. She was under the impression that he had died tragically, related to drugs or maybe suicide, but she didn't know for sure. She knew that her mother thought she, Aleda, was like him. Once, she tried that for an argument: "If I have to be careful because of Dylan's legacy, wouldn't it be better if I knew what it was?"

This caused Dinah to lift an eyebrow and look her straight in the eye and say, "I believe this is *casuistry*, Aleda. Or maybe *sophistry*. And since I'm sure you don't know what those words mean, go look them up."

Dinah didn't use a lot of big words, but she studied them and collected them, and taught them to the kids. They were a homeschooling family. Her mother said she wanted her kids to have excellent educations because she and Ray never went to college. Aleda was allowed to read anything she wanted published before 1900, Dickens and Shakespeare and even Rabelais, who was about as dirty as they come. Or rather, *bawdy*. Aleda liked words too. *Casuistry* meant "oversubtle reasoning," and *sophistry* meant "a plausible but misleading or fallacious argument."

Later, Aleda said to Dinah, "It wasn't a misleading or fallacious argument to say I wanted to know my heritage from Dylan. Maybe it was subtle, but I meant it. I need to know what he was like."

That time, Dinah simply turned away, and Dinah silent was far more formidable than Dinah telling you to go look up words.

It infuriated Aleda when her mother treated her like she was out to do evil. Aleda had never, almost never, done anything to defy her mother. Never a boyfriend, never a drink of alcohol. She helped teach the little kids and did her housework. She studied hard on her own education.

By the time she was fourteen going on fifteen, she did, it was true, have more conflicts with her mother. For example, she found herself very interested in the public high school. She liked animals and science, and sometimes imagined becoming a veterinarian and living in some place like Wyoming or Colorado. She pictured herself in denim with her hands on a sick horse. But how would she ever learn enough using the internet at public libraries? They didn't own a computer or a television. Information is free and plentiful on the internet, said Dinah. You just have to monitor it and know how to sift the wheat from the chaff. The libraries, of course, had sex-and-violence controls, but Dinah let Aleda and the twins look up things and read the news. You'll get a sense of how bad the world is, said Dinah.

But only at the library. And, of course, as soon as Dinah took Jakey to the bathroom or went off to nurse Benjie, Aleda and the twins, especially Zack, would switch sites on the internet. Zack usually went to the sports channels, and Aleda would do searches on her father's name. Even Sarah, who was the good little girl, occasionally looked at pictures of boy singers.

Except for searches for Dylan, Aleda didn't hide her research from Dinah. She had done a short paper on bawdy language in Shakespeare and Rabelais. Dinah rolled her eyes, but didn't stop her. She wrote an essay on cults and the dangers of groups that set themselves apart from the rest of society. She especially liked the polygamist Mormon sects.

Dinah, of course, read all their work and got the point. She said their family wasn't a cult, it was a family. Making your own clothes saves money, she said, and long skirts are modest and fashionable both.

And they set us apart, said Aleda. Plus it sets me and Sarah apart more than the boys.

Dinah drew her attention to a split infinitive in her essay, and Aleda *knew*, for a fact, that split infinitives were no longer considered ungrammatical. She had done an essay on that too.

Of course Aleda knew that Dinah's main interest was in keeping them away from sex, drugs, and alcohol, and above all to keep Aleda, who had long since passed puberty, away from boys.

She would wait maybe a week, and then ask again. "But exactly what was wrong with Dylan, Mom?"

She even asked Ray, who hadn't been there, and he said, "Well, Aleda, I never met him, as you know. He had fine qualities, though, or Dinah would never have loved him. And you're a fine girl, Aleda, so that's the proof of the pudding. Ye shall know him by his works."

Aleda didn't want Ray to go prophetic, so she said, "You're pretty sure they loved each other, Mom and Dylan?"

"Oh I'd say so," said Raymond. "Your mother has always been full of love. Ask your Aunt Grace," he said.

She *had* asked Aunt Grace about Dylan, the last time she saw her. Dinah had taken the babies to see Grace a couple of times since then without Aleda, and Aleda was convinced she was trying to keep them apart. Aleda knew that her mother worried about Aunt Grace and Uncle David and their girls because they weren't born again and maybe not even Christians, especially Uncle David who was half Jewish. "Why don't we see Aunt Grace and Uncle David?" she asked.

"We do see them, it just hasn't been convenient lately with them living down in West Virginia."

"They live in Raymond's hometown," said Aleda. "Shouldn't we go down and visit Ray's family and Aunt Grace at the same time? We never even met Ray's family. Isn't that weird?"

And this brought on one of Dinah's narrow-eyed piercing stares. She said, "Aleda, now I think you're *dissembling* and hiding what you really want."

"I want to visit family! We never see anyone but each other! We ought to visit your family and Raymond's family."

Dinah had said, "Don't try to game me, Aleda."

"There's no game!" said Aleda. "I love Aunt Grace and want to visit her." Mentally, she added, And I have things I want to ask her.

The last time she saw Grace was at the Interstate 81 rest stop, sitting at the picnic tables on the ridge. Dinah took the little kids to the bathroom, and Aleda grabbed the opportunity. There wasn't much time, so she plunged right in: "Aunt Grace, tell me some more about my father. Please."

"Dylan?" said Grace. She never brought her kids. They always had these get-togethers while the cousins were in school or daycare or wherever regular people put their kids. "Dylan was handsome and graceful. Everything you do with your body," said Grace, "he was good at: dancing, guitar, athletics. He was an incredible artist, too, you know. He could draw anything, but mostly he drew things from his imagination, creatures. He painted them all over the walls of the room they were going to use for a nursery before you were born. Mermaid-unicorn-dragon things, not scary, just very beautiful."

Her heart leaped in her chest. "I never knew that."

"Doesn't Dinah tell you?"

Aleda didn't know what to say. They were alike in some ways, Grace and Dinah. They looked alike in some funny way you couldn't explain. Dinah was almost blonde and sturdy, and Grace was darker and thin and moved a lot whereas Dinah was slow and calm. But they both had big eyes that narrowed when they were thinking, and smiles that stretched huge all of a sudden. Talking to Aunt Grace was a lot like talking to her mother would be, she thought, if her mother wasn't always trying to improve her.

She said, "I want to know it all."

Grace flashed the big smile. "Dylan was the loveliest boy in the whole gang. I don't mean a gang like an urban gang, I just mean our gang of neighborhood kids. He was racially mixed, you know, half-black, I think? And maybe something Asian? Was his mother from the Philippines? I can't remember, I'm sorry."

It took Aleda's breath away. It explained how everyone else in her family was pink, and she was an amber color. "So I'm mixed race too," she said. Little crystal doors had opened, and it made her want to laugh and cry all at once.

Grace said, "Mixed race means you're all American, and beautiful, like him. What else can I tell you. Dylan played all the same sports and games as the rest of the boys, but he was dreamy. I don't know how to explain it. He was an artist."

"Mom's afraid I'm going to be like him and do whatever it was he did."

"He didn't do anything," said Grace. "I mean he did drugs, like the rest of them. They all did that, nothing that hurt anyone but himself."

And me, thought Aleda. He hurt me.

"When we first knew him," Grace said, "he used to dance to music no one heard but himself."

"Was he crazy?"

"Just creative. And sensitive."

"Where is he now?"

"Oh Aleda, I have no idea. And I don't think Dinah does either, but you should ask her, not me."

Aleda remembered every word of that conversation. And she also remembered that while Dinah didn't hear them talking, she knew. Maybe Grace told Dinah, or maybe Dinah just saw it in their faces, but she didn't take Aleda on the trips to see Grace after that.

After that conversation, Aleda spent several long sessions in front of Raymond's shaving mirror looking for the African and Asian in her face. She researched the Philippines, and found out that most Filipinos are mixed race too. Chinese and Polynesian and Spanish. There was, Aleda thought, the tiniest upturn in her eyes, from the Chinese. Her skin was dark gold, especially noticeably when she put her arm beside Sarah's, or when she held one of the babies who were soft and chubby and extremely pink, especially when they'd just had a bath.

She liked how she looked, but it was all different now that she knew. Her hair wasn't kinky, but neither was a lot of black people's. It was more like dense, hard to comb. Her mother said it had a lot of body. She usually fastened it down at the back of her neck, but it never lay flat. And everyone else, Raymond, Dinah, all the kids, had blue or gray eyes. Even Zack, who took the most tan. Aleda's eyes were amber. She had looked up eye color, and her color was the rarest of all.

There was a feeling from Dinah and Raymond that something was going on. They had been in this little house in New Tripoli, Pennsylvania, for much longer than the last place. Aleda thought they were probably going to move again. Ray had lost a job and now had a part-time one. There were private conversations between Dinah and Ray in the daytime, not just their voices in bed at night.

The house in New Tripoli was small and musty with only two bedrooms, but Aleda didn't really want to leave. On their way to the library, they always passed the big consolidated high school. That was another reason she knew her mother was worried about her. One recent evening when Raymond was out at a little church he was hoping to pastor and Dinah was working at the sewing machine making more of the stupid gathered long skirts, Aleda said, "I was thinking, maybe the next time we go to the library, we could stop by the high school and get some information." The sewing machine went silent. "I've been thinking maybe I should take a class or two at the regular high school. With the labs, and languages." Zack and Sarah gaped. "Not full-time, but maybe taking science there, or conversational French or Spanish."

Dinah hadn't said no, but the next day, she took Zack and Sarah to the library, and baby Benjie of course, but left Aleda at home with Jacob, pretending he had a cold. She was also supposed to clean the kitchen.

It was as if Dinah smelled something in the air.

How dare you accuse me unfairly? Aleda cried out in her mind, scrubbing a stain on the sink. How dare you keep me from the library? She loved the library, its big windows, its computers which were also windows, the books and bright colors, the pleasant shared silence of strangers, mostly old people. She always wondered: Where do they live? Are they Christians? Might some of them be Muslims or Hindus or Jews? If they were Hindus, how could you pray to something made of clay? If you were Jewish, why did you reject Jesus? And what if that old man was an actual atheist? How could you live if you didn't believe everything would be made right after you died?

She doesn't want me to work on my comparative religion paper, either, she thought bitterly. She doesn't really want me to write that paper. She had appealed to Raymond when Dinah wasn't sure about comparative religion. He said it was good to study the other religions and look for how they fail to make the connection to Jesus.

"I don't think that's what she's doing," Dinah had said. "I think she's shopping."

"Mother!" she had yelled. "You have no faith in me at all!"

"My faith isn't in human beings," said Dinah. "I know what I was when I was your age."

So once again, it was all revealed. Dinah was afraid there might be boys at the library (although she couldn't imagine any boys who cut school on a weekday morning ending up in the public library).

She cleaned the oven and played with Jacob, who was perfectly healthy, with just a little crust in his nostrils. Raymond was out back between the house and the shed fixing something. The regular mechanic at the service station had come back from the hospital, so they were only giving Ray work occasionally. He was building storage boxes for the van, which was another sign that a move was coming. She went back to the kitchen and, since she was being treated like Cinderella, scrubbed the floor with her skirt tied up between her legs and rags on her knees. While it dried, and she went out back to ask Ray if soup and grilled cheese was okay for lunch.

He was always fine with food, and he was also always happy when he was making something.

Maybe they'll need me to get a job to help out if things get bad, thought Aleda. She had been thinking about a job if they wouldn't let her go to regular high school. Maybe she could get a bike. Ray could fix up an old bike for her, and she imagined herself biking to school or a job (would Dinah consider letting her wear jeans maybe? You couldn't really ride a bike in a long skirt).

She tested the kitchen floor to make sure it was dry, then let Jakey pick what kind of soup for lunch (he always chose tomato). Then she sliced some cheese and got out the butter and a pan for the sandwiches.

Someone knocked at the front door.

This rarely happened, so Aleda immediately felt a surge of excitement, as if this might be a sign that life was not completely passing her by. She figured it would be Jehovah's Witnesses again. They came almost every week. The last time, Ray had invited them in and spent an hour witnessing and arguing. Aleda had taken notes for her paper. She turned off the soup before going to the door, in case there might be a long discussion again.

Two men were standing on the concrete-slab porch, filling all the space: an old one and a young one, and definitely not JWs. The old one wore a sweatshirt, too short to tuck over his belly. The sweatshirt had the image of a rattlesnake and said, Don't Tread on Me, M— F—, only it spelled out the words. He had a gray ponytail.

"Hi there, pretty lady," he said. "I'm looking for Ray Savage." He was smiling, but his eyes slid past Aleda and took in Jacob and the dingy living room. "He lives here, don't he? I'm an old friend of his from Cooper County."

Cooper County was where Ray was from. Behind the old man was a taller and much younger and better-looking one with a glossy black beard and an enormous white smile in the middle of the beard.

She said, "Mr. Savage is working. Who may I tell him is calling?"

"Well," said the old one, "I have a kind of appointment with Ray. At least, he knew I might come back. Just tell him it's Poke Riley, and this here is my sister's boy Travis. We have some business to discuss with Ray."

"Pleased to meet you," said Travis, reaching his hand around Poke Riley. It was big and warm and thick and sturdy. It enclosed her hand totally, and she did not have a particularly small hand. It made a flush run through her body.

She took her hand back, and Jacob reached up and offered his hand.

Travis said, "Hey little man!" and leaned down to shake. They were all squished close together on the porch for a second, and Aleda could smell Poke Riley's tobacco.

"Well ain't this a polite young feller," said Poke.

She said, "Excuse me. Just wait here please, and I'll go speak with Ray."

She pulled Jacob inside and closed the door, turned the latch. She was being discourteous, but she didn't trust them. Travis had never stopped smiling at her as the door closed, and she was struck by how clean he was, especially compared to his uncle. Travis's sweatshirt was dark blue with gold letters for West Virginia University.

She half carried and half dragged Jacob and his blankie onto the rickety back porch. "Ray!" she hissed, "Ray! Some men want to see you!"

Ray blinked, took his time looking up from his tools. "Somebody named Poke Riley," she said, "he wants to talk to you. And his nephew Travis."

Ray grunted, like he knew who Poke Riley was and wasn't so thrilled he was here, but at the same moment, there was a crunching in the driveway, and here came Poke and Travis. They hadn't waited at the door. They should have waited! Aleda thought. It wasn't fair to trespass into the backyard like that when she'd told them to wait out front.

Poke had a kind of rolling to his walk, and called, "Hey Raymond, I thought I heard you back here. How you doing, Raymond? What's that you're building? Not a car engine. Nope, it looks like woodwork this time."

"Well, well," said Ray. "Look what the damn cat dragged in."

Oh, thought Aleda. Ray cursed.

Poke kept talking. He seemed to have a lot of words. "I told you I was going to come by. This biggun here is my sister's boy Travis. He's supposed to be a Davis, but he's a Riley through and through." He gave Travis a sort of half pat, half shove. "Look at the size of him. He's a football player."

Ray said, "That's my daughter, Aleda, and that little one is Jacob."

"We met," said Aleda, and she had an urge to explain that she was his stepdaughter, not his daughter, but she kept her mouth shut. It was all strange, Ray acting macho, the big-bellied Poke with the gray ponytail and too much talk. Travis. She sat down on the back-porch steps and pulled Jacob between her knees. He leaned back and started sucking on his blankie.

Travis kept grinning at her.

You better not bother me, she thought, and then, Maybe he'll come over and sit on the steps with me while they talk.

And meanwhile Poke had some kind of plan, something to do with a job for Ray. I knew it, thought Aleda.

"Yeah," said Ray, just standing there, with a short saw in his hand. "I didn't expect to see you up this way again so soon."

"Hell, Ray," said Poke. "You never expected to see me again at all, did you? Admit it, son." Poke went close to Ray and gave *him* one of those pat-shoves. "Let's go around to the truck and have us a conversation. I now have details on that sweet proposition I told you about."

Ray glanced at Aleda. She didn't know what that glance meant, but it looked just slightly embarrassed. "Well," said Ray, "to tell you the truth, I seriously doubt I'd be interested in it. It seems like it's a little iffy, the whole thing."

"You ain't heard the details yet, Ray." Poke followed Ray's eyes, to Aleda, and he said, "Yeah, let's go sit in the truck, and have a little conversation and leave these young people to enjoy the fresh air. Travis, can you entertain the young folks?"

"Yessir," said Travis.

Ray and Poke went around to the front of the house. Travis with the black hair and beard and teeth and thick hands came to Aleda and Jacob. He said, "I don't know what it's all about either."

Jacob said, "That's my sister!"

"Hey, guy!" said Travis. "I can tell by looking. The two of you look just alike."

"No we don't," said Aleda, wanting to get to her feet, but if she stood she was going to bump into Travis, who had leaned over her like a roof. "We're only half siblings. Ray is my stepfather."

"You are my sister!" said Jacob, with tears in his voice.

She hugged him close. He was so solid and smelled good too. "Of course I am!" she said. "I'm your whole sister, but half sibling."

Travis said, "I wish I had a sister and a little brother. I'm an only child."

"You can be with us," said Jakey, and Travis laughed and leaned down closer, and now Aleda could smell him. It was sweat, but it smelled like strength and activity.

She thought she ought to go inside and finish preparing lunch, but instead asked Travis, "So why did you come here today?"

"Like I said, Aleda, I'm not completely sure. I've only been visiting my uncle a week. He works for this guy he calls Doc, or sometimes Boss. We live way up on a mountain in a kind of bunkhouse. The food's good, and mostly we just drive into town and do errands for Doc. Uncle Poke says Doc's rich, which I believe. You should see where *he* lives. What a house. Poke says that hanging around Doc, you get ideas for how to get rich too."

There was a little silence then, so Aleda said, "Do you go to West Virginia University?"

He touched his sweatshirt. "Well, yeah, but I'm taking a semester off. I needed a break. I have a football scholarship, or had one. I started last fall."

"The beard makes you look older than a freshman in college."

"I'm nineteen," he said. "How old are you?"

She felt like she was making a fool of herself somehow, but she lifted her chin and said, "I'm in my sixteenth year."

"You mean you're fifteen?"

"I'm four," said Jacob.

Travis seemed to like Jacob a lot. "You're four, big guy?"

Aleda said, "I *yearn* to go to college someday. Why did you drop out?"

"I didn't drop out. I'm going back. Things didn't go right last semester. They weren't giving me any playing time, and I broke training and started cutting classes. You know. I fouled up."

She tried to sound disapproving. "I would never take college lightly, if I had the privilege of going."

"Hey, I admit it, I was totally immature. My mom is pissed. She's so pissed she decided to send me up in the mountains to do physical labor and be with a male role model, as she says. Some role model. Poke is—" He stopped.

"What about your own father?"

"Out of the picture," he said too quickly.

She shouldn't have asked, she could tell, but didn't care because this was the kind of conversation she had always wanted to have, with someone close to her own age, a conversation where she could take missteps and not be told it was bad. She said, "I think you ought to apologize to your mother and go back to college. And pray."

"I guess you're some kind of real religious people? I noticed the long skirt."

"We're just plain Christians, trying to live the way Jesus wants us to live."

Travis grinned. "How about if you pray for me?"

"I can, but you also have to pray for yourself."

"Maybe so. I'm doing okay. It's a little boring up there, but sometimes it's interesting, like today. They've got these Mexican people to do the real work. All we do is drive around in the trucks and patrol the property."

"Patrol the property! With guns?"

He lifted his eyebrows. "Sometimes I unload supplies for the cook. I don't know. It's way up there in the middle of nowhere. I hope your dad takes the job, so then I'd have some company."

She wasn't sure she heard that right, but it made her body heat up again. So this was about a job for Ray. But also about the family moving up there where Travis was staying?

Travis kept talking, "I mean it is *lonely* up there. It's on a mountain, and there's Uncle Poke and another guy and there's the cook and his wife, and the Mexicans who run away if you try to talk to them, and I've barely even met the boss. If you guys come up, I'd take Jake here for a ride in one of the golf carts they use to run around the place. Or the truck. Would you like a ride, big guy?"

"Wouldn't mind if I do," said Jakey. "The truck, please."

Aleda said, "I don't know that I would like so much isolation. I've been thinking of starting public high school. We're homeschooled. We study very hard, but I would like to have access to more facilities."

Travis said, and she was pretty sure he wasn't making fun of her, "I can tell you're smart. And well educated."

"I definitely plan to go to college. What are you majoring in?"

He grinned again. "Football. But seriously, that was the problem. I never got beyond wanting to play football. I have to figure out something better for when I go back, because I'm good at football, but not as good as I thought. I may go into business. Sports prepares you for business."

"Drive trucks," said Jacob, who never wanted to be left out of a conversation.

"Your little brother's smart too."

They were all silent for a few seconds, and Aleda had a fear that she was boring Travis.

But he said, "So tell me more about your family's religion."

"Jesus," said Jacob, sticking out a leg, not a kick, just like a touch, reaching for Travis.

Travis squatted down and grabbed the leg with both hands and gave a growl that made Jacob squeal happily and ended with Travis much closer to both of them. She could see the smooth pinkness of Travis's forehead and the skin between his eyes and the top of his beard. His eyes were brown.

She said, "I believe the same as my parents except my mother gets a little extreme with the modest clothing. She's afraid we'll all go wild."

He growled a little more at Jacob. "All moms are afraid their kids will go wild."

Then Jacob reached for him, and Travis picked him up. Jacob laughed and bent his body backward for Aleda to catch. She was holding his top half and Travis had his legs.

Aleda said, "We're just Christians."

Travis said, "Well, almost everybody's a Christian. We are, or at least my mother is. I'm pretty bad sometimes." He glanced at her. "I could use someone to set me straight."

"My mother thinks you have to be set apart if you're going to be a real Christian. And of course the homeschooling is okay for the little kids. If I go to regular high school, I might wear regular clothes."

She cringed, half expecting something embarrassing: either a laugh or a personal compliment, and all the time feeling the connection to him through Jacob's twisting body.

Jacob kicked at Travis.

"Don't do that Jakey! You'll get him dirty."

"I don't mind," said Travis. "I like kids. I never had little brothers but I like them a lot. So I don't suppose you go out much."

"Go out?" she said. "You mean like on a date?" She was amazed at how her voice sounded, something out of a book, like a sneer. "Don't make me laugh!"

He pulled Jakey away from Aleda and put him on his shoulders and galloped him around, and Aleda could finally stand up. She hugged the porch pillar and thought he was very kind and handsome, and muscular, and she liked the beard and he was good with children too.

Then she thought, He's showing off, like the display of the bird of paradise. They wear themselves out showing the females their colors and their strength and good health in hopes of mating. And in her mind saw feathers, curved necks, spread wings. The galumphing of Travis with his beautiful wide shoulders and brilliant smile in fine health, cutting his eyes in her direction and Jakey was so happy.

She felt a warmth stirring through her body. That's sex, she thought. That's my body reacting to his display. It's sex for sure. She was amazed that it could come this way, through a stranger playing with her little brother.

Travis came back, panting a little. "I have an idea," he said, "I'll tell you what, let's keep each other honest. You promise to go to regular school, and I'll promise to go back to college in the fall. If we promise each other, we'll be more likely to do it."

Could you do that? Make a vow with a stranger? "Okay," she said, feeling the thrill again. "I'll promise. It's going to be a struggle for me, to convince my mother."

He laughed, but not at her, she could tell now. He was laughing out of pleasure. He handed Jakey over, and she hugged him close.

Travis said, "Good. It's a deal." There was a silence, Travis on the ground, Aleda up two steps so they were eye to eye, with Jakey between them. Travis said, "I've never seen eyes your color."

"They're amber," she said. "It's the rarest color. I got them from my genetic father. It's like you, he's out of the picture. I know his name, but I never met him."

Travis said, "I met mine when I was little, but then he just up and left. It's harder for a boy, not to have a father."

She again had that feeling. This is a real conversation.

But the truck door slammed, and Ray and Poke came around the house, and it was over, the most important thing that had ever happened in Aleda's life.

CHAPTER 6

David met Grace when he was a resident doing an emergency-room rotation. She came in with one of her students who had taken a fall on a class trip and lacerated his knee. Grace's class had gone back to school under the care of the assistant principal, and she brought the child to the emergency room. David was immediately drawn to her neat figure and intensity. She kept her chin down, her mouth pursed, but her eyes seeing everything. She barely spoke to David, concentrating on the frightened eight-year-old. While they waited for the boy's parents, David came in and out of the cubicle as often as he could.

He asked her to stay and have coffee with him at the hospital cafeteria. It wasn't typical of him, to move so quickly. He joked about himself as having the grammar and personality of a man raised by maiden aunts, which wasn't strictly speaking true—Aunt Evelyn was a widow and Aunt Peg, he'd found out as a teenager, had a long-term boyfriend.

He had just come out of a painful breakup, and here was Grace, and he liked her a lot and he wanted more of her immediately. His shift ended, but getting away took longer than he expected and he was late getting to the cafeteria.

When he told her he was afraid she would have left already, she said, "I almost did. I didn't think you were coming."

He told her he would have been very, very sorry.

They drank coffee into the dinner hour, and then he bought them trays of dinner. A couple of nurses and residents David knew waved and smiled knowingly. He was irritated even to have to wave at someone else. He told Grace everything he could think of about himself, the bad and the good. He told about Aunt Evelyn and Aunt Peg. He said he'd always been serious and never knew the TV shows other people discussed.

Grace said she and her sister had created their own worlds growing up.

He told her that emergency-room medicine wasn't his favorite, but he knew this would be part of a family practice: the cuts, sprains, broken bones. He wanted to work in a community that needed a doctor, he told her. Not that he didn't want a materially good life, but he wanted his daily work to be important to a community. Ideally it would be in a place with hiking and biking available but close enough to urban centers that you could enjoy culture.

He told her he was a rationalist but also trusted his hunches. He told Grace she was one of his hunches.

They discovered coincidences: he grew up in West Virginia, and Grace's mother had been born in West Virginia. Grace had no family except a sister, and he only had his aunts. Grace was not in a relationship, and he had just left one. He said he was half Jewish, but, religiously speaking, an atheist. She said she thought she was an agnostic.

They began spending all their free time together, taking walks and hikes, buying wild salmon and fresh asparagus and cooking together. He visited her classroom and let the children listen through his stethoscope. He hit their knees with his rubber hammer, and their legs jumped. As time went on, they made excursions to communities that might need a doctor. They talked endlessly, easily, delightfully, silent only when they made love and sometimes for a peaceful interlude afterward, but not always even then.

Grace confessed early on that her father had been an alcoholic and her mother mentally ill. David told her his mother died of virulent early breast cancer and his father of a massive myocardial infarction at forty-five. "I'll always have that hanging over me," he said. "I try to stay lean, exercise."

"It's why you're a doctor, isn't it?" she had said with that wonderful widening of her eyes. "You still want to save them."

He avoided psychoanalytic explanations when he could, but he had thought of this himself, and he liked hearing it from Grace: "I think that's it."

His instincts, his hunches, his decisions had been good. He knew they had. The town they chose was Kingfield, West Virginia, in the north-central part of the state, only a couple of hours from his aunts, and within reach of her sister. They had considered the Midwest and Central Oregon, but this small county seat of Cooper County, West Virginia, seemed right. The local people always identified by county. There was a university hospital thirty minutes away, you could drive to Washington, DC, in three hours and even to New York City in less than a day. David's only real reservation was that it was the home county of Grace's religious-bigot brother-in-law, Raymond Savage. In fact, they first heard of the elderly doctor who was retiring because the doctor's nurse was an ex-sister-in-law of Raymond. And in spite of all the positives about Kingfield and the unimpeachable need for a doctor there, he almost didn't follow up because of the connection to Raymond.

He hadn't begun with an aversion to the man. He had been interested in talking to him when he heard he was some kind of born-again preacher. David had been raised to discuss everything, so he had been intrigued the first time Ray knitted his fingers over his belly and started talking about his best friend Jesus. David was always struck by how rational most people generally are, if you accept their initial premises.

David could even talk a little about the Bible himself, as Aunt Peg used to take him to Presbyterian Sunday school. She never tried to force him to join, because of his dear Jewish mother's feelings, she would say, but he read the Bible lessons and queried his teachers.

David had asked something, and Raymond replied, "Whoa there, Brother David. I don't intend to get in a fight with you."

"Of course not," David said. "I'm just exploring how this works, what you believe."

And Raymond closed his eyes and beamed up at the ceiling. "It's not about belief or debate, brother. It's just a simple thing. Jesus called me when I was lost in the darkness, and He led me out. It happened. There's nothing to debate."

David had been willing to accept this too, Raymond's premise, that he had had an experience, and built his thought system on that. David said, "But you study the Bible, don't you? You have biblical evidence for what you believe?"

Raymond said, "I know what Jesus tells me."

David said, "I suppose most of us study to support what we already believe. In science, though, it's dangerous. It's better to collect the facts first and build belief out of that."

And that was when it had fallen apart. Raymond had grinned in the most condescending manner. "I don't need facts, brother. I just need Jesus."

"But if you're sick—if one of your kids is sick—"

"I pray to Jesus," said Raymond.

At this point Grace's sister Dinah had broken in and said, "Oh Ray, you know we take the kids to doctors if they're sick."

"But we ask Jesus first," said Raymond.

David had been amazed, almost admiring of the purity of the insanity.

Raymond never broke stride. "You'll see, Brother David, one of these days, you'll see, He'll come for you. You'll be alone in your study or standing on a mountaintop—for me, I was in a prison cell, a prison cell, Brother David! And He showed Himself to me! The rest of it is just hood ornaments."

David had tried to keep it going, but Raymond smiled and said, "We're going to get you, brother, just wait and see. Jesus is going to reach into your chest and grab your heart. I seen this with my own eyes, brother."

But it was Raymond's good-old-boy teasing that had finally driven David up a wall. All that evening, every time David's face had turned in Ray's direction, there had been a wink and a grin, and from time to time, out of nowhere, Raymond saying, "Oh yes, Jesus will get you, just wait and see!"

David had never liked teasing. When he was teased, he would feel himself losing control, angry beyond reason. In the end, they stayed away, or rather, David stayed away. Grace and Dinah still got together.

It had been hard for David to accept the idea that Raymond might have something practical to give him—but he had been rational about it. When someone mentioned the connection, David would say calmly,

Yes, he is my wife's sister's husband. Like reminding himself of his father's bad heart. A fact.

Kingfield had been the right choice. He loved the people's low-key cautiousness and appreciation of kind treatment. He liked the town, too, nestled in the eastern Appalachians with state parks and national forests just miles away. Nestled, yet seeming to gather the hills to itself. The dense green hills of summer, bronze and golden gray in winter sun. He liked standing in the middle of town in front of the Masonic lodge and the bank and being able to see everything at once, the local hospital and the school complex on the flat by the stream, the churches and the granite courthouse. It was too far from the coast for hurricanes, too high for floods, mountains a barrier against tornados.

The negatives, aside from Ray Savage, were a limestone quarry at the extreme western edge of the county—a health hazard, but David had done the research and determined that heavy particles wouldn't be airborne this far east—and a federal penitentiary, like the quarry, many miles away. The people needed the jobs, too, from the penitentiary and the quarry. It was a region of mostly poor white people, many who lived in mobile homes and worked two or three minimum wage jobs and still fell behind on their bills.

When he took over, the old physician still made house calls. David didn't think house calls were particularly good medical practice, but he had an idea for a mobile clinic to go out to the remote hollows, called *hollers* around here.

The day they first drove to Cooper County, when Margaret was a toddler and Grace was pregnant with Ruth, Grace had said, "I told you, didn't I, that Dinah's and my mother was from West Virginia? She and our dad met at the university. He was from around Pittsburgh somewhere, she was from West Virginia."

He nodded. "But not from Cooper County, was she?"

"No, somewhere else. Maybe Webster County? She never went back home that I know of."

When Ruthie was born, Grace had postpartum depression. It was another fact that Grace had depressions. They got through it that time and they would again. He had given her a very low dose of Nortriptyline, a drug old enough to have been studied extensively for breastfeeding mothers. He didn't like prescribing for Grace, but it was temporary.

The depression resolved itself. They had a little ceremonial flushing of the leftover pills down the toilet.

He wondered now if it had been the moving that time more than the baby, because this time it was definitely moving from one house to another that set her off. She'll get better, he thought. She always does. This time, though, he was more irritated than he should be. Because he thought it was affecting the girls. Plus, she kept bringing in fast food, fried chicken and pizza, all the things they tried so hard not to eat. He knew it was her depression, her inability to plan a meal, but he felt deprived. He picked the breading off the chicken, the pepperoni off the pizza.

He was uncomfortably aware that at this point in time he enjoyed his hours with his patients more than his time with his wife.

He was this afternoon engrossed in an apparently intractable problem, Mrs. Betty Lou Shaw's uncontrolled hypertension. She was obese and, according to her latest blood work, slipping into type 2 diabetes. She had had a heart attack some years back and had been treated sporadically by the hypertension group at the university, but she often missed her appointments over there. She liked getting her medical care locally. She liked David.

The anomaly was that when she came into the office, her pressure was not always high, and was indeed sometimes shockingly low. And now she had begun to faint.

Infallibly cheerful, Mrs. Shaw always said she was feeling fine, and left it to the medical professionals—as many of the local people did—to figure out what was wrong. For some of them it was the conviction that diagnosis was the doctor's job, not theirs. But Mrs. Shaw seemed simply to believe in looking at the bright side.

"I haven't been light-headed hardly at all, doctor," she said. "Not since yesterday after church."

This visit was a scheduled follow-up after her last trip to the emergency room, which had also been after church, but he didn't think church was a significant factor because she was at church almost every day. She hadn't broken anything, but she had big bruises on her knees and elbows. She had just sort of faded away, she said, the same as at the grocery. But she insisted that she felt fine.

In the office, her pressure had been high, both as measured by his nurse Merlee Savage, and as taken by himself. After he had talked with Mrs. Shaw for a few minutes, he took her pressure again, and it was much lower. He called in Merlee, and she got the same lower pressure. Ten minutes later, it was high again.

Mrs. Shaw had been treated for her various problems, had been on several different hypertension drugs. She wouldn't lose weight, although she always promised to try. He was troubled by the fluctuations in the pressure, especially since the fainting had begun.

He took his time, resettled the position of his glasses, and said, "I understand you had another fall, Mrs. Shaw."

"Just a little one. Not like that last one. Did you hear my granddaughter got into the university?"

"Congratulations, that's excellent. Were you faint when you fell?"

"Oh I just guess I'm getting old," she smiled. "That's the way with old people."

"Not fainting," he had said. "Getting old doesn't mean fainting, Mrs. Shaw."

And she responded with a gay little smile that made her cheeks round. "I like that tie, doctor, did your wife get you that for Christmas?"

She was still on his mind after hours. He had had a dozen patients after her, a very full day, along with the worries about Grace at home, but he couldn't shake the puzzle of what was going on with Mrs. Shaw. It was time to leave. He could hear Merlee getting her jacket out of the closet. A beep from the front desk was Merlee checking that the phone message was on. He stared at Mrs. Shaw's chart, page after page, the hypertension group at the university hospital, the various times she had been to the emergency room, the broken wrist, the contusions.

Merlee came to the doorway of his consulting room. She was wearing a denim jacket over blue scrubs. She had graying hair that she wore brushed straight back and long. David thought she looked like June Carter Cash, the country singer. Her dependability and competence were another part of these mountains, along with Mrs. Shaw's fatalistic response to medical problems, along with the occasional wild craziness that seemed to sweep down out of the hollows, like the survivalist Mountain Militia in the news right when he and Grace were thinking of moving to West Virginia. That had almost changed their minds, too.

If Merlee got depressed, he thought, you never knew it.

"Everything okay, doctor?"

And he was tempted to say, No it isn't. Grace can't unpack the boxes. Grace is having panic attacks or anxiety or depression, or all of the above and I don't know what to do.

But he said, "I'm stymied over Mrs. Shaw."

"Betty Lou is a mystery all right. I sure don't know what to make of it. Why don't you go home and have a nice quiet evening in your new house and sleep on it. In the morning, you'll wake up with the answer."

Yes, he thought, that's a fine idea, except for not having a nice evening in the new house. He said, "The house seems to be taking a long time to come together."

Merlee nodded. "They say moving is stressful. I heard it on television, so it must be true." They smiled at each other. He felt better. Merlee kept talking: "I haven't moved in twenty-five years, and I expect they'll carry me out in a box. Why don't you take Grace and the girls out for pizza?"

That was the way Merlee was, cutting through with a caring, practical solution. He said he might do that. He listened to the sounds of her leaving, and for a few seconds felt lonely. Then he picked up the phone, punched the outside line. Grace, he would say, bundle up the girls and we'll go out for pizza. Not that you could bundle up the girls anymore, they were all legs and elbows and projects of their own. He punched the outside line, but he didn't put in the number. He wasn't ready for Grace's low, slow *hello*?

He turned back to the chart, but there was a blurring. Something happening to his eyes. He cleaned his glasses. He rubbed his eyes. He was tired, but he was always tired, and this was different, a block, something like tears too thick to fall.

I'm fine, says Grace, just like Betty Lou Shaw.

He was angry with Grace. He didn't like the feeling. He knew she was suffering, but if she didn't want to move, she should have said, Let's renovate an old house in town. Let's buy the cottage instead of renting it. Whatever.

He tried to reason with himself: it was an illness, a chemical imbalance. He had at one time wanted to go into psychiatry. He knew all the details of Grace's life, the mother, the father, the fiercely protective sister who went from small-time drug dealer to religious fanatic. In the end, he had done a family-practice residency *and* pediatrics. He probably should have done internal medicine as well.

He would prescribe something again for Grace. She needed something to get her through this. She had been so far away these nights. She wouldn't come to bed. He had found her wrapped in a blanket on the floor in the empty dining room, with her back against the ancient trunk that had been part of the security system she and Dinah created for themselves when they were small.

Three weeks since they made love?

He didn't want a depressed wife. He felt there was something bad growing in their house, like a cancer. Not a cancer, he said to himself, but something bad growing.

There was a pool of light in his mind. Not a cancer, but something growing:

It was a pheo. Mrs. Shaw had a pheochromocytoma, the rare but dangerous adrenal-gland tumor. Why hadn't he thought of it sooner? Why hadn't the renal group thought of it? It was a hunch, but much more than a hunch. It fit, it was all of a piece. The renal group would have been too focused on the hypertension, on the kidneys. And of course they didn't get the Sunday phone call from the emergency room after Mrs. Shaw had again sunk to the curb in front of church. That's what the general doctor gets.

He wanted to call someone, maybe Merlee, but first he would double-check, look up every detail. But he knew he was right.

He thought happily of how Mrs. Shaw's pleasant face would look when he told her. She wouldn't want surgery, but he would be firm, and she would finally agree: If you say so, doctor. He would call the renal group. He tried to hold down his sense of vindication: yes, I'm a general doctor, but the best general doctor is a specialist in the whole picture. Yes, I diagnosed it, not a big deal (but of course it was a big deal!). There are times when general knowledge trumps specialties.

He started through her chart again. He wanted no mistakes. He wanted to be absolutely sure. He was good at this part too, the checking and rechecking, leaving no detail unexamined, but just the same he knew he had the answer.

CHAPTER 7

Grace had loved teaching so much that it came as a shock to learn that being good with third graders didn't necessarily mean you were a good mother. She thought she had discovered exactly what her life would be, teaching, David, and of course having a family. She had assumed motherhood would be as Dinah described it, uplifting spiritually and physically satisfying. Dinah talked about how babies smelled, how you could travel with a baby and no equipment needed except a wet rag and a few diapers. Dinah sailed through pregnancies, considered childbirth to be labor but not pain, said breastfeeding was the greatest gift God ever gave a woman.

When Grace was honest with herself, she knew she had been happier when it was just her and David. She told this to no one, not to Dinah, not to David. She loved her daughters and would give her life for them.

But she had been happier before she had children.

After Margaret, it was just a little postpartum blues, but after Ruth, she had a full-blown depression. They had just moved to Kingfield, and she and David agreed having a toddler plus a new baby with all the hormonal changes plus moving had been too much for her.

Now it was happening again, but this time with only a new house. You wouldn't think that moving to a brand-new house within the same town would set off a depression. You wouldn't think she'd be standing here yearning for the damp old rental cottage with banging pipes and leaky windows and a little mold in the basement. During the move, they had all been stressed of course. Ruthie whined that Margaret got the bigger bedroom, Margaret stopped speaking to everyone because a particular tee shirt was missing.

Grace fell into the big hole the day the others went back to work and school. Alone in the new house for the first time, she hadn't moved from in front of the fish tank for a long time. She was in a gelid block of silence where she lost track of time. She remembered the other move, when she was nine months' pregnant, and Margaret was running around laughing, and playing, apparently delighted in everything new, and then, when they took her to bed in her new room in the new house had started shrieking, I want to go home!

Grace wanted to go home, to the smaller house, older house, familiar house.

She couldn't remember anymore why they decided to build in this barren development. She looked around at the large rooms, the echoing cathedral ceiling, the stacks of boxes, the smell of raw wood—and couldn't remember a single convincing argument in favor of this place.

If you were going to commit to a town, David reasoned, you needed to own not rent. She said she liked the clematis growing up the porch pillars, and he said yes it was picturesque, but it would be irrational to stay indefinitely in the cottage. Grace had agreed of course. They had been renting for nine years, and David would never have insisted if she had said directly she didn't want to move. She thought she *did* want to move. She thought she was thrilled. A guest room! Mexican tile backsplashes in the kitchen! Granite counters! Marble in the foyer!

She had fooled herself as well as him. She had been thinking of running for the board of education. The distance between that ambitious, active self and who she was at this moment made her cold with terror.

They were the first family to move into the new development. The other houses were just skeletons. There was no grass, and just boards laid over the March mud for the workers. It isn't safe here, she thought. She tried to convince herself she was premenstrual, she hadn't slept well. This was a comedown after the busy weekend. But her body was going silent and still. She felt as if she were encased in a metal jacket that didn't allow her to move.

She tried, inside herself, to find something to cling to: a thing to look forward to, a handhold for climbing out. But all she could see was the cottage floating away into the mountains. Her hands got clammy. A tower of panic rising in her throat.

That first day alone she did absolutely nothing except go out to pick up the girls and buy fried chicken for dinner. She told David that she'd been working on drawers, wanted everything done from the inside out. She was a good liar. She would do the big boxes last, she told them. Margaret slammed the door on her new room and unpacked her own things. Ruth couldn't find clean clothes, so Grace washed the things she had worn that day, and Ruth cried over having to wear the same outfit again. "You're in fourth grade, Ruthie," she had said. "Next year you can worry about wearing the same outfit twice." But Ruthie had whined and complained until David came home and read *Harry Potter* with her.

Grace wasn't exactly jealous of David's relationship with the girls, but she noticed how he and Ruth could go on at length about details of wizardry and how Margaret came to him with respectful questions about science. They saved their miseries and disappointments and demands for Grace. They'd be better people without me, she thought. But she stopped herself. Grace didn't go in that direction. That was too much like *her*, she would never be like *her*.

The second day alone, Tuesday, she managed to unpack Ruth's clothes before the paralysis set in. This means I'm getting better, she thought. Today I'll be okay. But except for Ruth's clothes, she did nothing but look out the window and take a long nap. That night, she could tell that David knew something was going on. David asked was she okay, did she need to take something. She kept smiling and saying she was fine, don't worry. Keeping her smile out there and her lies about what she had accomplished ("It looks like nothing now but it's going to be like magic suddenly everything in its place").

The third day, Wednesday, she walked from room to room and told herself, I'm feeling better, I can walk from room to room. But when she got to the dining room with the fish tank bubbling but the new table and chairs all covered with boxes, she thought: I'm having a breakdown.

And wondered, Was this what it felt like to her mother when she started to go under?

She pushed herself into the kitchen and chose a box in the center of the floor between the stainless-steel stove and the work island, and pulled it open, and stared at smaller containers. She wasn't hearing voices, she had never heard voices!—but everything else was wrong. She had thought she was happy, and instead, all the while, she had been tiptoeing on a tiny crust over a heaving volcano. She thought the only thing supporting her had been the old cottage. She was like the ivy that grew up the side of it: if you pulled its tiny ivy feet off the shingles, it collapsed in a heap.

She remembered watching herself all the time Ruthie was an infant, taking her own mental temperature—was she thinking of killing the baby? And answering herself, no not yet. No voices telling her to kill. She had, however, without any instructions from voices, considered killing herself.

She had come out of it that last time because the woman next door with the bright eyes and dark hairs on her upper lip had grandchildren who babysat Margaret and Baby Ruth. Grace had gone out to lunch with her new friend Fredda Crayton the realtor who had lived her whole life in Kingfield. Fredda made her come to a book discussion group even when she hadn't read the book. She came out of it because of good people and because she went to Margaret's nursery school and helped out once a week, and because the cottage had been small and cozy with its untidy backyard and front porch built right up to the sidewalk, its cut-out decorated eaves and corners, the old-fashioned clematis and blue hydrangea—everything the opposite of this barren yellow mud stretching before her now, exposed to the elements and the skeletons of other new houses.

The phone rang, and she almost didn't answer it. Then she couldn't find it, and when she did find it, hidden behind a box, it stopped ringing.

It rang again.

It was Dinah, and Grace closed her eyes in relief. It was a bad connection, but that was typical, Dinah always had a cheap cell phone with bad service.

"Grace!" she shouted. "It's me!"

"Are you okay?"

"We're okay! How are you? How was the move? You got to keep your same phone number!"

Grace closed her eyes, narrowed everything down to Dinah's voice. It was cheerful, but also too high-pitched. Something was wrong. She opened her eyes again. "You sound funny."

"Everyone's fine. How's the new house? Are you unpacked yet?"

Instead of saying, I'm having a breakdown, or trying to lie, Grace complained. "The deck isn't quite finished, and the convection oven doesn't work. We think it's the wiring. And the new furniture hasn't come, except the dining-room stuff. It's a mess."

Actually, telling it to Dinah did make her feel better.

Dinah said in the same high-pitched voice, "We're thinking about moving too."

"Where? Closer to us?"

There was a silence, as if Dinah had been cut off, then "Well, to tell you the truth, it's all up in the air. But we were thinking about coming down to visit."

"You and the babies?"

"All of us. Ray got some kind of crazy job offer, or maybe it's a business proposition, down in West Virginia somewhere. It's not totally clear, you know how vague he is about business. But it's a job with a ministry of some kind, in the eastern mountains, and, they're offering a house with the job, and we have to come down and take a look."

"That sounds great," said Grace, but something in Dinah's voice said that Dinah didn't think so.

"I thought we could stop and visit—"

The connection was wavering.

"When, Dinah? When are you coming?"

"Soon," said Dinah. "I'll tell you when I know. It would be all of us, Grace—I know there are a lot of us."

Grace said, "Of course, of course," the connection broke, came back, broke again.

Immediately, Grace felt a surge of excitement: something to look forward to. Dinah and Aleda and all of them! And with the little surge of hope, something happened inside her. She knew what she wanted. She wanted Dinah nearby, of course, but she always wanted Dinah.

But what she really wanted—it was suddenly perfectly clear—what she really wanted was the cottage back.

As she talked to Dinah, her eyes had fallen idly on the old trunk, that relic of their childhood. It had been in the bedroom closet in the cottage, and now it was lined up with the cardboard boxes along the dining-room wall, the oldest, most beat-up thing in sight. Dark green fiberboard, gouges in the panels, the lock stuffed with tissue because there had never been a key. The trunk where they used to store their safe houses and their emergency clean underwear if they had to run away or move.

Grace kicked aside a plastic bag of throw pillows and knelt in front of the trunk. A sigh ran through her body, a release of tension, the way she felt when she first smelled Dinah after a long absence. She opened it, shoved aside the stuffed animals, the coloring books, the loose crayons. She slid her hand along the back wall of the trunk to the one spot where the lining was tight instead of loose.

Where she had, many years ago, concealed what turned out to be $25,000 in cash.

CHAPTER 8

R ichie read *The Turner Diaries* by William Luther Pierce when he was a teenager in the early 1980s. His favorite author at the time had been Ayn Rand, and nothing in *The Turner Diaries* changed that, but he liked any story with ideas. He was, however, never interested in joining someone else's club. It had been business that brought him to William Pierce's compound in the mountains of Pocahontas County, West Virginia. Richie had been interested in investing some of the money his parents left him, and the most successful of his enterprises so far had been marijuana fields in the backwoods of West Virginia. Richie had wanted to buy more property, and, as it happened, the author of *The Turner Diaries* and founder of the National Alliance had land to sell. It had only been an afternoon, and what he took away, aside from some new acreage, was the desire to have a compound of his own, built to his own specifications, the way Pierce did.

Pierce himself was a disappointment. He said little and let his wife and assistants carry the conversation, but once or twice made short speeches with no relation to the topic under discussion. The man looked like a Midwestern banker, although at one time he had had thousands of members in his organization, a radio station, and a record company. It was all dwindling away when Richie met him, which is why he was selling property. The question in Richie's mind that afternoon was whether or not Pierce believed what he spewed, or pretended to believe it, and was there a difference? Pierce had been distant and distracted (and, as it turned out, dying of cancer). Richie wondered what would happen if Pierce announced to his followers that he had changed directions. If he told his thugs to become Christian integrationists or to commit mass suicide like Jim Jones did in Jonestown. Richie thought that might be the ultimate high, to change the path of thousands of people just because you could.

But Pierce was dead less than a year later, and Richie made his own medical discovery that would shape the rest of his life. His scope was drastically narrowed by the future of his body. Everything he had toyed with fell away except making enough money to have exactly what he needed to live as well as possible as long as possible. His full-time job—once he got over rage and denial and more rage—was organizing his life. He assembled a staff, built Mountain Dome, created what he needed to live with this final legacy from his father—an extremely unusual, early-onset, genetic variety of amyotrophic lateral sclerosis. He imagined that his father would have been pleased with this final proof of parentage.

Richie's worst times were when he was confronted by the specter of his father's long death in his vast bed in his vast bedroom snarling words no one could make out.

But mostly he focused on his project, a builder like Howard Roark in *The Fountainhead*. His wife hated the isolation at Mountain Dome and left after five months. Good riddance to wives, thought Richie. He had the Israeli commando brothers do his security. He built a helicopter pad and put the top neurologist in DC on retainer. He sold off the last of his marijuana interests and put organic vegetables in his greenhouses. He made mistakes along the way, primarily the wives, but the physical plant, Mountain Dome itself—his stronghold, his redoubt—was more than satisfactory.

The final stage, peopling Mountain Dome with the caregivers he wanted, would be more delicate. His plan was meticulous and time-consuming. He set aside long sessions to think it through, to look for flaws and prepare alternative approaches if problems developed. He was increasingly confident. The capstone to the structure would be bringing Dinah to Mountain Dome.

CHAPTER 9

The first time Grace knew she was good at lying was when she started taking the money that ended up in the trunk. At first, she moved a few twenties to the back lining just so she'd always have some available if she needed it. No one was supposed to go in Grace's bedroom except Dinah, but they did. They would walk in, not even knocking, Wolf usually, and grab handfuls of the loose cash to buy beer. Wolf would try to talk to Grace, who was always studying. They were expanding, he said, doing business with bigger guys. He implied it was dangerous. More cash came in, was dumped carelessly in the trunk. Grace transferred larger amounts to the lining, went to the bank and changed twenties for hundred-dollar bills.

Grace never even thought of what she did as stealing. Dinah was not in good shape that year, barely holding onto her job at the copy center while she slept with boys and used too much of the product. After a while, there was so much money, Grace rubber-cemented the lining to the wall of the trunk so she could keep it sealed.

Mostly, she kept her head down and studied. A few times, she heard arguments about missing money, but they were all so sloppy at business that no one ever knew how much was supposed to be in the trunk. Once, Grace even put some of the money back in the general pile, just to prove she could. Oh we were quite a family, she thought. Dinah in her bedroom with the boys, their father drinking himself to death in front of the television, and Grace stealing her sister's drug money.

Then Dinah threw Wolf out and stopped the business, and Dylan moved in with them. They lived on the money from the floor of the trunk, plus their father's disability checks and their jobs. Rent was free and there were still gifts from Richie's mother Sharon.

After a while, Grace stopped putting money in the trunk lining. She didn't exactly forget about it, but it made her feel queasy, so she ignored it and never even counted it. She did think about it when Dinah was working on finances for her to go to college. She thought she ought to offer the money, but she wasn't even sure she wanted to go to college. She thought there was probably not enough to make a difference.

She took the trunk wherever she went, a coffee table in her first apartment, the storage closet at the rental cottage in Kingfield. She knew it was there, but left it alone.

Thursday morning, as soon as David went to the office and the girls were off to school, Grace cleared a space on the dining-room table and spread out the money. She counted it three times. She divided it into four number 10 white envelopes, and put the envelopes in the very bottom of her shoulder bag, under her wallet and keys, sat down on the floor next to the phone, and dialed Fredda Crayton.

Fredda was delighted to hear things were going so well at the new house. She wanted to know if Grace cared to go out for lunch.

Grace made her voice something she hoped could be mistaken for cheerful, "Absolutely, really soon. But, Fredda, the reason I called is actually business. There's something I need you to help me with." She took a deep breath. "I want to buy the cottage."

Fredda was silent for a second, then laughed.

"I'm serious. I want to buy it."

"You mean the cottage you just moved out of and have been complaining about for years? *That* cottage?"

"That's the one."

Everything hung on whether or not she could make it sound reasonable to Fredda. Fredda said, with just that hint of the mountains in her voice, "You must be having a really hard time getting settled, honey."

Grace closed her eyes. Not to be thought crazy, that was the main thing. Not to be thought crazy or spoiled. "Well, Fredda, it was mostly

David who complained about the cottage. He doesn't like old leaky things."

"Who does. But, Gracie, moving is the most stressful thing in life after getting a divorce, or maybe it's having a spouse die, but either way, it's stressful. I'll tell you what, I'll come over. You put on coffee, and I'll bring some of Patty's homemade muffins." Patty was Fredda's assistant, and her cousin once or twice removed. They were always talking about putting a little coffee shop into the sunporch in the front of Mountain Vista Realty. "Besides," said Fredda, "I've already got someone interested in renting the cottage."

"Good. All the more reason, if I could actually make some money off it. I wasn't thinking of moving back," she said (liar, liar, she thought), "I was thinking about the income but mostly, the main thing is, my sister needs a place to live." Fredda made a neutral noise. "You've heard me talk about my sister? Her husband is a Savage?"

"Oh, yeah, Raymond Savage. He's the one who wanted to blow up the FBI place, right?" Fredda sounded just a little less suspicious.

"Well, I think he just got caught up in all that. But, the point is, they've got five kids, and they never seem to be able to get ahead. They're thinking of moving back, and I thought, if I owned the cottage. I could rent it to her, or eventually sell it to her."

"What does David say?"

"This isn't his money, actually, it's hers and mine, and she's going to need a place to live."

"I could rent it to her instead of to the people I was thinking about," said Fredda.

She squeezed her eyes shut. No no I want to own it, she thought. "That would work. But I was hoping I—we—could own it. It's just the right place for them, Fredda."

"Seven people? Wouldn't it be small—"

Grace bulled ahead. "Ray can fix anything. They'll put in sweat equity, when they get on their feet, it will be in great shape. You should see the kinds of places they've been living in."

Fredda had another house she thought might work better.

No, no, the cottage! "Oh Fredda," (tell as much truth as possible) "I love that cottage. It's like a home to me."

Fredda was still slow to respond, and when she did, seemed to be gearing up her professional voice. "Well, it does have that charming fretwork on the porch—"

"With the clematis!"

Fredda seemed to think it over. "The people who own it, I don't have a lot to do with them. It's all direct deposit, and I haven't spoken to them in a long while. Who knows, they might be ready to sell. I could tell them that at least you know what condition it's in. They live in Maryland. I could call them next week."

Now, thought Grace, call them now. "Well, if you could look into it, Fredda, at your leisure. Only, the sooner the better. Except for my sister coming down so soon, there wouldn't be any hurry at all."

And all the while, her mind crying, Call them now! The down payment's in my bag!

"Well," said Fredda. "Okay. I have no idea what they'll say. That house has been in their family for a long time, although I don't think the owners ever lived in Cooper County themselves. You aren't going to change your mind, are you?"

"Fredda, believe me, I love that old place."

She thought it had worked. It sounded like a crisis, to buy a house so suddenly, but Fredda thought the crisis was Dinah's, not Grace's, and maybe it was. Grace paced around the house. She unpacked some linens. She broke down cardboard boxes and laid them out in the front hall so David would see she'd been working. And in fact, she did work, steadily for the next two hours, amazed by how much she accomplished. And, then, like a prize for her good behavior, Fredda called back.

"You aren't going to believe this," said Fredda. It appeared that the cottage owners were having an illness in the family and were more than open to getting rid of the cottage. "It's providential," said Fredda. "You know I don't go around thanking Jesus every time the car battery turns over, but this is pretty amazing. They haven't even seen the cottage in years. They know it needs work, and I don't think they have any idea what it's worth. It's a steal, Grace, if you have the money. They're asking $75,000 if it's cash."

"I have $25,000 cash," said Grace.

"They want the whole thing. I guess you could get a mortgage."

Too complicated. Too difficult. David would be involved. She had CDs in just her name, from when she was teaching and on her own.

David had said just to keep them for the girls' education. "At the bank," she said. "I have $60,000 in CDs. It's just mine." Then she added, "Ours, I should say. Mine and my sister's together."

There was a trip to the bank, with Fredda. Handing over all the money, out of her hands. There would be paperwork and faxes. Blah blah blah. She had to wait, of course, let Fredda do it. This was where small towns worked best—Fredda would take care of the details, everyone trusted everyone.

When it was over, Grace went out for groceries, feeling euphoric and light. She came back and unpacked dishes and pans, she set the table hours ahead and made a salad, prepared turkey burgers with salsa and whole-wheat buns.

It was the best evening since they had moved, and she had a vague feeling it was the best in much longer than that. She felt David and the girls watching her out of the corner of their eyes, but she knew she was passing inspection with them as she had with Fredda. She asked questions about their days, and she said that Dinah had called and might be coming for a visit. Ruthie was thrilled, David didn't seem as disturbed as she'd feared, but it turned out he had something of his own to tell. He had made a diagnosis, figured out something the specialists had missed. He had been sure yesterday, but got confirmation today.

Margaret and Ruthie listened attentively, everyone on good behavior, and Margaret asked some questions about what you had to major in in college to become a doctor, and so then Ruth said she was going to be a doctor too, and Margaret was annoyed and said she never said *she* was going to be a doctor. Blissfully normal. A circle of orderliness, a glow around the kitchen, odor of cooked meat masking the plastic and wood.

She took a shower that night, feeling for the moment separated from what was bothering her the way you sometimes sense a pain cocooned away by medication. Margaret's music came faintly through her closed door and down the hall. Ruth was supposed to be asleep. She climbed into bed. She knew David was waiting, waiting to see what was going on with her. Waiting for her weather.

She rolled toward him, and he sighed and whispered her name. She wrapped her arms around his neck and felt his face, and after that, she didn't feel much at all, but she thought David was satisfied.

CHAPTER 10

nlike Grace, Dinah had never worried about going crazy, but she did worry about what effect her past might have on her children, especially Aleda.

Dinah had come back from their time in California with a grown-up body and a need for excitement, and things developed in a bad way. She had sex with a lot of boys for a while, and some men too. She couldn't remember what was in her mind at the time, except that sex was easy and made them grateful, and she liked it too. Even Wolf, that dumb meathead, became stupidly kind after sex and gave her presents she didn't want. They were lucky they hadn't all caught STDs, let alone AIDS, thank Jesus.

It wasn't that she was afraid Aleda was going to have sex. In fact, she longed for a safe lover for Aleda, for an opportunity for Aleda to meet a Christian boy and marry early and enjoy sex and babies in health and safety. She prayed about it with Ray, how to handle Aleda's adolescence. Ray was confident it would all work out, but Aleda was at the age when your body speaks loudest, when all you want is thrills. She wanted to tell Aleda, Your body is telling you to do things you *should* do, but not yet and not with the wrong people. She wanted to tell her to wait for the right man because having babies with the right man was the best thing in the world.

She sometimes referred to Aleda's father as her first husband, even though they never married. He was delightful and gentle whether he was high or sober. He used to draw on every surface, wrapping paper, menus, walls, sidewalks, stones. He would fill an entire sheet of paper and turn it around as if there were no top or bottom: snakes and flowering vines, faces and flaming swords. He had an idea to travel the world like Johnny Appleseed, leaving art in public places.

But her father had been ill and Grace saying she was going to stay home from college to help with the baby, and Dylan was making no move to get a job. Dinah told Dylan she couldn't take care of everyone. It took a while for him to believe that she meant it, and then another long while of his sadness and promising to get a job, and then a long time after that before he actually left.

When their father died, it left a bigger hole than she expected, and in the end, she let Grace take off that year and get a job, and help with Aleda, but she made her go back to college after that. There was a little insurance money from their father, and they lived on that for a while, and when Grace went back to college, Dinah started going to churches, and people helped her, and eventually there was Raymond.

Having babies was the best feeling she had ever known, to hold her children against her chest. It closed the circle, filled the space between her and the world. She loved all her babies, her living ones and her angel babies, who still came to her as she was falling asleep, after love with Raymond, when her body was spread out richly around her, merged with the bed, the walls, the tree outside the window. Sometimes they came to comfort her when troubles lined up, when she was feeling hard toward Raymond.

Why did he want to pull up stakes again and chase after this crazy job offer?

All the while, she was figuring out what to take, what to throw out, what to decide later. Five years' worth of living to squeeze into the van. Sarah and Isaac barely remembered any other place and this was Jacob and Benjie's only home.

It was the home of the angel babies, too, of course, who came after Sarah and Isaac and before Jacob and Benjie.

Amos, Rebecca, and Samuel. Amos and Rebecca had been called miscarriages, but Samuel had lived and died in an incubator, and he had clasped her finger once.

Dinah listed all her children in her mind, the lost ones and the living: Aleda, Sarah and Isaac, Amos, Rebecca, Samuel, Jacob, and Benjamin. I had eight babies, she liked to say, not five. I had eight babies. Eight tiny scrunch noses, squeezed-shut eyes, little sucking flower lips. Tiny fingers clasping and unclasping to the rhythm of her heartbeat. She yearned for them all, and wanted more.

Sometimes she mourned the babyhood of the ones who lived almost as much as the lives of the ones who died. Especially Aleda, the one who was gold instead of pink. Who was most emphatically not a baby anymore. Who was now physically capable of having babies herself.

Dinah had been most alive when she had babies. It was so much harder to keep them safe as they got older. Babies she knew how to care for, seemed to have known naturally, from the first time they put her sister on her lap and she was herself only Jacob's age. She had always known that babies were the best thing, the most physically satisfying and morally clear thing in the world. You hugged them and fed them, you loved them and cleaned them. You made them laugh and they made you laugh. You formed your body in a protective arc around them and made them a safe place.

Her arms and breasts did not call out to the big children the way they did to Jacob and Benjie and the angel babies. She prayed to be as clear-sighted with Aleda as with baby Benjamin, but she found herself impatient with Aleda and her talk about high school.

The first miscarriage had been very soon after she and Raymond resumed relations after the twins were born, and she hadn't known what was going on, had flushed Amos away, and still had nightmares in which she went to the toilet and one child after another was sucked to oblivion. Sometimes she woke in a sweat and had to check each bed to make sure the remaining ones were still alive.

The doctor told her that was her body rejecting pregnancy so soon. She said it wasn't a pregnancy, it was Amos.

She knew what was happening when the cramps and blood came and then Rebecca. This time she stayed away from the toilet and took the baby to the hospital in towels and plastic bags. Raymond had a job as a night watchman then, so after she wrapped up Rebecca she had to wake Aleda and the twins and take them all to the hospital. The doctor told her the fetus was malformed, and this was nature's way of preserving only the healthy.

"It was a girl, wasn't it?" she said.

The doctor said it was female.

"Rebecca," said Dinah. "Her name is Rebecca, and it is God's will not nature."

The doctor had walked away, but the nurse said, "That's okay, honey, I named the ones I lost too."

The doctor came back and told her, "You have three beautiful children, and you're not even thirty. And the record here says this is your second miscarriage this year. Why don't you give your body a rest? Isn't three enough?"

"No," Dinah had said. "Three is not enough. The Lord gives and the Lord takes away. Blessed be the name of the Lord."

The nurse, who was as black as King Solomon, raised her hands and said, "Yes, Jesus!"

The doctor scowled at both of them, and they put Dinah in a twilight sleep while he cleaned her out. She didn't trust the doctor, drifted under saying to the nurse, "Don't let him tie my tubes, don't let him cut anything out."

They sent her home with napkins for the bleeding and some antibiotics.

It was two more years before Samuel, long enough that she worried the doctor really had done something without telling her. But then she got pregnant, and Samuel was born at home, and very easily, because he was so small, but limp and blue, so they all went to the emergency room again, and little Samuel was whisked to the incubators and stuffed with breathing tubes and saline solution and drug drips, and once they had examined Dinah and given her stitches she didn't want, she was finally allowed to go to him, and that was when he grabbed her finger as if he didn't want to let go. She stayed with him for three days, never left him except when the doctor sent her to a social worker. The social worker was from India and had that lilting way of speaking that sounded at once educated and condescending. It made Dinah want to say, Listen here, lady, I found my sister a scholarship to college, and I found Jesus, so who are you to look down?

The social worker said, "Mrs. Savage, you have three children, two miscarriages, and now this premature birth."

"I want," said Dinah, "as many babies as I can bear. It is the only thing you can be sure of." She had meant to say she wanted as many as God willed her to have, but she said that instead.

The next baby was Jacob who was not so easy to get out, but that was because he was big headed and thick bodied, never in a hurry, and the healthiest, hungriest baby she ever had. Of all her children, the one most like Raymond: light in color, a little short of hair, big and strong.

She was half-afraid Raymond would love him more than the others, but Raymond loved without prejudice, like God, she thought. He shed his smiles equally on the skinny brown-haired twins and little Benjamin when he came along, and Aleda who was not even his own.

Dinah's challenge was going to be when there weren't babies anymore.

She knew exactly what the littlest ones were going to need for this trip. Benjie would need diapers and Dinah's breasts. Jacob would want his special blanket and his stuffed animals. And snacks. Plenty of snacks. She had already warned Sarah and Isaac to start thinking about which books, which board games. She was probably asking them too soon, putting some of her anxiety on them. Isaac-who-insisted-on-being-called-Zack frowned and stated that he only needed his handheld electronic game, carefully chosen by Dinah for no guns or fighting. Sarah wanted to know how many bags of fabric swatches and art supplies she could take. Aleda, though, seemed perfectly undisturbed. "When it's time to pack, Mom," she said, "Just give me a box so I know how much space I have, and I'll decide then."

Of course Aleda was old enough to make her own decisions about what to take, but Dinah didn't like it. She watched Aleda out of the corner of her eyes, feeling there was something not right. It would have been so much easier if they'd had a house at the other end of the journey instead of this great dim abyss of the mysterious church on a mountain, or was it a lighthouse, or maybe a radio tower. Still, she would have everything of value with her in the van, including the three lost angel babies deep inside her chest.

CHAPTER 11

Richie checked and rechecked the little house where Dinah and her family would live. Her husband had taken the bait, was coming for the interview, and now there was the waiting, the obsessive flipping of light switches and testing the thermostat. It had to be so perfect she couldn't say no. He tried to imagine Dinah breaking out in a smile. *It's wonderful, Richie!*

He also imagined her hand on his forehead.

Shhh, Richie, she would say, *everything's going to be all right.*

Not it isn't, he'd say. *I'm going to die horribly.*

I'll hold you, she would say.

He didn't want the cottage oppressively hot, but certainly not damp and chilly. One of the new evergreens outside looked dead, so he called the greenhouse and told them to replace it. They said they didn't have another quite the same size, so he told them to replant the others so it didn't look like anything was missing.

Back at the big house, he went to Enrique in the kitchen and talked about treats for children. Enrique suggested cupcakes with *Sesame Street* faces. Richie said fine, but make cookies too, just to be sure. And lots of fresh fruit in case they weren't allowed to eat sweets. Hot dogs for lunch maybe? Enrique was insulted. He knew how to prepare meals children would like, he said.

Then Richie went to the safe room and scanned the surveillance monitors. The gardeners were already digging up the dead evergreen at the cottage. Enrique was sautéing something. Poke's nephew was in there too with a plate, always eating, that boy. Enrique's wife Maria changing the sheets in Richie's bedroom. He mostly slept in the safe room these days, preferring the compactness of everything.

He couldn't find Poke and Bobby Mack at first, but one of the perimeter cameras had them sitting in the back of one of the trucks, talking. Smoking too, which they weren't permitted to do in or near the main house. He wished he could hear them, but there were no microphones that far out. He thought about calling Poke's cell phone to give him a jolt: Big Brother is watching you. It wasn't that he particularly did or did not trust them. He knew they stole a little now and then, but he was confident they weren't creative enough to do anything big.

He had a necklace for Dinah in the safe to the left of the computer and house monitors. He rarely bothered to lock the safe, because the safe room itself was more secure than any safe, and he didn't keep anything irreplaceable there anyhow: cash, and extra cash just before payroll. His best watches—the Patek Philippe, the Ulysse Nardin chronograph. The pearls.

He thought she wouldn't accept the pearls, but there was something about the touch of them, a neutral temperature, the attractive spherical shape of each one. He imagined laying them around her neck, fastening them, his fingers on both the pearls and the skin at once.

He rolled the chair to the left of the safe, to the half wall of corkboard where he kept his snapshots. The newest ones had been shot with telephoto lenses by the per diem operatives: Dinah carrying a baby into the house, Dinah standing next to her tan-skinned daughter, Dylan's half-black kid with the weird light-colored eyes like Dylan.

But he was most attached to the old pictures, the ones that went with his memories: Dinah, Grace, and him as little kids dressed up for Halloween. He was a pirate, Grace a princess, Dinah a gypsy. There was a snapshot of him and his mother. He was seven or eight in that one, wearing one of the ridiculous outfits she spent large bucks to buy for him: khaki pants and a shirt with plaid trim to match an absurd faux-Scottish cap. The kind of clothes that assured he would get maximum bullying. What had she been thinking. He had one other picture of his mother on the corkboard, and that was at the big Christmas party just after his father died. In that photo, his mother was extending a flute of champagne toward the photographer and wore a Santa hat, dress cut deep between her big tits. That party had been the first time he saw Dinah and Grace after they came back from California.

He looked at his favorite picture last. This one was Dinah alone, and he had taken it himself. She was asleep, curled on her bed, hands flat together. Hair spread out, face relaxed, tee shirt, breasts. They had all been high, as they were most of the time, hanging out at the carriage house. They usually hung out in her bedroom, with the music, the posters. Her father in the living room, ostensibly the chaperone. He took the picture one evening in the spring when he was on break from school. He had come over to Dinah's with a shopping bag of stuff, music, his new camera, joints in foil, a bottle of Southern Comfort. He found her and Dylan and Wolf in her bedroom. He offered to share what he had, and they did some uppers and then were smoking grass to mellow out, sipping Southern Comfort.

After a while Dinah was lying on her side on the bed, the others on the floor, propped on pillows. Grace stopped by, on her way out, to the library no doubt. She seemed glad to see Richie, but Dinah made her leave because Dinah had this big game going on that Grace didn't know about the endless partying. Everyone, even Wolf, pretended. Dinah had made that congenitally stupid oaf Wolf more of a player than he would have been alone, and she kept Dylan semioperational far beyond his allotted time.

That day, desperately wanting to make an impact on her, somehow, Richie suggested a game.

"Fuck that," said Wolf.

"What kind of game?" said Dylan.

"Everyone tells the worst thing they can think of."

"That's a game?" said Wolf. "What kind of game is that?"

Dylan answered first. "The worst thing would be not to be able to do art. And to be stuck inside. Never go outside."

"Like prison," said Wolf.

"Yes," said Dylan. "I'd die if I couldn't be where the sky was overhead."

Well, that worked out for him, didn't it? thought Richie.

"Shit," said Wolf. "What kind of shit is that. Fuck that." Good old Wolf, always a master of language.

Dinah's eyes were closed, but she said, "My worst thing would be having something bad happen to Grace."

Richie remembered being impressed that Dinah and Dylan had both known exactly what they feared most. He asked Wolf for his.

Wolf tried first to get a laugh. "Dropping the soap in the locker room," he said. "You know, having to bend over? In the locker room?"

"We get it," said Dinah. "But what, really?"

"Being an old fart nobody respects?"

And then they all were silent, because that was true too, and then Dinah said, "What about you, Richie?"

He must have known he wanted her to know, or he wouldn't have started the game. "Never seeing you again."

"Never seeing who again?" said Wolf.

Dinah opened her eyes. "Poor Richie," she said.

That's how it had been: when she finally noticed him, she would be devastatingly, painfully kind. That time, he remembered, she made Dylan move so that Richie could sit on the floor next to the bed, and she laid her hand on his forehead, as if he had a fever.

That was it, now he knew. It was that hand on his forehead that he imagined sometimes.

After a while she seemed to go to sleep, with her hand still cupped over his skull. Richie closed his eyes too, but only halfway. Dylan and Wolf started whispering and glancing at him, and he realized they were going to take something from his bag, and they did, they pulled out all the joints. He could have said, Hey, stop it, or, Fine, go sell it, bring me my 60 percent. But he wanted them to go so he could be alone in the room with Dinah, listening to their feet retreating, to the door closing.

And after a while, when it was so quiet, and no one was there, he took her hand off his head and held it and kissed it. Then he laid it beside her, and took the picture of her. And sat on the bed. "Dinah," he whispered, "I meant it, what I said."

She stirred and opened her arms, and he became alert and thought it was an invitation, was it an invitation? Was she saying, Don't be alone, let me comfort you? He moved himself horizontal, everything stiff and stiffening. She seemed to go back to sleep. He could smell the

Southern Comfort on her breath. He began to touch all the soft parts of her body, her breasts, her throat, and finally, like someone getting home very late at night, he had let himself in as quietly as he could, trying not to disturb her.

He sometimes wondered if she was awake, aware at all. If she knew, if she remembered. But more often, he remembered the deep sleep afterward, wrapped up with her, pressed against her chest, a deep dreamless nourishing sleep, the safest he had ever felt in his whole life.

He never slept long anymore. The misfiring nerves kept him semi-alert and semiexhausted. For an instant he allowed himself to lay his forehead against the photo and even that made him quieter, safer. She'll come, he thought. She'll come to me.

CHAPTER 12

The year they came back from California, Grace prayed for snow. Grace's efforts at praying rarely worked out, but this time, she got what she wanted. Not a lot of snow, but enough to make pools of white around the evergreen bushes at the big house. Enough to find a drift at the side of the carriage house clean enough for snow ice cream. Grace was twelve, but she clung to the delight of things they had done before they went away. She made a family of tiny paper dolls. She made safe houses for them.

Dinah, though, was more interested in Sharon Lock's Christmas party. The Christmas party had been the excuse for coming back. Mr. Lock died, and Sharon called to say she needed them, meaning their father of course. The carriage house was waiting for them, and whatever had happened between their father and Sharon was forgiven. Everything, like registering for school and hunting for a job, was put off till after the party.

Sharon had chores for everyone, decorating wreaths, addressing envelopes, choosing a caterer, picking wines and champagne. As it turned out, helping Sharon would be their father's job for the next several years. He tried to sell insurance for a while, but there was so much to do for Sharon, the legal details of the estate, then spending money—repairing the big house, planning and accompanying her when she needed an escort. It was, he said, a full-time job.

During those first weeks back, Grace figured their father and Sharon would get married, and Richie would come back from school, and they'd all live happily ever after as one family. Dinah, however, was skeptical. Even if they do get married, Dinah said, they'll spend all their time on cruises. We can't depend on them.

Their dad often slept over at the big house. If the carriage house got creaky, Grace called Dinah to come into her bed. They spent time at the big house, too, eating takeout while their dad and Sharon had drinks and Sharon talked about what she called the first real goddamn party of her whole life because the cheapskate—pardon me—the dear departed would never let her invite anyone over.

"Sharon was always a good sport," Dinah used to say, when they were grown. "She always wanted one of us to marry Richie."

It had been the Saturday morning a week before the party. Sharon showed up at the carriage house at 7:30 a.m. wearing a purple velour running suit and carrying a shopping bag with eggs and orange juice and champagne. Grace and Dinah were still in their nightgowns, and their father had not, apparently, undressed before going to bed. He always looked neat, though. Grace remembered khaki pants and soft flannel shirts. New flannel shirts Sharon had bought him when they got back with their Southern California clothes.

Sharon brought in clouds of cold air. She said she had awakened before dawn and started cleaning out her clothes closet, and she'd found some great things for the girls to wear for the party. Their father made mimosas for him and Sharon and coffee with his special French press that was the one thing he never forgot to pack when they moved. Sharon had planned scrambled eggs and English muffins, but she'd forgotten the muffins, so Dinah used the eggs for her special butter-batter pancakes, and Sharon did a tour of the carriage house and said she was going to fix up the leaks, just as soon as the lazy bastard carpenters finished with the big house.

They ate pancakes with too much syrup, and Sharon said the only thing missing was her darling Richie.

"He's going to love how beautiful you girls have become," she said. "I've got it all worked out, kids. As soon as the rest of the money comes through, we're going to put in a swimming pool and a workout room and we'll have a big staff and parties every week, and maybe you'll all move over to the big house, god knows there's plenty of room—and one of you girls will marry Richie, and we'll have the biggest wedding ever."

"Which one of us?" asked Grace, immediately embarrassed, knowing she sounded childish.

"It's a little soon to marry them off, don't you think?" said their father, smiling.

Sharon got out of her chair, pressed her stomach against the back of his chair and hugged him from behind, resting her breasts on his head for a moment. "It's never too early for love," she said.

Then she dumped out the shopping bags of clothes, and Dinah picked a wine-red velvet dress that fell to ballet length on her. It had elastic at the neck and could be pulled off shoulder. Then there was a metallic sweater that was supposed to be an oversized top for Sharon, but it looked great as a dress on Grace once Sharon cut out the shoulder pads. That morning was a bubble of happiness in Grace's memory.

Richie didn't come home till the night of the party. Grace and Dinah had spent the day adding tinsel and jingle bells to the flower arrangements. The caterer brought two bartenders and four waiters, two boys and two girls, and they did most of the set up. Sharon rearranged things, and the waiters taught Grace and Dinah how to make fancy napkin folds.

Then they went home to dress. Their father made Dinah wear his blazer to cover her bare shoulders. Grace's metallic mini and silver tights covered a lot more of her, but she felt sexy anyhow, as if this were the beginning of being a teenager.

They walked between patches of snow, around to the front door where there was an outrageously large wreath of evergreens with white lights. There were cars parked in the driveway and on the street, and they all three looked up at the lights and peered at the bustle through the windows, heard Sharon's shriek of laughter from inside.

Their father smiled gently and said, "Poor Sharon." He was always gentle and admiring of Sharon when they were together, but sometimes, when they were away from her, he seemed condescending. "She takes her party so seriously."

He gestured for Dinah and Grace to go up ahead of him. Dinah gave him back his jacket and led the way in naked-shouldered glory.

The unfinished wing of the house was closed off, the part where Mr. Lock had stayed and Richie had his trains. The part that was open had fresh paint and refinished mahogany and a recarpeted main stairway. The girls had been in the house just an hour before, but it was all different once the party began—the waiters had put on red cummerbunds, the glittering balls hanging from the chandeliers, the tables of food, and in the second parlor an enormous Christmas tree.

In the first parlor was a round table sprinkled with silver confetti and loaded with fruit and cheese and olives and stuffed grape leaves and dips. The bar was in there too, and waiters were walking around offering trays of hot-cheese pastries and glasses of champagne.

Their father selected two flutes of champagne and advanced toward Sharon, visible in the dining room wearing a Santa hat and a lot of gold jewelry. She was surrounded by friends, but saw him immediately and reached out to take a glass, even though she already had one in her other hand. She kissed him and drew him into her circle.

Dinah and Grace stood by the food table. Tiny miniature quiches came by and they each took a couple.

"We should get plates," said Dinah, and then, "I'm going to drink one of those glasses of champagne later."

"You better not!" said Grace.

Dinah pointed at one of the waiters. "I'm going to tell him my father asked for one. But not you, Gracie. You haven't reached puberty yet."

Grace was about to argue, but at that moment Richie Lock appeared. It was unmistakably Richie, although Grace wasn't absolutely sure how she knew because he looked so different. He was no longer fat, but he still duckwalked. He had grown his hair long in a sort of floppy, slightly greasy pageboy, and he was wearing a gray velvet smoking jacket with a fleur-de-lis pattern shaved into the nap. No glasses, but it turned out he had a pair in the pocket of the smoking jacket.

He stopped face-to-face with Dinah and said without preamble, "Come. I have something to show you," and turned on his heel.

Grace and Dinah exchanged glances, but followed, of course, to the staircase, up one flight, then half a floor more, where he stopped on a broad landing with a window seat.

Richie raised his left hand in a gesture that meant halt. He looked up and down as if to make sure they were alone, and then he turned around and kissed Dinah.

His hand was already up, and he laid it on Dinah's right shoulder and pressed his mouth into hers. He was taller than Dinah now. She had stopped growing at exactly five foot one.

Grace felt a giggle rise out of her stomach.

Dinah pulled back. "What was that supposed to be?"

Color rose to Richie's cheeks, but his expression remained the same. He took out his glasses. "I've been wanting to do that for a long time."

Dinah crossed her bare arms over her chest, and said, "Well, I haven't! We don't even know you anymore, Richie Lock, so you had better not try that again!"

"You look stunning," he said to Dinah.

Dinah scowled. "What about Grace?"

He didn't even look. "Her too."

Grace crossed her arms across her chest just as Dinah had done. Her breasts had only started to get puffy, and she hadn't had her period yet, but she wanted to be like Dinah.

"I mean it, Richie," said Dinah in her rich deep voice, always deeper than other children's. "I don't know what's gotten into you, but I don't want any nonsense and not toward Grace either. Especially not toward Grace."

Richie said, "Not nonsense, it's part of my strategy. I plan things now. I've been planning to do that for a long time."

"Planning to *kiss* me?"

"I feel," he gazed out the window into the dark, "that we are inextricably linked."

"Well I don't. I haven't given you one thought since we moved away."

Grace said, "We've been in Los Angeles for *years*. We lived in Santa Monica and Venice Beach."

Richard turned his eyes on Grace for a moment, then pulled a book out of his pocket and sat on the narrow wooden window seat. "Have either of you read this?" He held it up so they could see the title, *The Virtue of Selfishness*. "It's a summary of Ayn Rand's philosophy." He opened to a page with a dog-ear and read: "No philosopher has ever given a rational, objectively demonstrable, scientific answer to *why* man needs a code of values."

"Oh my god, Richie," said Dinah, "Someone turned your switch to On tonight."

"You turn me on."

"Oh shut up."

"In other words," said Richie, "everything is validated by logic and only by logic, and everything starts with self-interest. I've made this the basis of my personal strategy in the world."

Dinah said, "Is that what they teach you at that prep school where your mother sends you? Because it sounds to me like an excuse to do whatever you feel like."

"Not an excuse, but a philosophy for strong men. I've started reading Nietzsche too." He put the book back in his pocket. "Here's what they teach at Perthie." He scooted to one side and opened a hinged section of the window seat. He pulled out a canvas bag, closed the seat again, and spilled out the contents on the lid. There were aluminum-foil packets, prescription containers, and an old person's plastic vitamin organizer with units for each day of the week. "School is *drek*." he said. "That's Yiddish for shit. At one time I was thinking of becoming Jewish because Jews are like the ultimate outsiders and very smart, but they have way too many rules, and they're also into groupthink. If you're an objectivist you can't be following someone else's rules." He snapped open the pill organizer, showing different pills in each section, all colors—dark purple and banana-colored tablets, tiny pink and white and chartreuse pills. Then he unrolled the aluminum foil quickly and in it were thin cigarettes, twisted at the ends.

Grace turned her eyes to Dinah to see how to react. Dinah sat down on the other side of the display and said very calmly, "You do drugs, Richie?"

He wiggled his butt a little on the seat. "Not so much personally. I'm an entrepreneur. People want to buy this stuff, so I sell it. It's in my self-interest."

Grace said, "People get hooked on drugs!" Dinah and Richie ignored her.

Dinah said, "You convince people at your school to buy this stuff?"

"Are you kidding? Convince? No one needs convincing. I never even heard of drugs till I went to Perthie. The guys at school have been doing drugs since they were in kindergarten. They learned this stuff at their mothers' breasts. I'm in it for the money."

"Can you make a lot of money selling this stuff? What about getting caught?"

"Nobody gets caught. Half the kids at Perthie have dads who are lawyers."

Grace was disturbed by how Dinah wasn't telling him to stop being a drug dealer. She said, "We could turn you in to the police, you know!"

Dinah frowned, and Richie's glasses glinted so you couldn't see his eyes at all. He said to Grace, "Would you? Would you turn me in?"

"I might."

Dinah said, "Of course she wouldn't. Gracie, you don't want to use this stuff, but it doesn't mean you turn in your friends to the police. So what are these anyhow?"

Richie became more natural. With his glasses on, he looked more like his old self. "I try to keep a little of everything on hand," he said. "Bennies, Georgia home boy, special K, ludes. I got blotter, microdots, roofies, and tons of blunts. General merchandise." He had always been Mr. Encyclopedia, the one you turned to if you needed state capitals and which Star Wars movie first had Boba Fett. "And this," he said, "is just my traveling kit. I have more at school. Anything I don't have, I can get."

Dinah gazed at him a long time. "You're doing something dangerous, you know. Probably stupid."

He got agitated, pushed his glasses up on his forehead. "That's where you're wrong! I know what I'm doing!" His voice rose. "I studied this for a long time! I watched what the guys were doing, and who was doing what, and how much they were paying for it and who got drugged out and why they got caught—"

"You don't need the money," said Dinah. "You're inheriting all the money you could want from your father. Sharon said so."

"I consider myself on my own. I don't have access to that money, and she has no idea if she can afford all this champagne and shit—she doesn't have the cash to pay my next semester school bill! I don't need her or his money either—I'm going to be like John Galt—he's the hero of objectivism. From *Atlas Shrugged*. This stuff, this—candy!—it's just"—he waved his hand over the drugs—"this is just a means to the end. I'm going to build an empire, do big things. I'm going to do such big things that the little people will never even know that it's me doing them."

Grace kept watching Dinah for the signal to march out and leave Richie alone with his illicit drugs, but Dinah seemed more interested than she should have been.

Richard closed up his little store, except for the foil-wrapped ciga-rettes he put in his pocket. That's weed, Grace thought. People used to smoke it all the time at the beach.

"For later," he said. "If we need to smooth out the edges."

"Not we," said Dinah. "You."

Richie slipped the rest of it back into the canvas bag, back in the window seat. "Objectivism has changed me," he said. "I always imagined I would step in front of a bullet, give my life for you. But don't expect me to take a bullet for you now. That kind of altruism isn't who I am anymore."

"Nobody asked you," said Grace. "That's stupid. Isn't that stupid, Dinah?"

"I don't believe in giving my life for someone else now," he said.

Grace said, "Well I would. I would"—she really liked the phrase— "take a bullet for Dinah!"

"Oh stop it," said Dinah. "Both of you. This is about the most ridic-ulous conversation I ever heard. If Richie wants to be selfish, fine. Who cares? Everybody's selfish."

He moved ahead of her, blocked her way down the steps. "But I want you to be there with me. You and I belong together. I don't belong at Perthie anymore than I belong on the street with Wolf and Dylan."

"Are those guys still around?" said Dinah, shoving past Richie.

"They're coming tonight. I invited them."

"How about Eric and James?"

"They moved." Richie patted the pocket where he'd put the mar-ijuana. "We're going to have our own party up in my room," he said. "You're invited."

"Maybe," said Dinah, "but not Grace. She's going to go to college and be a doctor."

Grace was startled: she knew about college, but it was the first time she'd heard about becoming a doctor.

Richie glanced at Grace. "Is she smart?"

"She's very smart," said Dinah. "You ought to see how hard she studies."

"Then she's a good candidate for college," he said. "People who are really smart don't need college. Institutions are created for mediocre people. The really smart people, the ones who do things, ignore conven-tions and social expectations and don't need degrees."

"Oh Richie," said Dinah, "You are so full of shit."

Richie took them into the kitchen where he snagged a bottle of champagne from an ice bucket behind the back of the catering staff. Grace was feeling sulky. She hadn't had enough to eat, and she didn't understand Dinah's reaction to Richie.

They went into the front parlor with all the food, and that was when they saw Wolf and Dylan on the other side of the food table, mouths full of sandwich and trying to be cool, but grinning when they saw Dinah.

Wolf was heavier and hairier than when they last saw him, dressed in black jeans and tee shirt, just what he had been in eighth grade except larger. Dylan, they decided later, was the one who had changed the most. He had grown muscles and wore a gold earring and his hair in little braids tied together at the nape of his neck with a thin strip of leather. He looked, Grace thought, like a golden pirate. She fell in love with Dylan.

Dinah, apparently, preferred Wolf's motorcycle boots and chains.

Wolf glowered at her bare shoulders and décolletage. "I remember you."

Dinah glowered back. "So? I remember you too."

Richie made an effort to stay in charge. "Well, this is Dinah, and here's little Grace, only she's not so little anymore either, and they've been in California, and they're living in my carriage house—" He stopped talking. He may have been planning his kiss for years, but he didn't seem to have planned this part. He dropped to the flats of his feet from his toes, and shut up, stepped back from the heat between Dinah and Wolf.

"California, huh?" said Wolf.

"Yeah," said Dinah, crossing her arms under her breasts again and lifting them higher.

Dylan dipped slightly, like a great exotic crane. "I'm going to live in California someday."

"Sure you will," said Wolf, never taking his eyes off Dinah in this stupidly obvious way, and Grace didn't understand why Dinah didn't stop him.

Richie jumped back in. "All right then. Who wants to sample my supplies upstairs? I've got a private party up in my room."

Grace had understood from the beginning that all three boys were centering their attention on Dinah, that there was no reason to think

86

she might get one for herself, especially beautiful golden Dylan. This made sense to her, and she was more than willing to be part of the circle admiring her sister. But when Richie invited everyone to his room upstairs, and Dinah said, "Okay, but not Grace," she was wounded.

"Why not?"

"Let me check it out first," said Dinah. "I'll see if it's okay for you. If it is, I'll come back down and get you."

They're cutting me out, Grace thought. She stared at Dinah's face as a person going under anesthesia stares at the lights on the ceiling, paralyzed and cold but unable to take any action to stop what is happening.

"You hang around down here," said Dinah over her shoulder. "I won't be gone long."

"I'd rather just look at the Christmas tree anyhow," whispered Grace, but no one heard her.

She stood where she was for a while, next to a radiator with a bowl of cashews on it. The knees of her tights had begun to sag, and she carefully lifted her skirt behind and tried to get the tights pulled up. Party sounds swirled and clattered around her. She made a circuit of the first floor of the house, watched her father and Sharon and the other people for a while. She went back to the parlor with its table weighted down with food. There was a beautiful crystal punch bowl full of eggnog, and she thought they had maybe just put it out, because no one seemed to have taken any. She used the special dipper, clear plastic, not crystal, but the cup was crystal. She drank it off quickly, delicious and sweet. It had an unexpected sharp taste under the cream and sweetness, and she took another cup, and thought: What if there's alcohol in it?

Rum, she thought. They put rum in eggnog, but she had never tasted rum, so she couldn't be sure.

The second glass she drank with deliberation, and decided that she liked it a lot, especially because it wasn't just sweet. She thought this was a sign of growing up, to enjoy what was not only sweet.

Her father had gone somewhere, and Sharon had other men gathered around her. Grace thought that Dinah was doing the same thing upstairs, a kind of trick to make them cluster around you. Then you take your pick.

I'd pick Dylan, she thought.

No one else seemed to have found the eggnog, so she had two more glasses, which lowered the level in the bowl a surprising amount. Next, she struck some poses that were like Sharon's, with an arm slightly outstretched, her body angled back. With her shoulders against the wall. She was feeling interesting opposites: visible and invisible, huge and tiny, floating and also very meaty.

An old man was in the doorway, looming over her, blocking her from the rest of the party. She smelled dampness and cigarette smoke rising from his wool turtleneck. He said something, and laughed in a way that showed crooked yellow teeth. He was talking about what a nice party it was and how pretty she looked, and she rolled away from him, under his arm, through the doorway, and she made the entire circuit of the downstairs again. When she came back to the room with the eggnog, he had moved on, so she got a large plate that she filled with cookies plus two brand new cups of eggnog and another cup that she carried in her left hand and she crossed the hall, balancing carefully, to the Christmas-tree room.

There she made a nest between the tree and a big easy chair, her back against the chair, and she finished one eggnog and then sipped another and ate cookies and hummed Christmas songs and stared up into the heart of the enormous tree with its vast green interior and the huge red balls that reflected herself with a big nose or a big forehead, whatever she chose. After a while, she realized that it wasn't the balls going around, it was her head.

She went to get more cookies and eggnog, and it was hard to walk, and everyone laughed, but she realized it had nothing to do with her, that no one was watching her at all, and she picked up the entire eggnog bowl and carried it to her nest under the Christmas tree. Eggnog sloshed on her dress and the floor.

"Oops," she said, and looked around, but still no one saw her. So she sank back next to the tree with the bowl in her lap, drank as much as she wanted, enjoying the dizziness. She let her head fall sideways and looked up into the lights and sometimes she closed her eyes and watched the colors inside her head which went from green and red to a quavering neon green and pink.

After a while, the dizziness in her head seemed to sink down into her stomach, and she began to wonder if this was how she would always be for the rest of her life, invisible and dizzy, and a little sick.

Some time passed, and a familiar voice said, "Oh no!" It was Dinah and the boys, and they had come looking for her just as she was beginning to feel sick.

"She's drunk!" said Dinah, and then the boys were laughing, and Grace knew everyone could see her again, but she couldn't see anyone, and Dinah told Dylan and Wolf and Richie to help stand Grace up, and the next thing she knew it was dark, and the dark was above and below and then she was throwing up in the bushes.

Dylan carried her the rest of the way home, and that was so nice, Dylan was long and strong, and he sang songs to her with no words. He laid her in her bed, and Dinah washed her face. She heard Richie say she should drink water, and then she heard Dinah making them all leave.

She woke much later, and found that the room was still going round, but that Dinah had crawled into bed with her. "I got drunk," she whispered.

Dinah was still wearing her wine-red dress. She said, "You little dope, didn't you know there was rum in the eggnog?"

"Did you drink champagne?"

"I didn't do anything," said Dinah. "I can't believe I didn't do anything and you got drunk. I just watched Wolf and Dylan and Richie."

"Don't do drugs," Grace said. "And don't drink either. It's sickening."

Dinah shook her head. "There I was with those boys, and you were passed out under the tree. And I thought I was taking care of you. We have to preserve your brain, Grace. Alcohol is bad for your brain."

She didn't like getting sick, but she remembered liking how the Christmas tree pulsated. "Daddy doesn't get sick," she said.

Dinah stared into the slowly revolving blackness of the night. "You get immune to it," she said. "The more you drink, the more immune you get. He's in the immune stage."

Grace was starting to fall asleep again. She was sick, but it was okay because Dinah was taking care of her.

CHAPTER 13

Richie stood at the window in the great room looking out over the gorge, trying to breathe naturally, not to notice the tremors. Around him, his house, the curved driveway, the heliport, barns, greenhouses, bunkhouse, garages, machine shop. He could see what he had built in his mind, without the monitors. He had lost patience with the yoga instructor, the meditation specialist. He knew what he needed. He needed Dinah. He didn't believe she would cure him, only that when she was within reach, his breathing would be calmer. Even the possibility of having her calmed him. The view was of national forest. Not a cell tower in sight.

The restlessness in the back of his shoulders was not a twitch, he decided, but rather impatience. The trunk of the body came later, extremities trembled first. Relaxation was supposed to slow the progress of the disease, maybe. He thought it was probably a weakness, his belief that having Dinah nearby would relax him, would slow his decline. But it was a weakness he was willing to accept. Whether or not her presence slowed the organic irritability in his hands and feet, the creeping suffocation, he believed it would make more light in his dark days.

No one except his doctors knew exactly what was wrong with him. He never told his mother. He came close once, at the very beginning.

He said to her on the phone, "You always made it a big secret what he was dying of."

Sharon had said, slurred speech, not long before her fatal fall. "He didn't want you to know. He didn't want anyone to know. It isn't genetic anyhow. And you're fine, aren't you, Richie?"

He didn't spare her because he was altruistic. He had held back because hurting her didn't seem useful. Hurting randomly, out of anger, was as bad as doing good for its own sake.

He had thought, but didn't say to her: You didn't do your homework. About 5 percent of the cases have a mutation of the enzyme superoxide dismutase 1 that can be passed down. The old man can rest in peace knowing I'm really his son, because I got the mutation.

And I hit the jackpot and started having symptoms at the young end of the continuum.

"Richie?" his mother had said. "Are you still there?"

But he had said, "I'm fine, don't be ridiculous."

She was so pathetic there was no point. And then it was too late: drinking too early one morning, she slipped on a rug, banged her head hard, wasn't found until her brain had swelled too much and she died.

Mountain Dome had no rugs. A few carpeted rooms, but no rugs. You shouldn't have rugs if you drink in the morning, he thought. Or if you have neurologically impaired balance.

For the moment, he could still do without the cane most days. He had a physical therapist twice a week, he had the yoga person in from time to time. Occasionally, he called in a medical psychologist who ran him though exercises for visualizing himself living beyond his actuarially defined five years. He flew doctors in twice a month for checkups. He went out twice a year for a full workup, to have the medications adjusted. He had all his plans made, financially, a twenty-year plan, in spite of the actuarial tables.

His favorite of the many ironies in his life was that he had been fat and self-indulgent with single-malt Scotch and multiple sex partners and oceans of blow, and he was now drug-free, slim as a riding crop, eating only grass-fed no-growth-hormone steer meat no more than twice a week and organic vegetables from his own greenhouses and fields, tended by Enrique's so-called cousins who were required to wash their hands several times a day with not-too-dilute Clorox. ALS, Richie Lock's no-fail weight-loss and healthy-living secret.

It clears your head too, he thought. He knew exactly what he wanted, and he was patiently going after it. He had laid his bait. Poke had asked permission (unusual for Poke, to ask permission: he and Bobby both liked to think they were putting one over on the boss) to take his nephew with him to talk to her husband, and that turned out to be a bit of serendipity. Richie considered it rational to accept good luck as well as bad. Poke's nephew, Travis, a handsome boy, an athletic college dropout. Young Travis had hit it off with Dinah's daughter.

Dinah and Dylan's daughter. Why, he wondered, with a definite spasm in his left hand, why had she picked Dylan to have a child with? He spread his fingers, gave it his attention, got back control of the hand. Not that he wanted children, but it meant something that she'd chosen Dylan.

Poke said Travis liked the girl, and Richie asked if the girl liked Travis. Poke said, "Who the hell knows what's going on in a girl? I don't think she even goes out with kids her own age. That's part of what Travis liked. All unspoiled." Sound of sucking teeth from Poke, the idea of despoiling a virgin.

Richie asked what they talked about.

"Don't know, Boss. I was pitching the radio show to Ray. I told him there was a housing opportunity that went with the job."

"Just a 'housing opportunity'?"

"Well, Boss, you don't want to scare these people off, do you? I'd say start slow and let them see the setup, and you know the little lady's going to love that house. The place they were living was pretty run-down. They're going to be in pig heaven when they see what you're offering them up here." Poke said he practically grew up with Raymond Savage. He insisted he knew how to talk to him. Maybe. Poke was shrewd in his own way.

Richie said, "So you think there was an attraction between Travis and the girl?"

"Two good-looking kids, boss? What do you think."

"I saw the surveillance photos from earlier. It looks like she's pretty."

"Hell yeah she's pretty. She's a little *overbaked* in the skin-color department, if you know what I mean, but exotic, like one of those Asian girls. Travis liked her *a lot*. Hell, Doc, *I* liked her a lot."

Richie wondered if the husband had told Dinah. At least Poke had followed instructions well enough not to go when Dinah was there. She would know that someone had come and talked to her husband. That the husband had made an appointment to come and interview for a job. Would the girl tell her about the good-looking boy? He liked the possibility that she hadn't told. He liked his chances on this one, especially since nothing really depended on it. Luck comes, good and bad. Although in his experience good luck is small, incremental droplets and bad luck is a tidal wave.

It is called the cruelest disease because the mind and senses stay fully intact and the victim observes and feels exactly what is happening. Richie wanted to be alert to the end. He thought he could deal with it, if he had Dinah nearby.

It's going to be okay, Richie.

CHAPTER 14

It had been a good weekend, their second in the new house. Monday, as he saw patients, he had that feeling that the ground of his life was almost steady again. Grace was much better. Between patients, he spoke with Mrs. Shaw and her family by phone to set up the surgery. He talked again with the hypertension group at the university, accepted their praise with what he hoped was humility.

His first appointment after a sandwich at a desk full of paperwork was Fredda Crayton, the realtor, the first person they'd met when they came to town. She was having trouble with her knee, which would be healing much faster if she would lose some weight. He was following her for mildly elevated blood pressure and cholesterol levels. She wore colorful scarves and a shawl. She liked to make jokes about being a tenth-generation hillbilly, but she was proud of her university degree, her trips to Europe, and her theater excursions to New York.

She sat on the table fully dressed, and he palpated the knee. The effusion from the twisted knee was mostly gone. He had removed the fluid himself. He asked if she was doing the exercises he had prescribed.

"I try to. Sometimes. I appreciate that you didn't march me off to the surgeons. Seriously, David."

He released her knee. "And I won't, if you do the exercises and continue to improve."

"And lose weight," she said, "I know. Do you want me in the other room?"

He usually had a final few words with people fully dressed, in the consultation room. It gave the patients a moment to gather themselves, to meet him with more equality, possibly ask better questions. Fredda had never been undressed, though, so he was going to tell her she could leave, but she said, "I'll be right in, as soon as I get my boot back on."

Merlee was in the hall trying to aim him at examining room two, but he said he was going to talk to Fredda Crayton for a moment.

Fredda came in and shut the door behind her. "The whole town is talking about how you saved Betty Lou Shaw's life," she said. "I mean, it would be on the noon news if we had a TV station!"

"It's nice to know good news travels fast too."

"She's my first cousin once removed," said Fredda, settling in with a big smile and eye contact.

He nodded, and waited for whatever she wanted to ask about.

"Thanks for not weighing me again," she said. "Merlee already did it. That was plenty of bad news for one day."

He glanced at Fredda's chart and Merlee's note. Up three pounds.

"The holidays," said Fredda. "I know it was three months ago, but I'll be better, I promise. We've been testing Patty's muffins. We're thinking about starting a coffee shop in the little sunroom at the office."

He said, "I'll call you when the bloods come back, and we'll see if you need anything adjusted. And the exercises for your knee."

"My pressure was good," she said.

"Not bad," he said. "Any other issues? Anything you need to discuss?"

She smiled and shook her head. He closed her chart.

"Everything okay with Grace and the girls?" asked Fredda in a light voice. "Moves can be so stressful."

"We got a lot done over the weekend."

"I make a living selling houses, but I'd probably make more money treating people's nerves when they move. And then all this with Grace's sister. It's too bad about him losing his job. Raymond Savage, I mean. Did you know I was in high school with him? He was always on the lazy side, not very interested in school. I remember him taking off more days than anyone else when it was deer season. He used to say he had to get in shape for hunting and then recover afterward. But, you know, it's good when family supports each other like Grace and you and her sister. Although I don't know why it couldn't be the Savages helping."

He said, "Yes, we'll be seeing them in a few weeks."

But Fredda still wasn't finished. He was trying to remember who the next patient was. He heard Fredda say "support" and "helping out," and then something pulled him back.

"Cottage?" He repeated the last word he had caught.

"I guess it makes sense," said Fredda. "For Grace to buy the cottage for her sister. I mean, it seems like the rainy day they were saving for has arrived. And it was a nice coincidence all around that the owners were willing to sell, more than ready, they would have sold five years ago if anybody had wanted the cottage. I was surprised though, I have to say, when you had just moved out."

It seemed supremely important to David that Fredda not know he had no idea what she was talking about. In the back of his mind there was an image of Grace that had to be protected, a statue of Grace, gold, with her arms tight at her sides, like an Oscar award statue, something for which he was responsible.

Fredda said, "As you well know, it has its problems, but Grace says Raymond is handy. Well, it's tremendously generous, putting down the money for the cottage."

Putting down money?

Fredda finally stopped talking.

He had an excuse to get away from her, a perfect excuse, his patients. He was at least half an hour behind, but he waited. He held very firm, unmoving, and he outwaited her.

She said, "It was funny, because I had this crazy feeling it was related to—her stress. Wanting to buy back the cottage. But then she told me it was for her sister. But, of course, you know all about it, didn't you?"

That was her final thrust, the direct question.

Very carefully, as if he were explaining an extremely serious diagnosis, he said, "Yes, it has been a stressful time for all of us. Very stressful."

Merlee opened the door. Thanks be for Merlee. "Hi Fredda. Doctor, I just wanted to check—if you need anything."

He stood up. Fredda stood up, saying goodbye, offering to do anything she could do to help.

Merlee stayed and watched Fredda go out. She said something about the patient in room two, but he waved her silent. "I need a minute," he said. "I have to make a phone call, if you could close the door." He picked up the phone, then put it down. What did he want to ask? Grace, did you buy a house and not tell me?

He called the bank instead. It took a while, and he had to get out his account card, even in Kingfield, to identify himself. Which meant he had to be extra careful with what he asked.

"We're afraid we might have overdrawn the account," he said. "I need to know if there was a large check in the last few days. Or a cash withdrawal. It's just sloppiness," he said. "We moved last week, you know."

There had been no unusual activity, they said. They would fax over the statement, if he wanted, but the fax machine was with the staff.

No, no, no fax.

Maybe, he thought, it was some money of Dinah's. That somehow Dinah had asked Grace to do this. How much was it? A few hundred dollars? A thousand? More? If Dinah turned over some money to Grace, to hide it from Raymond, that would make sense. Only Grace hadn't told him. And when had she said they were coming? Had she said they were moving to Kingfield? It must have been Dinah's money, but whatever it was, Grace should have told him.

Merlee came back again, and he realized a lot of time had passed. She could have looked at any phone and seen that he had been off the line for a while. "Doctor?" she said.

"I'm fine," he said, even though she hadn't asked.

She didn't move away immediately. Her arms crossed over her chest. Merlee was at least fifteen years older than he was, not quite old enough to have been his mother, but he yearned to comfort himself by pressing his face into her scrubs.

"Doctor?" said Merlee again.

He said, "Yes, I'm ready." But he couldn't quite move yet.

Merlee lowered her chin. "Fredda told me about the cottage. She said Grace handed over a lot of money in cash."

"Who else did Fredda tell about this?"

"Oh, I think just me," she said.

He didn't believe that, but if someone had to know, better it was Merlee. Somehow Dinah had convinced Grace not to tell him. Somehow, he was sure, it was because of Ray Savage. Not Grace.

CHAPTER 15

Buying the cottage made everything seem possible again to Grace. Over the weekend they watched a movie and filled the kitchen cabinets. David taught Ruth how to hang a picture without cracking the plaster. It was all beautiful and normal, and there was no opportunity to tell David about the cottage.

She stowed the paperwork in the lining of the trunk where the money had been, adding fresh rubber cement to make sure it stayed closed. As soon as everyone left on Monday morning, she checked it again, took out the papers, read them over. There were things she still had to do, papers to sign (tell David, tell Dinah), but everything would be all right.

She washed her hair, dressed, made a shopping list. Before going out, she decided to tackle the one unsorted box left in the kitchen so the kitchen would be done. The missing scissors were in the box, magazines to recycle. A bag of twisties from old bread bags. At the very bottom was the folder with the information about running for board of education. She had already filled out the application. There was the sheet of notes she'd taken. How many names you needed on a petition. A scribbled line for a speech: "Our children in Cooper County, West Virginia, deserve the same technology as children in the best schools in the biggest cities and most affluent suburbs in the nation." She was moved by her own words. I was right! she thought. To her surprise, the deadline hadn't passed yet. Of course she wasn't going to do it, the new house and the cottage and Dinah coming. Just the same, it pleased her that the deadline hadn't passed yet, that door hadn't closed. One of the secretaries at the school had said, "I was hoping you'd run, Mrs. Siefert. Somebody needs to run against them."

Them being Caliph Savage and his cronies, the antitax, black-boards-and-chalk-were-good-enough-for-me faction.

She was still going through the folder when the phone rang. It was Dinah with another bad connection. Something about sleeping bags and blankets, they would sleep on the floor.

"Don't be silly—there is so much space. When are you coming?"

Dinah said, "We have almost everything in the van already. It's just for the night, Gracie. Just for one night, then we're going down for this job interview for Ray. We're coming tomorrow. I know I should have given you more notice—then we go down to see about this job."

Grace was thinking, I have to tell David now. That they're coming tomorrow. About the cottage.

Dinah went on. "We'll be out of your hair by the next day," she said, and then paused again. "Or—I was thinking—it's a lot to ask—I thought I might leave the kids with you. Just for a day. I'd leave Aleda too, to watch them. Not the baby, of course, I meant Jacob and Sarah and Isaac. They're really well-behaved, Grace."

Grace didn't think she'd ever heard Dinah quite so frantic. She said firmly, "I'd *love* to have your kids for a day. I'd love to have them for a month!" She was going to say, I want you to live here. She was going to tell about the cottage, but Dinah kept talking.

"Maybe I won't even go. Maybe I'll stay and visit with you and let Ray go look at this job alone. I don't know. No, I have to see it too. It's in the middle of nowhere, it's Pocahontas County, do you know anything about Pocahontas County? There's a house that goes with the job."

Grace didn't mean even to hint a criticism, but she said, "That's what you want, isn't it? To have your kids far from everything?"

"This is really isolated, Gracie. Are you sure it's okay for us to come? We won't be in David's way?"

So she never told Dinah about the house.

She started thinking about food as soon as she was off the phone.

She hadn't asked if anyone was a vegetarian. She'd make two pots of chili, one meat, one fruit-and-nut vegetarian. Maybe she and David and the girls would move back to the cottage. This place, this echoing house in the empty development with the relative isolation and all the space would be perfect for Dinah and Ray and five children. She thought she had better call David. He always needed to prepare himself mentally for Ray.

Somehow, though, with all the figuring out what to cook and where everyone would sleep and shopping and more straightening, she didn't get around to calling, and then school was out and Margaret on her cell phone asking Grace to pick her up later at the library, and Ruth had to be taken to gymnastics class.

Usually, David called to say when he'd be home, but this evening he arrived without calling. She didn't hear the door either, because she and the girls were in the kitchen. He seemed to materialize from the hall, was suddenly in the kitchen, his face a strange gray color, and she immediately thought he had one of his rare but terrible headaches.

Ruth launched herself at him: "Daddy daddy daddy," she screamed, and he smiled the smile of someone in pain. "Daddy!" cried Ruth, "Our cousins are coming tomorrow! We haven't seen them in *years!*"

She should have called. She said, "Ray has a job interview down in the southern part of the state."

David looked past her, at the refrigerator. "Were you going to tell me?" he said, and didn't wait for an answer. "Fredda Crayton was in the office today."

It took a second for that information to organize itself in Grace's mind. Meanwhile Ruth was jabbering about how she was giving her room to Aunt Dinah and Uncle Ray, and Margaret would have their big cousin Aleda in her extra twin bed, and Ruth and the other kids would sleep in sleeping bags on the floor.

Fredda had told him. Fredda had told him about the cottage.

All through dinner, he talked only to the girls. He answered anything Grace asked him, but he never looked at her.

Grace thought: Fredda had no right. Grace was the one who was supposed to tell him.

Ruth wanted to know if she could watch Margaret's vampire show with her. Grace nodded yes.

As soon as they were gone, she said. "I'm sorry I didn't call you as soon as I knew they were coming—"

David said, "Come in the bedroom."

She had never seen him this angry, she thought, and glanced longingly at the pan waiting to be washed. She wanted desperately to clean out the grease before she talked to him.

He stood at the window in the bedroom looking out. She closed the door. She put on the light too, but then was sorry, thinking this would have been easier in the dark.

He spoke with his back to her. "I talked to the bank today, so I know you didn't withdraw the money from our bank account. Where did it come from?"

At some level, she was still insisting to herself that this was about Dinah and Ray coming. "They gave up the house where they were living, and they need a place to stay. I'm sorry, I know I should have called you as soon as she called me—I didn't know they were coming so soon until she called today."

He finally turned around and she flinched.

He said, "Fredda Crayton told me you bought a house."

She said, "The cottage. Where we used to live."

"I know which house. I want you to tell me you bought a house with Dinah's money, not ours. Without so much as mentioning it to me."

Because that cottage saved my life once, she thought, but said, "It was money from when Dinah and I were teenagers. And those old CDs you had me keep that nobody was using. From when I was teaching."

"Old CDs that nobody was using." He sat abruptly on the bed, shielded his eyes from her with a cupped hand. He made a choking sound.

Poor David, she thought, looking down as if from very far above. And realized for the first time how strange it must look. She said, "I always thought of that money I put away from teaching as Dinah's money. And the cash was money I took from her and just forgot about."

"How much cash money?"

"Twenty-five thousand dollars."

"You forgot about $25,000. You had a secret bank account?"

Oh yes, it looked very crazy. "It was in the old trunk. Hidden in the lining. I forgot it was there."

"You forgot about $25,000 cash in that trunk you have been dragging around your whole adult life? *You forgot about it, Grace?*" He lowered his shading hand. His face seemed to be in pieces, eyes wheeling like tires off a crashed car. "Tell me," he said. "Tell me the whole thing. In order. How you bought a house without telling me. Tell me where the money came from."

"In high school, you knew, Dinah sold drugs. And I used to hide some of the money in the trunk for a rainy day. Just little bits so she didn't know."

"Twenty-five thousand dollars of little bits?"

"Yes, and later, I worried about her, she never had much money, and before I met you I saved from teaching, for Dinah."

"We agreed the sixty thousand was for the girls' education."

"We have plenty," she whispered.

He made a strange chopping wave of his hand, as if he would erase her. "I don't even know what to say. It's so completely crazy. I thought I knew you. I thought we talked about everything."

"We do!"

"Everything except the $25,000 you kept in the trunk and the certificates of deposit we were holding for our daughters' education that you decided to cash in to buy a house without telling me."

"The money was really Dinah's." She couldn't stop whispering. She knew she was trying to disappear, when what she needed to do was to say something, to convince him, or do something, to offer to have sex. "I haven't been thinking clearly. I've been depressed."

Now she could hear herself not whispering, but whining.

He chopped the air again and got up. "I can't stay here," he said.

He turned away and went down the hall and out the door. Rain struck the window and ran down in rivulets, in sheets. She thought: He's taking a walk to cool down. In the rain. He isn't leaving me, is he? He wouldn't leave the girls.

Ruth came in. "Where'd Daddy go?"

"I think he went for a walk."

They heard his car start. Ruth ran and looked out the window.

"Mom!" she said. "What's going on?"

"I don't know," said Grace.

Ruth ran out yelling for Margaret. She could hear their voices in the distance, then, after fifteen minutes, the phone rang, and then Margaret came to the bedroom door holding the portable. Ruth was behind her.

"It's Dad," said Margaret. Grace reached for the phone, but Margaret said, "He's already off. He said to tell you he's staying at the Mountain View Motel tonight."

Grace felt it like a blow. That was what he wanted of course, that she would feel a blow as he had felt a blow. She said, "He's mad at me. Not at you girls, at me."

"How long is he staying at the motel?" said Ruth, and started to cry. "You're getting divorced! We're going to be a broken family!"

"No, no," Grace said. "He needed some space."

Margaret said, "Right, that's what people always say when they start divorce proceedings." She shoved Ruth out of the room.

Grace knew she should go take care of them, but her limbs were too heavy. She sat on the bed until the house was completely quiet, and finally got up to go to the bathroom, and while she was in there, cleaned her teeth. The girls had gone to their rooms, or maybe both of them in Ruth's room, she wasn't sure.

She broke up some more cardboard boxes. She cleaned the pan. She kept thinking she should be dealing with this, with the fact of David sleeping in a motel. She could drive over to the motel. But every time she tried to focus on it, something would distract her: an empty glass to put in the dishwasher. Crumbs on the table.

Dinah is coming, she thought. Everything will be all right.

CHAPTER 16

That night before they left for West Virginia, Dinah had one of her rare visits from Jesus. Everything in the house was in shambles, of course, Jacob especially anxious about forgetting important things. We won't forget, she told him, although she felt the tension too. We've done this before. The twins were anxious too. Sarah carried a backpack filled with her art supplies room to room, occasionally adding something. Jacob tucked stuffed animals in his bed and covered them with his blanket. Aleda didn't even have a bed tonight: her mattress was already rolled and tied to the roof of the van.

Boxes of food staples and canned goods were in the lowest strata of stuff in the van. Dinah's sewing machine was packed and Ray's best tools. Ray was leaving the big table saw for the landlord to cover the missing rent. It made Dinah shake her head. If they had only planned better. We got too low on funds, she thought. She had been frugal. She was always frugal. Well, she thought, maybe something will come of this job. She didn't think it was likely, but maybe. And if not this job, something else in West Virginia. Why not live near Ray's family?

Jacob asked her to count his teds, which was what he called all stuffed toys. She said, "You can count them Jacob, you're a good counter."

But he shook his head. "I'm only four, you count."

So she counted teddy bears and stuffed animals. And found Sarah's favorite blouse that had somehow got in with the sheets and towels after the last wash. And kept wondering about the job.

"You've got all the information that I have," Ray had said. "Poke works for some rich fellow who's building a media center. He wants some Christian programming."

"Why you, Ray? Why come all this way looking for you?"

"Because Poke knows me. Maybe he feels like he owes me something. I don't know. And according to Poke, this rich man doesn't have a lot of church connections."

She knew Ray always told the truth, but not necessarily every part of it.

"What's his name?"

"Poke Riley."

"No! The rich man!"

Raymond gave a sheepish little shrug. "It never came up. It seems he's a private sort of individual, living up on a mountain like that. Eccentric, you know."

"Are there other people trying for the position?"

"I don't know that either, Dinah," said Ray, "but that isn't my business. My business is to ascertain if this is the call. If Jesus is telling me to pick up my bedroll and go."

Some bedroll. Five children and Dinah and a vanload of worldly possessions. She had shut her mouth. She had long ago chosen to submit to her husband. And that meant not only cooking spaghetti twice a week because he liked it best, but also submitting to what she didn't like. Submission was when you bent your will to the other's.

I chose this, she told herself. I chose to bend my will.

They ended the day with a prayer circle. It calmed everyone. Jacob prayed aloud, almost shouting: "Oh please don't let me lose my teds!" and then he named all his stuffed animals to the point that it almost sounded like he was praying to them instead of to God.

While the others prayed, chores dodged and flickered like bats in Dinah's brain, but then Benjie started nursing, and God's wonderful natural nursing drug flushed her body, and the bats faded away. Benjie fell asleep and she felt at a great distance from the soft voices.

That was when Jesus showed up. She'd been drifting, so sleepy, reaching inside for her angel babies, but suddenly He was there, in the center of the circle, mysteriously close to her when the rest of them were far. Wearing a red tunic, toddler sized but sinewy like a man. He crossed his arms over his chest and raised a finger and shook it at her.

What? she said. What do you want?

Jesus didn't say anything. Just shook that finger, and then he was gone.

Not a warning, she didn't think. A caution. Be careful.

He was always so clear to Raymond, and so ambiguous to Dinah.

On the handful of previous occasions when she'd seen Him, she'd never been sure if it was her imagination or a real visitation. This time she suspected Jesus was warning her that Ray was too hungry for the opportunity, that there was reason to be suspicious. She had been afraid from the beginning that there was a catch, something Ray was refusing to see.

What is a media center anyhow, she wondered. What did that mean, a private radio station with some Christian programming? Something over the internet? What was it?

The visit from the little red Jesus made her feel more sure of herself. She had to be vigilant. She had to take care of Ray as well as of the children. Everyone was always in peril, all the time. Aleda from the burgeoning animal urges, Ray from his ambition. Well, she thought, at least we'll all be together, in the van, with each other, and I'll get to see Grace.

She had asked Ray once about the little red Jesus, who had first come to her when she was pregnant with Aleda. That time Jesus told her Dylan must go away. She asked Ray if he thought it had been real. She was sure it had been real, but she wasn't sure it was Jesus. She hadn't been saved yet, at that time, and it wasn't exactly a spiritual experience, just very vivid. She asked Ray if he thought she had been fooled by the devil.

"By His works ye shall know Him," said Ray.

"He told me that I had to end it with Dylan, and he did this little dance and then *poof!* he was gone."

Raymond nodded.

She said, "So do you think it was the devil or Jesus?"

"I think Jesus was telling you to save yourself and the baby. That Dylan had his own path—"

"To perdition," she said.

"We don't know that," said Ray. "But you had your path, Dinah."

"But was that little red thing Jesus?"

Ray didn't know. He smiled and touched her. She thought that if it was Jesus, it was a kind of waste of a special visit because she had already pretty much decided to make Dylan leave on her own. Raymond got visits at least twice a week, messages and sometimes complete sermons. Ray said, "Sometimes we don't know for a long time, the meaning of the calls."

Or if they're real calls, she thought, feeling cynical again about Raymond's upcoming job interview. Benjie's milky mouth had long since popped off her nipple, and Raymond embraced each of the children in age order, sending them to bed. He ended with Benjie, and of course embraced Dinah too.

She put Benjie in his carrier next to their bed, tucked in Jacob with his blanket along with Ted and Big Ted and Little Ted and Yellow Ted and Rabbit Ted and all the others, said goodnight to the ones on the floor and couch.

While she was tucking in the kids, she heard Raymond go out back and put some more things in the van. She laid out paper cups and napkins for breakfast and packed away the last of the clean dinner dishes. Did her teeth, washed her face, decided the bathroom would have to be given a light cleaning in the morning, but not until everyone was finished, no use to do it now, and she went to bed.

She lay in the dark for a long time, expecting Ray, but he continued to clatter distantly outside. Finally he came in. She heard him in the bathroom, checking something in the front room, maybe to see if the kids were asleep. Finally in the bedroom. He closed the door, undressed. He made a small grunt as he sat on the bed, she felt the shift, felt his warm presence blocking space on that side. She waited for him to reach for her, and when he didn't, was disappointed. She could have reached too, but she was tired, a little grouchy. Usually, when he didn't roll toward her, he fell asleep promptly, slept well and without worry. He was a good sleeper.

Time passed, and she began to drift off herself, pulled out just a little to think, Oh I'm going to go straight to sleep for once, but then Ray stirred, and she realized he was awake. He rolled toward her, pulled her close. It always excited her, his body. Her whole life, she had always liked sex, body to body, but no one had ever worked her from the inside out the way Ray did. The smell of him excited her, made her receptive. Her body arched, she felt she was a smile, she curled against him, his bulk, his heat.

Afterward, she was calm but wakeful.

Then Raymond surprised her. He still wasn't asleep. There was something on his mind. "Dinah?" he said. "Are you awake? I need to tell you. About why I went to prison," he said.

"Now?" she said. "You said it wasn't murder or rape, and that's enough for me." Unless, she suddenly thought, it has something to do with this job, and then, immediately, she was sure it did.

"I got involved with some bad people," said Ray. "I was bad too, I know that, but I was bad in the normal way, you know, wild and careless, drinking my way into the wilderness. Figuring I could make some easy money. But these people had ideas about making war on the government, and not just the government, but people who were—you know, diverse."

"Black?"

"Black, Jewish, Chinese. Whatever. I was just in it for the money, but I'm not exonerating myself. I listened to them. They had a false god, and at first it sounded to me like a god of freedom, and I thought all I wanted in life was freedom. I had no idea that submitting to God, going where Jesus tells you, is the real freedom."

"Oh honey," she said. "You're a different man now. I know you are. Believe me, I wouldn't be here with you if you weren't a different man."

His hands stirred a little under the blanket. He said, "Do you remember back in 1995 or 1996, there was that Oklahoma City bombing?"

"You weren't involved in that?"

"No, thank you Jesus I was never tempted to hurt babies and little children!"

In her mind, Dinah did a roll call of where her children were: Benjie here, Aleda on the couch, Jacob, Sarah, Isaac. The angel babies deep in her heart. She could find everyone if there was a fire.

"No," said Ray, "I'm just telling you about what those times were like. It was after the first Iraq war and before the second one. People were talking about the New World Order that was going to take away our freedom. So there was this bunch running around in camouflage fatigues, playacting, if you ask me, but they had plans to pull back into the mountains, to strike a blow at the government if things got bad. They called themselves the Mountain Militia, and they were getting nervous about the FBI building that big facility down in Harrison County. It was supposed to be computers for checking fingerprints for the whole country, but these people were convinced it was a front for controlling everything. And they decided to blow it up before it went into operation."

Dinah finally remembered, very vaguely, a newscast, a headline. "It sounds a little familiar," she said. "But they got caught before they did anything, right? Were you part of that?"

Raymond said, "I drove trucks for them. I'm not trying to pretend I was innocent, but I was only involved in the petty criminal end of it, hauling stuff."

"Hauling what?"

"We never knew, but I'm pretty sure it was explosives."

"Oh Ray."

"I hadn't met Jesus or you either, Dinah. It was a bad time, and I thank Jesus every day that it was stopped before anyone could be harmed."

She said, "So you're saying you went to jail for aiding and abetting this Mountain Militia thing?"

"Prison," he said, sounding a little drowsy now. "The FBI had been watching this damn Mountain Militia all along. Hell, they probably suggested blowing it up themselves, to catch them out." His breathing slowed, and for a second, she thought he had gone to sleep, but he added, "This fellow Poke, he was never very interested in it either. Poke is sorry he was part of it too. He's just another one of the lazy people always looking for a way to make a quick buck. That's what we were like then."

"What's he like now, Ray? You don't know him anymore. This isn't Mountain Militia stuff again, is it?"

"No, Poke was real clear about that. I asked him that right up-front. You know I wouldn't get involved in that now. Poke's settled down too, and his boss is a legitimate businessman."

"So he says."

"That's what we're going to check out, Dinah. I don't even know if this boss is a Christian. Poke says there's something wrong with him, I mean physically, he's sick with something. I figure maybe he's getting scared and maybe he's looking to be converted. Maybe that's why Jesus is sending me, to help save this man."

She waited for more, but a tiny half snore came instead, and he was asleep, and she was wide awake at 2:30 a.m. and Benjie would wake hungry anytime now and then it would be morning and the kids' breakfast and clean the bathroom and put the chairs on top of the van, stuff in the last bags of toys and teds and toothbrushes—it all trotted out in front of her in a gray rehearsal, making her tired and anxious.

But at least she knew what the warning was about. Raymond loved stories about changes of heart, about this sick rich man to bring to Jesus. She wished she had been here the day Poke came by. Her brain wanted to see him, to hear his words. But there had been two men, Ray said. Who was the other one?

She started locating the children again. Benjie in the carrier beside her. Aleda on the couch, Isaac and Sarah on the floor in sleeping bags, Jacob buried in teddy bears not wetting the bed, she prayed. It would be light soon.

Rebecca and Amos and Samuel.

CHAPTER 17

David was stunned and appalled by the yellow overhead light and the shadows cast by the humps in the ceiling. The floor was covered in vinyl, the bedspread printed with an imitation antique quilt pattern. There was a staleness in the air as if they didn't get a lot of customers at this time of year. Who came to the Mountain View Motel in Kingfield ever? The gas heater under the window came on and blew dry hot air at him.

He had a creeping sensation on the back of his neck. He hadn't sat down yet, and he was imagining vermin. He had no rational reason to think the room was dirty. He knew the Patels. He did school checkups for the children, he had treated Mrs. Patel for vague abdominal pain that went away, Mr. Patel for an infected toe he had waited too long to treat. They were people who ignored pain, always worked. It was racist to doubt that their motel was clean.

People could see his car parked outside. Humiliation ran over him in waves and he couldn't sit down. He wondered if the gossipers were already calling from house to house: Did you see? Dr. Siefert's car is at the Mountain View? Is someone sick? Did Dr. Siefert sleep at the motel? He could leave now and hint to people that he had made a house call to the Patels.

He had known it was all wrong even as he pressed the bell taped to the counter in the motel office. Mrs. Patel had come in from the apartment, fixing her scarf, a faint whiff of cooking in her clothes. Her careworn face had lit up to see him, and she said, "Oh Doctor!" and then the smile shut down. Just like that: her cheeks sagged, her lips tightened, her chin lowered. She became *discreet*. He supposed there was some unwritten code among innkeepers. But of course she wondered: Why did the doctor need a motel room?

He had always been so careful, worked so hard. Like the Patels.

He had, by ringing a bell, by saying, Good evening Mrs. Patel, I need a room, taken a step down in everyone's eyes.

Everything around him was abysses and quicksand. He was undermined. His new house was undermined. His marriage. His ability to perform his work undermined. *Undermined*. A word with a literal meaning in Cooper County. There wasn't much active mining now in the county, but there were old mines, small private mines, long worked out and deserted, and sometimes they collapsed on themselves. Patients had told him of houses with sudden cracks in the foundations, or outbuildings that disappeared in the night.

He didn't take off his glasses, he didn't turn off the light. He sat on the edge of the bed. He thought about Grace, about mental illness. This was a kind of mental illness, of course. He had known from early on that Grace was a depressive. When she had the postpartum depression, after Ruthie was born (a new house that time too), he had been frightened, but he gave her antidepressants. Why hadn't she asked this time? Why hadn't he seen the extent of it?

She had done so well for so long. She had been outward oriented, full of plans. He had forgotten that she was a depressive. He felt a flash of the anger again: How dare she!

And then turned back to his mistakes: missing what was going on with her. Walking out of the house and coming to the motel. To be seen by Mrs. Patel, by any passing truck. He didn't believe rationally that there were bedbugs, but his body was itching.

There was a crack in the wall next to the little closet with its plastic folding door. It was an enormous crack, possibly structural, plenty of room for mice as well as bedbugs.

Maybe all his choices, his whole life, had been a series of terrible mistakes, one leading to the next. All their discussions and plans. Had it been their plans or his plans? If he mentioned Vancouver, Grace said, Great! If he said something about the ocean, she exclaimed how much she loved the ocean and when he said, Yes, but hurricanes, she said, No, you wouldn't want to be where there were hurricanes.

Had she always been thinking about her nest egg, her secret: $25,000 cash in a beat-up footlocker? The insanity of it was raw and exposed in his mind. Was it all a trick, she never really cared about their lives, was always ready to run with her $25,000 and the CDs in her name?

He lay down, on top of the covers, leaving the yellow lights on, leaving his glasses on. He thought he had read somewhere that bedbugs didn't come out unless it was dark. He rolled to his side, pulled his knees up, folded his arms. The itching crept up the back of his neck again, and he leaped off the bed. He would park at the bottom of the driveway so they didn't wake. He would sleep in the car.

CHAPTER 18

Grace was awakened by the front door opening just before 6 a.m. She tracked his footsteps into the kitchen, then up the stairs to their bedroom. She kept her eyes closed and held very still. He opened drawers, he opened the closet. No effort to be quiet. He's packing, she thought, he's leaving.

But then he went to the shower, and she decided he hadn't spent enough time to be packing. He was just getting cleaned up for work. He came back in, dressed. With her face deep in the bedclothes, she dropped off again, woke again, this time to coffee and frying butter and voices floating up out of the kitchen. It wasn't seven yet, but she could hear Ruthie, and she thought she heard Margaret too.

She rolled back the comforter, combed her hair, went to the bathroom still damp with David's shower, went barefoot down the carpeted steps, then over the cool tiles in the hall. In the kitchen, Ruthie in her flowery nightgown, Margaret in flannel pajama pants and tee shirt, eating French toast. David with his tie tied but tossed over his shoulder, at the stove.

The girls looked up at Grace. David offered Margaret another slice. Margaret shook her head no, but Ruthie accepted it. He knew, of course, that Grace was there, but didn't look at her. Just the same, he was here. He was making breakfast for the girls.

He took the empty pan to the sink and started to wash it.

Ruthie said, "Daddy, what if Mommy wants some French toast too?"

His shoulders stopped moving.

Grace said, "Oh that's okay, thanks, I'll have something later."

He went back to washing the pan.

Margaret kept her face down at her plate, but Ruthie was relentlessly communicative. "Daddy went to the Mountain View Motel last night," she said. "Amina Patel from my class lives there. But he didn't stay, he slept in the car in the driveway."

David placed the clean pan in the drainer with his familiar precise movements, exactly enough to do the job, no flourishes. He kissed Ruthie on the cheek and Margaret on the top of her head. He had to walk past Grace to get his briefcase. She held perfectly still as he sidled past.

"Daddy," said Ruth, as he went down the hall, "what about Mommy?"

They heard the door close.

Ruthie said, "He has a very busy day."

Margaret got up and put her plate in the sink. "I'm going back to bed."

"I'll wake you for school," Grace said.

Ruth took more syrup. "Daddy's French toast has vanilla," she said. "Do you want a piece? I have an extra."

"No, thank you, honey. Are you going back to bed too?"

"I don't know. I'm not sleepy."

"Maybe you should check your homework?"

"Everything feels strange," said Ruth, staring at her.

Treading carefully, Grace poured herself some coffee and said, "Daddy's angry."

"Why?"

Grace's impulse was to explain, but she stopped herself. "Did he say if he'd be home in time for dinner with Aunt Dinah and Uncle Ray?"

"I think he said he might be late."

She nodded. She hadn't been thinking of him. That was not why he was angry, though, he was angry because she'd betrayed him by acting like a crazy person.

But some tiny part of her wasn't sorry for buying the cottage.

Later, she stood on the small front porch (not a porch for sitting on: no rotting swing like at the cottage, no clematis growing up the posts, no hydrangea in summer) and watched until the mist-flattened rectangle of yellow school bus stopped for Margaret and Ruth.

She thought: I never should have married. I should have insisted on staying with Dinah and Aleda. She thought she had been weak her whole life, depending on David, depending on Dinah.

She failed everybody.

One time, Dinah had failed her.

It was Grace's last year in high school, and Dinah was working at a copy center as well as selling drugs. She had also started researching college and scholarships for Grace. We're sending you to college, Dinah would say over and over. We're taking care of you first. And at the same time, their father had been having health problems. After a lifetime of cigarettes and Wild Turkey Kentucky Straight, the deterioration of his various organs was accelerating. There were trips to the emergency room for pneumonia, and when he was home, he rarely left the Barcalounger. His presence had no effect on Grace and Dinah's activities, except that they tried to have someone home most of the time, in case he couldn't breathe.

Dinah broke up with Wolf, but he still came around. Grace would come in from school and find Wolf sitting in front of the TV drinking with their father. Sometimes he brought friends she didn't know with him. The bathroom smelled of beery piss. She found a crowbar in the garden shed and angled it floor to door to block her room when she was inside.

That winter, their father spent six weeks in the hospital, and just before they brought him home, there was a burglary at the big house. They heard about it when Sharon called from her condo in Boca Raton. There was a scene with Wolf. Dinah screamed that he and his stupid friends were supposed to stay away from Lockwood, what did he think he was doing.

"Shit fuck," said Wolf. "It's just sitting there full of shit."

Dinah said, "You said you'd leave Sharon's house alone—and not only that, you were too stupid to close the front door so it got reported right away, you jerk! That's it, no more. I don't want to see you and I don't want to see your knuckle-walker friends. Ever!"

Wolf tried to make himself big and threatening, but Dinah never seemed to have any physical fear for herself. She dared Wolf to touch her, and screamed at Dylan that he had to choose between her and Wolf, and their father actually got up out of the Barcalounger and lurched toward them with his pants almost off his hips he was so thin.

"You go back and lie down, Daddy," said Dinah. "We're just working something out."

"Let me help you sit down, Mr. Mackey," said Dylan.

Grace locked herself in her room, but she heard Dinah say, "Listen Wolf, the cops are going to be watching this apartment now, don't you see? You've fucked up everything. This whole thing is over. We can't do anything out of the carriage house anymore."

Wolf said, "We can use my grandmother's house, she's out most days."

"Your grandmother!" said Dinah, "Now you want to get your grandmother into it. No, it's over. I want it over. I'm sick of it."

Daddy called weakly, "You boys listen to Dinah, she's the one with the brains around here."

Dinah said, almost sadly, "If I really had brains, I would have thrown these jerks out long ago."

After the burglary, Grace shifted larger and larger amounts of money to the back of the trunk. Once she heard Dinah accuse Dylan of taking it, and he may well have slipped into Grace's room, but it was mostly Grace, lining the back wall of the trunk with the largest bills she could find.

The police came, as Dinah predicted. They came twice, once when it was just Grace and Daddy home, and once when Dinah was there too. They always asked for Wolf, and Grace really didn't know anything about his whereabouts, but Dinah, who did know, lied like a dream. Her face lit up with her big easy smile and said, "Oh my God officer, I knew that boy was in some kind of trouble. I feel so bad about Mrs. Lock's house, when she's been so good to us. Do you think it was those guys who did it?"

Less than a week after the police, the thing happened that Grace always felt secretly was Dinah's betrayal. Dinah, who had always promised to take care of Grace. It was a cold Saturday morning, and Dinah had stayed out all night and wasn't home yet. Grace was sitting in bed reading her European history text and having trouble keeping her hands warm because they had to be outside of the covers to hold the book and turn pages.

She heard sounds from the kitchen and thought maybe her father was having a good day. She got up and moved aside the crowbar and went out in her nightgown. Dinah's room was empty, their father in the Barcalounger, eyes closed, and for a second she thought he was dead, but he coughed.

Out of the corner of her eye, she saw a movement, in the kitchen, which was separated from the living room by an archway with no door.

A man was standing with his back to her in front of the open refrigerator. He was heavily built, like Wolf, but older. A big butt in jeans. He turned around, holding a fruit yogurt container as if it might explode, and let the refrigerator close.

He said, "You the little sister?"

She had never seen him before. He was wearing motorcycle boots with dusty square toes turned up slightly, buckles at the sides. She crossed her arms over her chest, aware of the thinness of her nightgown and missing buttons.

"Who's the old guy? Your dad? He is in bad shape. Where's Dinah?" he said. "Where's that stupid dipshit Dogboy?"

She didn't look directly at him, but she knew he had a shaved head, a ring in his ear, a leather vest over a bubble-knit undershirt and a big belly, "Don't say much, do you?" He started opening cabinet doors and drawers, which he left open. He found a spoon, ripped the top off the yogurt and ate. "I hate this fricking stuff. Haven't you got anything to eat here?"

He tossed the container and the spoon in the sink and leaned back and looked her over. She kept her eyes fixed on the motorcycle boots. There was a crust of dirt around the soles. She felt him taking it all in, her nightgown with the missing buttons, her dad in the Barcalounger, the portable oxygen tank.

"You don't have shit in here, do you?" he said. "Not a beer, not nothing. That TV looks like it belongs in the trash. What a shitty place to live."

Then go away, she thought.

"So I'm looking for Dogboy. That's what I call him, but you know who I mean. He owes me something."

In those days, her fear was of outer things like shouting and being hit. Of this fleshy big man in denim and leather.

"Can you talk?" he said. "What are you, deafanddumb? Or just dumb? Wolf's got something of mine that's supposed to be here and I want it."

"My sister broke up with him."

"So where's your sister?"

"I don't know. At work. Or with Dylan."

"Who's Dylan? Oh, the weirdo. Well I'm looking for fucking dipshit Dogboy who has something that belongs to me."

"He doesn't come here anymore."

"So maybe your sister has it."

Grace thought he was looking at her breasts even though she had her arms crossed over them. There were goosebumps on her arms. She said, "Wolf took all his stuff."

"Dogboy," said the man. "Call him Dogboy."

She whispered, "Dogboy."

He opened the refrigerator again, drank directly from the milk carton, opened the cheese drawer and took a block of cheddar cheese and shoved it in the pocket of his vest. Slammed the door.

She said, "He's maybe at his grandmother's. I don't know where that is, though."

He said, "I ought to rip this place apart," he said.

"My dad is here," she said.

"Oh, that's scary."

He'll go soon, she thought. As soon as he goes, I'll throw out the milk container he drank from. I'll eat gingersnaps. He didn't find the gingersnaps. She'd make gingersnaps with icing. She thought there was a can of vanilla icing in the cabinet, and she pictured the front door locked and the crowbar against it and a plate of iced ginger snaps.

"You should go now," she said.

"I should, should I? You're standing there peeing your pants and you're telling me I should go? I'll leave after I get goddamn *something*."

His boots thudded on the old linoleum, crushing a dried crumb of cake or bread, smashing it to pieces under the sole of the boot. Now his leather jacket and underwear shirt filled her field of vision, and her body jerked because he was clamping his hands on her arms up near the shoulders. He was so close she could smell something sour from his body and wanted to say, You smell like yogurt.

He gave her a little shake, and she knew she had said something wrong. I shouldn't have said that, what I said. But she couldn't remember what she said.

The voice was rumbling above her now. "I don't leave without something. What will you give me to make me leave?"

His rigid leather jacket and his sour smelling shirt pressed up against her face, and now her right arm wasn't being held but her breast was, lifted up and down, flopped, held, through the nightgown.

"Not bad for a little girl," he said.

He wasn't touching her skin, just the outside of her nightgown.

She whispered, "You can have some of Daddy's whiskey."

He had a tattoo of a cross on his neck. Not a Christian cross, one of the short thick ones more like a swastika. He pressed her breast back against her bones and was rubbing it in a round movement. She'd never seen that big a tattoo on a neck before, a square cross with a thorny rose between two deep creases in his skin. And more of the sour smell, she didn't know where it was coming from, from his mouth, from his shirt, from the circling thumb from her nipple under the nightgown.

"I don't know," he said, "do I want whiskey? Nah, I've got my own whiskey. I don't need any old-man whiskey. What I really want is the money goddamn Dogballs owes me." He dropped her breast so he was only holding her by one arm.

He was a little farther away from her. Her arm started to hurt.

He said, "You're not going to cry, are you?"

He started pulling at the buttons on her nightgown, popping the ones that weren't already missing. He slipped the hand that wasn't gripping her arm inside and it was cold, his knuckles cold pressed into the skin and fat of her breast, the right one he'd already held and now the left one too.

"Toaster oven," she said.

His hand stopped. "What?"

"You can have the toaster oven. It's new."

He pulled his hand out of her nightgown and let go of her arm so he could use both hands to spread her nightgown wide open and stare. "Are you offering me a toaster oven? Are you trying to buy me off with a toaster oven?" He shook his head. "You're a weird little sister, that's all I can say. You need a new nightgown. You want to be my girlfriend? I'll get you a sexy nightgown."

She pulled back, and he let her go.

She said, "We hardly ever used it, I just cleaned out the crumbs." She grabbed the toaster and held it up to him. Between her open nightgown and him. He took it.

"Piece of shit," he said, rotating it in his hands, but tucked it under his arm. "Listen, tell your sister to tell Asshole Dogballs that Carl was here looking for him. And make sure he knows it's Big Carl, not Little Carl." He had released her, it looked like he was leaving, but Grace couldn't move. He looked around the kitchen and took the two bananas lying on the table too. "You've got frickin' shitty stuff here," he said. "Tell him that he had better find Big Carl and pay what he owes or else if Big Carl finds him first, he's going to be sorry. No, he's going to be *fucking* sorry. Can you remember that?"

He left the door open, and she felt the cold air coming up from below. She stayed in the kitchen awhile, afraid it was a trick, that he wasn't really gone. Then, she locked the door and got the crowbar out of her bedroom and propped it against the apartment door. Her father's eyes were still closed. She thought he was pretending to be asleep because there was nothing he could do. Then she had to pee, and after she peed, she went to her room and heard her father began to stir around. She didn't offer to get him toast and tea as she usually did. There was no toaster oven anyhow. After a while, she heard the television click on.

Grace got dressed and moved all of the remaining money to her hiding place. There were many many dollars, maybe thousands, far more than she had ever moved before. Then, when she had done all these things, she sat on her bed and waited for Dinah. It was nearly two hours before she heard her trying to get in the front door, pounding.

"What's going on?" said Dinah when Grace had moved the crowbar. "I have to go to work. What—" then saw Grace's face, glanced at their father and pressed Grace back into her room. "What?" she said, closing the door behind them. "Oh shit Gracie. What happened?"

Grace sat back down on the bed. "He didn't do anything," she said. "He just took the toaster oven."

"Who?" said Dinah. "Oh shit Gracie. Who? Who came here?"

"Big Carl."

"Big Carl came here? Oh my God. Did he do something to you?"

The first time she said it, it came out unvoiced. She said it again. "He touched my breasts."

Dinah sat down and hugged her. "Oh shit Gracie, I'm so sorry Gracie, it's my fault, I should have been here. What else did he do? Did he do anything else?"

Grace discovered she could lie as smoothly as Dinah. "He took all the money in the trunk, but he wanted more."

"We're leaving," said Dinah. "We're really leaving. The money doesn't matter, are you okay? He didn't do anything else?"

"No. Except for the toaster oven. He took the toaster over."

"What an asshole! That's really the end, Grace, I promise, no more of this shit. This is over."

And the more Dinah apologized, the more Grace pulled inside herself. She thought: Dinah said she would take care of me and she didn't.

All these years later she wondered about herself. She had thought she was a victim, but she had taken Dinah's money. The purest thing in her life, her relationship with Dinah. What kind of a person, really, would betray her sister?

And her husband?

But, oddly, the badness at her core shone like a piece of polished coal. It was solid, dependable. More dependable than people, maybe.

She moved the flattened boxes to the basement. She baked brownies. She washed her hair and did laundry. It was a skyless kind of day, fog and the clouds meeting up in the hills so you couldn't tell which was which. Objects flattened like the boxes, colors grayed. It made it easy to concentrate on one thing at a time.

Toward time for the kids to get back from school, as she was shredding cabbage to make slaw, there was a distant broken-vacuum pop of a car door. She hurried to the window that overlooked the driveway.

The van had mattresses on top and two wooden chairs, like the Okies in the Depression, she thought. Like Dinah and Grace and their father going to California.

Ray Savage was out first, big shoulders, the bald spot on top. He opened a sliding door, and a girl got out. Grace thought it was Aleda, but when a boy the same size came after her, she realized it was the twins. Then Ray lifted out Jacob. She knew Jacob. Then Dinah, on the other side, wearing some kind of spring-green rummage-sale raincoat. Someone handed her the baby, and finally another woman got out, but it wasn't a woman, it was Aleda, full breasted and golden colored.

CHAPTER 19

As soon as he could get away, Ray drove up to visit his mother. Dinah hadn't been happy about it. She had said, "She wants to see these kids, Ray, why are you going without the kids?"

He couldn't explain. It was something about being home after so many years. Jesus had told him, with no fanfare, that he had to go and make things right with his mother.

The hills looked good, a sprinkling of buds turning to leaves. He opened the window so he could smell the mud and the green. He said: "Wherever You're leading me, Jesus."

Job or no job, it was time to be back.

He felt calm, all the roiled waters of life lying a little smoother. He started to hum an old song as the van climbed the rises: "Are we weak and heavy-laden, burdened with a load of care? All because we do not carry everything to God in prayer." He had old-fashioned taste in music. He'd been turned down as an assistant pastor at a church near New Tripoli because he spoke against their rock-and-roll music. He hadn't opposed it, only said he thought the church needed to pray about it, not just assume they should try to appeal to modern taste.

There was a shearing of the clouds above from the mist below, and a clearer view of the wet trees on the hills. He shifted to a lower gear, and light broke through. "Look at that," he said aloud. "The silver lining!" He didn't believe in writing down sermons, but he was always casting around for ways to bring people closer to Jesus.

He sometimes wished he could show the old troubled Ray who he was now. Old Ray would scoff at silver linings. Old Ray wanted to make some money so he could carouse. He could preach that too: I know some of you men are scoffing as you sit there, scoffing at fancy phrases and calling out to Jesus! Oh I wish you could feel what I feel! You *will* feel what I feel! I believe it! I believe Jesus has his hand on you right now!

Thinking about Old Ray, Poke Riley came into his thoughts. Poke had insisted he was changed too, but he had said things, sitting in the truck in front of the house in New Tripoli, that made Ray wonder. Some kind of plan to make a lot of money.

I just want a job, Ray had said. Not interested in a big score.

This is a job! Poke had said. Just a job, a legitimate job, hell yes, Ray, you are going to want to snap this up. This is a salary and a house, a really big opportunity.

But Ray kept remembering how Poke's eyes, which never were very big, disappeared altogether in his grin. A lot of opportunities, Ray, he said. The boss ain't going to last so long, and the ones of us who are around, the ones who help him out—I'm just saying, there's some good opportunities.

That was all he said, and Ray had no reason to think it was something evil or illegal—it sounded like maybe he was expecting the boss to leave a legacy. But it stayed with him.

I'll see for myself, he thought. I'll meet this poor sick man who is thirsting for Jesus, just as we're all thirsting for Jesus, whether we know it or not.

The turn for Savage Run came up suddenly, and he almost missed it, not expecting it to be paved. Well look at that, he thought. He drove a little too fast, and the oil pan scraped. That was the same, anyhow. A road that was hard on vehicles.

As he drove, he felt his heart climbing into his throat. In spite of what he'd said to Dinah, he knew his mother was going to be PO'd. He should have come back sooner. He should have brought his kids to meet her.

Scenes of home flashed around him: spying with his brothers on whoever drove up this road. Once they threw rocks at Uncle Caliph's car and Uncle Caliph got out and chased them with a switch. More like a branch. Caliph made his money in little dog mines, not that he ever went in them himself, and later he sold his mines and bought trucks and worked for the county and managed to make money there too, and then bought an auto-parts store. Ray's father used to call him King Caliph of Cooper County.

The only rich Savage in Cooper County. The family allowed that there might be other rich ones in other counties, but not in Cooper County. Caliph married, but never had children, which was considered a strange thing about him, and his wife died early and Caliph didn't remarry. Ray's father had been all the opposite, a generous spendthrift, always wanting to bring everyone he knew to his house. Ray supposed that was hard on his mother, seeing as how there was never much to be generous with.

He pulled into the yard next to the house. No other cars, except his dad's 1959 Chevrolet Impala convertible under a tarp. The tarp had collected rain and sticks. Nobody was taking care of his father's pride and joy. He got out of the van and went over and pulled a couple of sticks off and drained off some of the water. He'd like to take the engine out, take it apart, get it purring. Repaint the body, get it a new soft top. He waited for a moment, asking if this was something he was supposed to do or would just enjoy doing.

No answer, so he looked up at the house. He figured by now his mother would be watching him, assuming she was home, so he squared his shoulders. The house looked good, the stilts under the porch had been framed out and covered with lattice, and there was a garage now. The house had vinyl instead of the old asphalt composite they used to repair every summer till it was a multicolor patchwork of other people's leftovers. It was clean looking, clapboard style. Double-glass replacement windows and porch posts made out of something white and wood textured, PVC, probably. A rocking chair with a pad and a pot for flowers. He wondered who was taking care of it so good. Probably Verna.

But it wasn't me, Ray thought. I wasn't here helping her. I'm the one, Raymond thought, who did time in prison and used to send her a pitiful little few dollars twice a year but not even that the last couple of years. They were going to be hard put to buy gas to get to Pocahontas County tomorrow. I'm the prodigal son, only knowing my mother, there won't be no fatted calf.

Mother, he thought, all I have to offer is Jesus!

He felt the calming presence of the spirit in his lungs and went up on the porch. He raised his fist to knock, but before the fist struck, she opened the door.

He saw the glitter of her glasses first. Taller than Dinah but shorter than he remembered, thin in the shoulders, and her head forward, hair cut short and curly gray. Mouth turned down. She was wearing pants. He always thought of her in a dress.

But it was still his mother, and he felt himself smiling. "Hello, Mama," he said. "The prodigal son done come home." She stepped away from him, hugging herself, not him.

"Where are they?" her voice as thin and tight as her mouth.

She never knew Jesus, he thought sadly. "We just got in about an hour ago, Mama. They're in town at Dinah's sister's house. We'll bring them over."

"Dinah's sister is the doctor's wife. Verna goes to that doctor." Still blocking the door, like she hadn't decided to let him in or not.

"How's Verna?" he asked. "Is she taking care of you, Ma?"

"I take care of myself," she said. "Verna stays here because she needed a place to stay, her and that fat son of hers." His mother did a thing with her head, sort of a toss or a shy, and then stepped out of his way. "You might as well come in, Raymond. Come on back to the kitchen. Wipe your feet, I just mopped."

There was a mat outside and a rag rug inside. He wiped in both places. The floor was wood laminate, nice looking and easy to take care of. He thought Dinah might like that someday. "The house looks good, Ma, new siding."

"Skip the soft soap," she said. "Don't expect smiles from me."

"I don't expect one single thing, Mama, except to see you. I'm a sad sinner. Lost for a long time, till Jesus found me. I'm full of sorrow for what I've done wrong, including not coming to see you, full of sorrow and regrets for where I've failed but also full of the rich and freely given love of Christ."

She spun around in the kitchen door, and he almost bumped into her. "Turn it off, Raymond. They told me you went for a preacher, and that's well and good, but if I want to hear preaching, I'll go to church."

She used to rail against the hypocrisy of preachers all the time. She was one of the ones who always said you could worship God just as well in the garden as in church.

Raymond relaxed and sat down. Maybe a scolding from his mother was just what he needed. She used to scold all of them all the time. The big boys, Junior and Duke, then Ray and C.T. and all of them. When she scolded C.T., he used to grab her and make her do a little two-step with him. She never stopped the scolding, but she danced at the same time.

She said, "I expect if you're a real preacher you like some coffee."

"Yes ma'am," he said. "I'd like some coffee."

She turned on the burner under an old tin pot. There was a Mr. Coffee machine on the countertop, but she was using what looked like the same pot from when he was a boy.

She said, "Why didn't you bring them straightaway? Is your wife too fancy for the house where you grew up?"

"Now, Ma, don't blame Dinah. Dinah wanted to come right over with the children, but I wanted to see you myself first." She shook her head. He added, "I was afraid you'd be angry after my long years of absence, so I wanted to come and tell you how sorry I am."

"You should have brought those children, Raymond! You knew I'd want to see those children. All those years. And your wife too."

Yes, he thought, a scolding from your mother, that's a better thing than diamonds and rubies. The selfless love of mothers. "I should have come back long ago. I was wrong not to come."

"I suppose you're hungry too."

"Dinah's sister just fed us lunch, and she's got a big dinner planned."

She brought half a pound cake over, iced with chocolate, and started putting out a plate and fork. She cut him a big slice. Poured his coffee, got out the cream and sugar.

Thank you Jesus, he thought, feeling cared for, feeling all the familiarity of what may not have been the best childhood, but had been better than he deserved. He and his brothers ran all over the hills building forts, eating blackberries, catching black snakes, passing around the .22

to shoot at rabbits. Wrestling and spying and fishing and never catching a damn thing in those poisoned creeks.

"I've never been a good son," he said, "but you and Daddy gave us a good childhood—"

She dropped into the chair, heavily for a thin woman. "You were a perfectly passable son," she said, "until you decided to stop coming home. I never cared what you done, all I ever ask was to see you from time to time. Here I am an old woman and two of you boys dead already, so I'll never see them again. And don't you dare start spouting about meeting on the other side, Raymond. Do you prefer Sweet'n Lo?"

"No ma'am, sugar is fine." The sweetness of the cake and icing, the bitterness of the coffee. The sweet and bitter of this old life, but only sweet to come. He had an impression of cheerfulness from red and white curtains. "Everything spic and span, Mama."

She said, "Verna has been putting some money into this place since she moved in. She's a manager at the bank. I bet you didn't know that. She divorced her husband and moved back up here."

It was crowded in the old days with her, and his father and six boys plus Verna. Where did Verna sleep? He couldn't remember. Half the time there were cousins too. He said, "Is it just you and Verna then?"

"And her boy who takes up space for two."

He couldn't remember Verna's boy's name. "How old is he now?"

"He's a freshman in high school. He's a good boy, just lazy."

Raymond thanked Jesus that even if he couldn't remember the boy's name, Jesus had vouchsafed him to come home and see his family once more. He said, "That's about the age of my stepdaughter."

"You all move back here, and she can go to high school with Kelvin."

Kelvin, thought Ray. That was Verna's boy's name. "The cake is real good, Mama."

"Store-bought, but my icing."

She stopped talking, her loose-skinned hands lying in front of her on the table. From time to time she worked the wedding band around her finger. He said, "I saw Daddy's car under the tarp outside. It needs fixing up."

She snorted. "Junior's too busy working on other people's cars to fool with that. That boy Kelvin says he's going to work on it, but he's all talk."

"I might work on it if we stayed around," he said, and her eyes flashed at him so quickly he was sorry he'd said it. "I'm on my way down to interview for a job in Pocahontas County—"

"Pocahontas County!"

"It's a preaching job, Ma, which is what I am all about now. I go wherever Jesus sends me to share the good news."

"Well don't share it with me."

"I know you and Daddy were bitter toward the church," he said, wondering if this was the time to speak to her, "but it isn't any human church I'm talking about, it's Jesus—"

"Raymond," she said with her eyes narrow and her mouth. He heard her all the way through his shoulders and chest. "I'm asking you one more time. You're my boy, but you walked out on your mother and ain't been back in twelve years, so don't presume to preach at me."

He said, "Okay, Mother, not this time, but I'm going to be spending more time with you."

"Not if you go to Pocahontas County."

Jesus told him not to argue. He would have to prove himself to her. Fair enough.

He had a memory of being on her lap, and she was rocking him, some little hurt, an elbow, a knee, and she was whispering privately to him, making a tent of her arms around him, Shush, shush.

She said, "When, Raymond?"

"When what, Ma?"

"You know what. When are you bringing those children over for me to meet? And her. I want to meet your wife too."

"We'll come over day after tomorrow. How's that?"

She made a gentle snorting noise. "I want to have something sweet for those children. You could stay here, you know. We could make room. But I suppose the doctor's wife has a better place. Pocahontas County is farther off than Pennsylvania and all those other places you didn't come to visit from. I thought maybe with her sister here you might move back."

He said, "I might. If this doesn't work out. Maybe that's Jesus's backup plan for me."

She kept complaining in a comfortable way. "You never even come for your Daddy's funeral or C.T.'s either."

"I'm here now, Mama," he said, feeling himself wallow in regret like a great rich mountain of chocolate icing. "You know where I was when Daddy died—"

"I know. All the things you boys did, but I never thought you'd be the one to go to prison. Duke was a straight arrow, for all the good it did him, so I figured if anyone ever served time it would be C.T. I never figured you'd be the one, and I never figured you'd go for a preacher either. I know there was bad blood between you and your father. You Savages. I never knew what happened."

He could hardly remember. His father raised his hand to him. Thank you, Jesus, I don't remember what evil happened between me and my father.

He said, "You're a Savage too, Ma."

She sucked her teeth. "Not hardly. By marriage don't count. I never had any idea what it would be like having Savage boys for children."

"Now Ma, you always was a strong mountain woman."

She stared at him a long time. "And what is that supposed to mean, Raymond? That's a big pile of horse cake. I was a little bitty teenage girl your father decided to marry, and all of a sudden I turned around and here I stood in this very kitchen only it didn't have Corian countertops then and half the time the well was coughing up air instead of water, and here I was with seven children and a pail full of diapers and your dad expecting this strong mountain woman to put dinner on the table for however many friends and family he decided to bring over and you big boys screaming bloody murder and running out in the woods and getting ticks and broken arms and Lord I had no idea in the world how to make the bunch of you mind. You just ran wild and I stood there with my mouth open catching flies."

"You're exaggerating, Ma."

"I was ignorant. If I'd knowed a little more, you might not have ended up in jail."

"It's all worked out. Jail is where I met Jesus."

She rolled her eyes. "You're not going to tell me it's Jesus's idea for you not to come home, are you?"

It made him laugh. "Oh Mama, for a long time I was ashamed, and then I was trying to get my footing, and then, well, Dinah and I have a lot of love but not much money. Just one thing led to another. I always meant to come."

She shook her head. "You never were one to think very far ahead, which is strange because you're smart enough. It's not that I needed your help, Raymond. Verna never went far. Kenny, he tries hard, but that Kester, he'd be in worse trouble than you if he wasn't so lazy. C.T.'s wife Merlee stays in touch, even though she divorced him. Oh, it's not like I'm alone. I'm not complaining, Raymond," she said. "But I missed you! Each one of you is something special to me. And I always thought you'd bring me my grandkids to see."

He felt tears in his eyes. "I want that too, Mama. You don't know how much I want that. I promise, just as soon as I have this job interview." All the evil he had done, the pain he had given her. Jesus had promised him joy, but not that he'd never feel remorse. "I promise you, Mama, if I live, I'll be over here as soon as I have that interview, I'll bring you your grandkids to see."

He would have liked to pray with her, but Jesus said, Give her space. She poured more coffee, cut more cake.

He said, "You're not as tall as you used to be, Mama."

She snorted. "You're getting bald."

The last thing she said to him as he went out the door was, "Once you're as old as me, Raymond, you'll see that the only thing left is babies."

It was what Dinah thought too. If the Lighthouse of the Cross radio station didn't work out, he'd see what Jesus had in mind next for him. You just let me know, Jesus, he thought. You know I'm listening.

CHAPTER 20

That morning, David arrived at the office long before the staff. He sat down and set his breakfast in front of him: a large McDonald's coffee, black, and a plastic-wrapped pastry. He had had three hours of sleep, most of it shivering in the car. He had finally gone inside the house, showered, made breakfast for the girls, and then left without eating anything himself. The sweet roll's icing caused him to wince. His eyes fell on the print from *Water Lilies* on the wall, and that turned his stomach. He felt like one of his fibromyalgia patients saying, Doctor, I hurt all over.

He went out to the front desk and brought back some charts, laid out last night. He flipped through them, but couldn't concentrate. Once the day was in progress, he thought he would be okay. Once the phones were ringing, faxes coming in, once he was listening to murmuring heart valves, looking at throats, palpating bellies. Once he was called to action, he'd be fine. It just all felt bleak now. He closed his eyes, and Grace rose up inside his eyelids, her chin lowered, her eyes enormous, silent. What did she think? What was all this doing to their family? How could he go on taking care of patients, taking care of the girls—and having to watch his back with Grace?

He took off his glasses, laid them on the desk and rubbed his eyes. Drank coffee, forced himself to take a bite of pastry. Finally someone came in the front. He thought he recognized Merlee's step. He felt a little flag of hope. Merlee would help.

The footsteps hesitated outside his door, then a knock. "Doctor?"

She was fuzzy to him without his glasses, but he could see the lavender of her scrubs, and how they were pressed out by her chest. It was hard not to notice Merlee's breasts. She didn't dress to emphasize them, but they were always there. He still wanted to bury his face.

He put the glasses back on.

"Are you okay?"

"I went to the motel," he said, "but I didn't stay."

Her forehead wrinkled. "You and Grace had a fight."

Part of what he wanted was just sympathy. "A fight? What's there to fight about, Merlee? She bought a house and never told me. How can I ever trust her again? How can you live with someone who buys a house without telling you?" It felt good to say it aloud.

Merlee nodded. "It was a pretty crazy thing to do."

He felt a big baby sob in his throat, but swallowed it down.

In the distance, voices as the others began to arrive. Merlee stepped all the way in and closed the office door. "Do you need us to cancel patients?"

He shook his head, got up from his desk. He had a vague impulse, a memory of sitting on someone's lap with his face buried. "No I need to work. It's the best thing, maybe the only thing."

When he said that, he felt even more sad and needy. He took three steps from behind the desk, closer to her.

She said, "Doctor?"

He didn't look at her face. He laid a hand on each of them, through the scrubs, like a stone wall, not soft at all. He lowered his face toward the speckled V of soft skin between. He knew her odor, as if he'd been breathing her in for a long time, a little soap, an undercurrent of skin oil, no perfume.

She took hold of his wrists and removed his hands, forced him back. "I don't think you want to do that, Doctor."

"Actually," he said, "I want to very much."

"I think maybe you're a little crazy too, Doctor. Like Grace."

He was a little crazy too. Merlee said so. Just like Grace.

She pressed him back, and he thought: I just grabbed my nurse's breasts. I did something sexually inappropriate. Grace wasn't the only one who could go crazy.

She said, "I know you don't mean anything by it." She backed him to his chair. He felt himself drop into it. She stepped back and said, "You need to straighten it out with Grace, Doctor. That's what you need. Let me tell you what's going to happen." Please, he thought. Please tell me. She placed herself all the way back against the door again and said, "You're going to be mad at Grace for a while, really mad, because she did something she should have talked to you about first. And after a while, you won't be mad, and then the two of you are going to make up and go on. That's what people do."

"You got a divorce."

"From C.T. Savage! Of course I did! That was the only thing that ever made him sit up and take notice. You and Grace are different people. And besides, divorcing C.T. never got him out of my life. I think I saw more of him after we got divorced than I did before."

They were getting louder in the front, the staff. He said, "Please accept my apology for my behavior. It was inexcusable."

Merlee waved a hand. "The only real question is, are you up to seeing patients? Maybe you ought to cancel the morning and take a nap on the exam table."

He shook his head no. "I want to see patients."

"Okay." She opened the door. "Would you really want to be married to someone who never surprised you a little? Would you want to know everything about her and have her know everything about you?"

I thought I did, he told himself. He thought yes, that is what he wanted.

But he didn't want her to know about Merlee's breasts.

He put in a full day. There were no major crises, but enough happening to keep him awake and reasonably alert. Someone went out for sausage sandwiches for lunch. Merlee insisted they all eat together in the little kitchen, David too. Everyone knew about the cottage, of course, but nobody mentioned it.

In the midafternoon, Merlee came in person and called him out of an examining room to tell him Grace was on the phone. Her sister and family had arrived. What time did he want dinner?

He hesitated. "Tell them not to wait for me?" Merlee frowned, so he added, "I'll be there, but I may have to go to the hospital first."

Merlee accepted that, and presumably so did Grace.

As she left, with the others, buttoned up in her denim jacket, she put her head in his office. "You'd better do the hospital rounds tomorrow," she said. "Go home and be with your family. Tell my evil old brother-in-law Ray Savage hello for me. He always was a piece of work."

"I'd rather be late. That way I'll miss him praying over dinner."

Merlee laughed. "It's hard to picture Ray a preacher. I swear. Tell Ray that nobody around here believes a bit of it—I don't mean God, I mean about him turning into a preacher." She started to leave, then turned back. "You make it up with Gracie tonight, all right?"

"Merlee," he said, "I'm sorry—"

"Shush," said Merlee. "I said it. Everybody goes a little crazy sometimes."

He felt weariness beginning to catch up, sleep gathering like a midnight blue pool. He almost dropped off, then came awake thinking about his girls. He didn't want them alone in the same room with the religious fanatic. Merlee was right: the patients in the hospital were all stable. He could go later tonight or early tomorrow. He imagined himself protecting his family, chest to chest with Ray.

As he stood, his foot brushed the bag under his desk. A sack, in West Virginia, not a bag. It had been there for two weeks, a gift from the staff for the new house. Two bottles of wine that he kept forgetting to take home, or maybe not forgetting, but having nothing to celebrate. He took that with him, a weapon against the fanatic.

CHAPTER 21

Grace's two girls flounced and tossed their heads and sighed and gestured. But Dinah's children were polite and didn't squabble. She wondered if it was because they were guests or because they didn't watch television or play computer games.

She was especially glad to see Aleda, so grown-up and beautiful. She had been the first baby Grace ever knew, and she had loved her with no mixed feelings, no postpartum depression, no terror over making mistakes. The year after Aleda was born, Grace had worked in a flower shop to supplement Dinah's welfare and took some community-college classes. She had been cheerful and purposeful and sure of what she was doing. But Dinah found an obscure scholarship at the University of Delaware for an orphan girl who aspired to be a teacher of young children. None of Grace's arguments in favor of staying with Dinah and Aleda had changed Dinah's mind.

Grace went, got her degree, got a job in the school where she had done her practice teaching, met David, and never spent much time with Aleda again. She thought how sad it was she hadn't seen her grow up, had hardly known Dinah's other kids. How sad that Margaret and Ruth had missed knowing them and Dinah too.

Grace wished it could be dinner with just Grace and the kids, that Raymond would stay at his mother's, that David would go to the hospital instead of coming home. She didn't even feel guilty about her wish. She wanted just them, her sister and herself and their kids.

The twins and Ruth plus little Jacob got umbrellas and went for a walk around the development. Margaret and Aleda went up to Margaret's room. Grace chopped cabbage and apples for coleslaw, and Dinah nursed Benjie to sleep. There was a golden silence in the kitchen.

Now, thought Grace. Now I can tell her about the cottage.

Benjie dropped off, and Dinah kissed his forehead. "I'm in a rotten mood, Grace. Yelling at Ray about going to his mother's."

"You didn't yell."

"Yes I did. Raymond is the kindest man in the world, but I've never understood about his mother. All these years, all these kids, and she's never seen them. I've just been so irritable lately. I shouldn't be giving him a hard time. I've been praying for a way for him to have a ministry, and now we get this chance, and all I can think about is objections." She flashed a big smile at Grace. "Human nature, right Grace?"

Grace said, "You never met any of Ray's family?"

"His brother C.T. came through once on a motorcycle. That was a long time ago."

"The one who was married to Merlee?"

Dinah nodded. "Raymond always calls his mother at Christmas, and then he shoves the phone at me. So I've talked to her, but never met her face to face. She always names my kids like she's memorized them, and asks about each one. Then she wants to know when we're coming to visit, and she makes a point of saying Raymond's stepdaughter is welcome too. She says exactly the same thing every year." The baby jerked awake again, sucking before his eyes opened, then pounding a fist on the broad slope of Dinah's breast. "This guy has a voracious appetite."

"I miss nursing," Grace said. "It's the best feeling. If you could put it in a pill, no one would ever be depressed again."

"Have another baby. This house has plenty of room."

"I'm finished."

"Having babies is the best thing in life," said Dinah.

Without planning, it just popped out of Grace: "David and I are having a fight. We never had a fight like this before."

"Oh Gracie, that's too bad."

"I've been depressed over the move, and I did something that hurt him."

Dinah made a soft noise.

"I bought a house. I bought the house we lived in before we moved here. It's just a cottage, and everything's old, but we were so happy there. I bought it for you, Dinah."

"In Kingfield?"

"I went into some kind of panic and bought the house we just moved out of and didn't tell David. If you lived there, you could still homeschool your kids. Or we could trade houses and you could live up here and we'd go back to the cottage."

"Wait, back up. You didn't tell David?"

"I was half-crazy. And it wasn't his money, Dinah. It was money I had saved when I was teaching that was supposed to be for us, and the other money, that I stole from you."

"What are you talking about, Gracie. When did you ever steal from me?"

"The money you made selling drugs. When I was still in high school. I stole it over months and months, for years. It was in the trunk."

Benjie was asleep again, Dinah buttoning her dress and pursing her mouth. "Drug money?"

"You used to put it in the trunk for safekeeping, in my room, and I would slip part out and put it in the lining of the trunk."

"I should never have involved you at all."

"Well, you did. Do you remember when that man came to the house and I told you he stole the money? I took everything that was left and hid it. I should have given it back to you long ago."

Dinah was quiet for a while, then said, "I don't want that drug money."

"I used it to buy the cottage. Plus my savings, none of it was David's."

"No, Gracie, whatever a woman and a man have, it's theirs together."

Grace plunged on. "You haven't seen the cottage. It saved my life right after Ruthie was born and I was depressed, and then when we moved up here, I wanted to go back to the cottage. So I bought it. I know it was crazy, not crazy like *her*, just a kind of craziness. I wanted the cottage back so much I couldn't live without it, and now, I see I'm okay in *this* house if you'll live in the little house."

Dinah's face was very still. "Gracie, Gracie. You can't plan for other people. We have this job interview down in the mountains."

Grace didn't think she could bear it if Dinah said no, so she didn't wait for an answer. "But the worst part is David found out from someone else. He didn't sleep here last night. He went to a motel."

"Oh Gracie."

It felt so good, the sorrow in Dinah's voice. The very exhalation of the air it took to tell her made her feel better. "I had to have the cottage."

"Then you and David should go live there."

"No, Dinah, I see now it wasn't the house, it was home. I want a home. You're my home."

Dinah lowered her face and kissed the baby's forehead. "Conflict between husband and wife is like the opposite of a blessing."

"I have to have you near me. I want my girls to have cousins. It wasn't David's money." It was so clear to her, at least for the moment, that this wasn't about David. Not really even about her marriage.

"You offering me a house, Gracie, that's so sweet. It's just like you. But—"

"Just think about it. We can talk about it after you get back. Why don't you leave the kids with me tomorrow, and go find out what this is all about, and then you can stay here in this house or in the cottage, as long as you need to."

"I might leave the kids with you. Not the baby, of course. I might take Aleda to help me take care of him. This place—this radio show or church—we don't even know what it is. It's hard to trust and obey—I do trust and obey, I don't care where we are, Gracie, honestly I don't, I just want to be settled. And safe."

Grace smiled, thinking, You can be safe in the cottage, here in Kingfield, with me.

The kids came back, cheeks pink, voices excited over nothing and everything. Grace asked them to set the dining-room table.

"We're going to use the *dining room?*" said Ruth. "What about the boxes?"

Grace told them to stack the boxes along the wall. Aleda and Margaret came down, cloth napkins were folded. Ruth explained to the twins about saltwater fish tanks and freshwater fish tanks. Jacob talked to the fish. They were bringing out chairs and stools when Dinah said,

"Oh, there it is, The trunk. When Grace and I were small, we always kept it packed in case we had to move."

Margaret glanced at Grace, "You never told us that."

Ruth said, "You never told us *anything!*"

Dinah told the story of the trunk and how each of the sisters kept a change of underwear in it and packages of peanut-butter crackers and coloring books. Just in case.

Grace said, "I thought anything we put in there would be safe. Once I got in it myself when I thought there was a tornado coming."

Zack and Sarah looked thrilled. Dinah opened it, and everyone gathered round. There was the ancient apple, a couple of board games, Monopoly on top. Coloring books, decades-old crayons scattered on its floor.

"We kept the safe houses in here," said Grace.

Then they had to tell the kids about the safe houses. Ruth said, "I wish the safe houses were still there."

Sarah said, "Do you think we could play Monopoly?"

"Of course!" said Grace.

The Savages looked at Dinah, and she said, "I don't see why not."

So all the children, the big girls too, took the game into the living room and began discussing the rules for the ones who hadn't played. Benjie woke up again and Raymond came back. He had his big smile on and filled so much space.

"Need help, sister?" Ray asked Grace.

Dinah said, "Don't let him help, Grace. He's a danger in the kitchen."

"Now Dinie." He leaned over and touched the baby's head with his lips. "That's just how they raised us back then. Dividing up the responsibilities. Not that I was ever very responsible, always tried to get out of my chores."

"How was she?" asked Dinah.

He took the baby. "She scolded me for not bringing the kids."

"We should have gone with you."

"We'll go," he said. "As soon as we get back."

They put out dinner, meat and vegetarian chili, coleslaw, jars of pickles and chow-chow that Dinah had made. The oven buzzed for the corn bread. "I think that's everything," said Grace, everyone standing around, waiting to be told to sit.

Before they could sit, the front door opened. "He's here!" Ruth cried and ran to the door, returned carrying David's briefcase.

Dinah's kids went into size-order again to meet David, who looked strange to Grace: his hair damp, his cheeks pink. His face determined. He had said he'd be late, but here he was. Carrying something, a paper bag, clutched to his side, and he didn't put it down. When it came Jacob's turn to shake hands, he turned away and clung to Dinah's leg.

Dinah said, "Oh dear, I forgot. We told him you were a doctor, David. He's fascinated by doctors. He had a broken arm last year and had to go to the hospital."

Jacob rubbed his face on his blanket and stared at David.

"And you were brave, yes?" said David.

"Yes," said Jacob. "This arm."

David squatted down and felt the arm, commented on how well it had healed. David had to put down his sack to examine Jacob and then to wash his hands, but he carried it with him to the table, slipped it under his chair.

Grace kept watching it. It seemed to carry some meaning. She told herself it was a good sign he'd come home, but she had felt more sure of herself when he was absent. Then she realized what was different about him. He wasn't wearing his glasses. She had noticed his hair but not the missing glasses.

Dinah said, "Ray's mother ought to come and see you with her arthritis, David. Ray says she won't go to the doctor at all."

Ray said, "My sister Verna Burns and her family are your patients."

David nodded without smiling, always so circumspect about patient confidentiality, even though he was the only doctor in town and everybody was his patient.

Grace lifted a plate of cornbread to start passing, but Ray cleared his throat. "Before we begin to enjoy these good things, I'd like us all to pause and offer thanks to the One Who Provides."

Grace didn't look at David but made her own prayer, to him: Please don't make a fuss, just let him say what he wants.

The Savages folded their hands under their chins, and after a pause, so did Ruth, but not Margaret. Ray started with thanks, and how much he and his family appreciated the hospitality of their beloved sister and brother-in-law.

Grace kept her eyes open to watch David watching Raymond.

"Yes, Jesus," Raymond went on. "I can see before me the lighthouse of the cross, a beacon for the lambs lost at sea! Let me be your instrument Jesus to sail the lost lambs home."

David's mouth was getting tighter.

"All these little bleating lambs, Lord! Walking to the slaughterhouse! All stumbling toward the bloody shambles! Yearning to be saved and never knowing it! Yearning to be saved from the great knife with the edge as sharp as a razor!"

Ruth's eyes popped open.

Raymond's jaw went stiff, and he made a clicking sound in the corners of his mouth between words, and his head jerked as if he were having a seizure. Ruth pushed back her chair and scuttled around the table to Grace, who hugged her close, smelling her damp hair.

"The great knife with the razor-sharp edge, Lord!" cried Raymond, clicking. "Jesus Jesus! He gave it all to save us!" Louder and louder, the shouting and the clicking. "Buckets of blood pouring out the doors of the great slaughterhouse! Oh save us, Jesus!"

By this point, everyone's eyes had flown open except Ray's, and Dinah shouted, "Amen!" Then added, "And thank you Jesus for this delicious food that's starting to cool. Thank you Jesus for feeding the children, they're hungry now. It's time to eat. Amen. That's enough Ray."

Raymond blinked, saw them all staring. "Amen," he said, softly. "God bless our loved ones. Amen."

"Amen!" shouted Sarah and Zack and Jacob. Ruth clung to Grace for a few more seconds then went back to her place between the twins.

"Well," said Raymond, in his normal voice, although his forehead was still sweaty, "I got the spirit there, didn't I? Don't this look fine!"

David stood up. "I'll be right back."

What? thought Grace. What now? She said, "That chili is vegetarian because Margaret and Ruth—"

Then David came back with the corkscrew and four wine glasses. "I'm going to open a bottle of wine," he said across the table to Raymond. "I hope you aren't offended."

"Not at all, brother!"

David pulled out two bottles of wine from the mysterious sack. "It was a housewarming gift from my staff, and I thought this would be an appropriate time to celebrate. Now, who'd like some?"

"Me!" shouted Zack, and after a look from Dinah, said, "Sorry, just joking!"

Dinah said, "You go ahead, David. We don't want any, but you do exactly what you always do in your own home."

"We don't usually have wine," Grace said.

David said, "Raymond, will you have a glass?"

"I don't mind if I do," said Raymond, causing the entire Savage family to stare.

"All right!" said David. "Excellent." He didn't ask Grace, but poured one for her. "Dinah are you sure?"

"I'm sure, thank you."

Ruth said, "Can we have coke because it's a celebration and drink coke from wine glasses?"

"Of course," said David.

Dinah said, "We stay away from—"

"It's a celebration, honey," said Raymond. "We're celebrating being with family in their beautiful new home."

Margaret went to the cabinet for more wine glasses, and Ruth got out a liter bottle of cola from the pantry. She showed Zack and Sarah how to use the ice maker on the refrigerator. For the moment, the novelty of coke for dinner, the ice maker, and the beautiful big-bulb wine glasses, and then eating, seemed to occupy everyone, and just for the moment Grace thought it really would be okay.

Raymond said, "I never was a wine drinker, it was always beer and the hard stuff for me."

Aleda said, "They're beautiful glasses, Uncle David."

David smiled at her. He liked young people.

Raymond said, "Sometimes we used to get 'shine from down in Webster County when I was a boy."

"Moonshine?" said Margaret.

"You never told us that," said Sarah.

Ray shrugged and knocked back his wine. "It's just homemade liquor," he said. "No better or worse than this."

Dinah said, "Except that it's illegal."

David said, "Let's have a toast. Raymond prayed, now I'd like to make a toast!"

Everyone paused and lifted the glasses. Even Dinah had taken some coke and ice.

David raised his glass toward the chandelier. "A toast to life," he said. "To the drinking of wine and the laughter of children. To enjoying life and preserving it. *L'chaim*."

"That was a beautiful toast," said Dinah, after everyone had sipped.

"Thank you Jesus," said Raymond. He finished off his second glass, and David emptied the first bottle into Ray's glass and opened the second bottle.

Grace took a good long sip. Whatever happens, happens, she thought.

There followed a discussion of what was the secret ingredient in the vegetarian chili: raisins, nuts, apples, beans, tomatoes and—"Cocoa!" cried Ruth. "Mexican food uses unsweetened chocolate and cocoa."

Ray complimented Grace's cooking. David complimented Dinah's homemade pickles. Zack whispered something that made Jacob giggle, and Sarah reached behind Ruth to poke Zack.

The wine was creating a glow around the table, and for the first time Grace liked the dining room with its brushed brass chandelier and enough space for so many. She thought if she had Christmas here, she could fit in everyone, including David's aunts. I can live here, she thought, if Dinah is nearby. In the cottage.

Grace didn't think she'd ever seen David drink so much wine. Raymond she had assumed didn't drink at all, and he was ahead of David.

There was a conversation about hospitals, how David liked the Kingfield Community Hospital, but also the nearness of the university's teaching hospital.

Grace started the coffee, the baby began to pull at Dinah's dress. "Excuse me," said Dinah. "We'll just go in the kitchen."

Grace said, "You can nurse him here, Dinah."

"Please," said David. "It's one of my crusades, to make nursing an everyday thing. To have women nurse longer."

"Oh, we nurse a long time, believe me," said Dinah. "I won't miss a thing from the kitchen."

Raymond said, "She likes privacy for that."

David turned slowly toward Raymond.

Grace felt it coming, and she was almost glad. Get it over with, she thought.

He said, "You know, don't you, that breastfeeding is absolutely the best thing for the baby's health and the mother's well-being?"

"Absolutely," said Raymond. "Dinah nursed every one of them for as long as she could."

"Except me," said Aleda.

The men looked at her but didn't seem to see her.

David said, "Part of my crusade is to encourage it publicly as well as in private."

"Well, brother, I don't see it that way. After all, there's plenty natural that we do in private. Things between a husband and wife. Bathroom things."

"You're not comparing nursing to defecation, I hope."

Dinah called from the kitchen. "Okay, that's enough of that. The baby and I like privacy."

David was totally concentrated on Raymond, the kids totally concentrated on the match shaping up in front of them.

Ray said, "It is surely natural to feed a baby the way God meant it to be done. I just prefer my lady to step away from the dinner table. That's all."

David said, "Why is it that you feel a breast at the table is wrong, but you have no problem with images of violence at the dinner table?"

"But the words aren't mine, Brother David. I am just an instrument when I pray."

"Your god tells you to frighten little children?"

Raymond said, "Oh, Brother David, Jesus loves them all. He just wants to save them. I'm filled with a great sorrow, whenever I think that you and your beautiful family haven't found Jesus. Jesus suffered more than any of us can ever know, and he suffered to make a place for you and me and all you have to do is accept it."

"We don't need saving, Raymond," said David. "My family and I are making our way without your interference. Without buckets of blood."

"I'm praying for you, Doctor. I'm praying for all of us sinners, but especially you and your family. You're the lost lambs, David."

David had his hands flat on the table, his eyes wide, and without glasses his whole face was open as if in the wind. "Not lost," he said, "and not lambs."

"Amen?" said Jacob.

Raymond turned his eyes up to the ceiling. "If you see a man in a burning house, wouldn't you try to drag him out?"

David said, "My house is not burning. This is my home, and you are welcome here, but not welcome to frighten my children."

Grace thought suddenly, This is what a warrior does. David is protecting. He's trying to keep us safe.

Dinah came back in buttoning her dress. "Aleda, take Benjie." She went and stood behind Raymond and laid her hands on his shoulders. "Raymond, just tell them again how grateful we are for their hospitality."

Ray blinked. "Absolutely. We appreciate your hospitality. I never had a better bowl of chili in my life."

"And the corn bread," said Dinah.

"The corn bread was outstanding," said Aleda, jiggling baby Benjamin.

"And the salad," said Sarah.

"And the coke," said Zack.

"And dessert?" said Jacob.

The Savages were ready to move on, and Grace's kids were smiling with relief, but Grace found herself wanting to stand behind David as Dinah stood behind Ray. "David does more good for other people than all the rest of us put together!"

"Oh Gracie," said Dinah. "Let it go."

"Sister," said Raymond, "Brother David is a fine man and the best doctor these poor lost souls are likely to ever have. But Jesus isn't about our—accomplishments."

"I give up," said Dinah. "Pass me the corn bread. I'll just sit over here and quietly have another piece of corn bread with jam. The rest of you argue to your hearts' content."

David said, "I respect your belief system, just respect mine, that's all. Listen as well as talk."

But Dinah hadn't really given up. She said, "So, David, did you hear that Grace and I both made brownies?"

"It's a brownie competition," said Margaret. David blinked.

Margaret could always call him back to himself. "A competition for which sister makes the best brownies."

Dinah said, "Ray I thought you wanted to go over to your brother's tonight. You should go and get back because we have to get up early and drive a long way."

David stood, reached for his briefcase. "I have to go to the hospital anyhow. I didn't make rounds yet."

"What about the brownies?" asked Ruth.

"I'll take one in a napkin," he said.

Grace followed him to the door. "Do you want me to drive you to the hospital? Are you sure you're okay to drive?"

He paused with the door open, facing out, into the evening. The rain had stopped, but it was still cold and wet. "You mean the wine?" He didn't sound particularly angry.

"Well, that, and the fog—"

"I'll drive very carefully, and when I get to the hospital, I'll sit in the parking lot a while before I go it. I don't want to cause any more scandal."

"David," she said as he opened the door. He paused, back to her. "What about your glasses?"

He took them out of his pocket.

Possibly without reason, she felt hopeful.

CHAPTER 22

Richie had insomnia long before he knew he had ALS, so it was no surprise that he would have insomnia the night before Dinah came to Mountain Dome. In the absolute darkness of his safe room, he tried to breathe himself to sleep. In the end, it would be the breathing that got him, the creeping paralysis that finally affects even the automatic systems. But not the senses. His senses would stay sharp: vision and hearing and also intellectual function. Eye and bladder muscles the last to go, and oh yes, sexual function and sex drive can continue unabated to the end. In the end you are left with nothing but desire.

It was enough to make you believe in god, he thought: a malevolent god who sat around planning the worst for each human being. Which disease will cause the maximum suffering for Richie Lock? All the senses alert for maximum suffering? Amyotrophic lateral sclerosis? Perfect.

When he was a little boy, he used to be afraid of falling asleep and forgetting how to breathe. He had slept better once he had Dinah and Grace in his life. He would, in the dark of night, imagine them on his toy shelf next to Luke Skywalker and Obi-Wan Kenobi. Their miniature legs would be swinging back and forth above his head. It was always both of them, but Dinah was the one with the Force.

He would hear her voice: Oh just relax, Richie, could you just calm down already? Where's the switch? Can we turn Richie Off for a while? Her voice was always an unchildlike alto. Practical and no nonsense.

All he wanted, he believed, was her presence so he could fall asleep. He didn't care if she lived in another house, if she had sex with her husband. He didn't care if she kept having babies. He believed he could sleep if Dinah was nearby.

When he was a teenager, away at school, he used to lie awake imagining her having sex with someone else. He remembered coming in one weekend and dropping his bag at the house and going straight to the carriage house looking for Dinah, but only Grace was home, and probably their father, too, but no one noticed him. Grace had acted the hostess, made tea, served a plate of cookies. A regular little tea party. We haven't seen you for so long, Richie.

He wasn't surprised that Dinah was out, he didn't remember details, just that he had come looking for her, and she had not been there.

Richie remembered he talked too much to Grace, couldn't stop boasting about something, money girlfriends big plans. At some point, he had said Dinah never respected him, Dinah used him.

That roused Grace out of her hostess mode. "Well that's ridiculous, Richie. Dinah wouldn't use you, she never even thinks about you"— which of course was far worse. "Besides," said Grace, "I thought you were in favor of using people. I read those books too, you know, *The Fountainhead* and *Atlas Shrugged*."

He had asked if Dinah read them, and Grace said no, Dinah didn't like novels. Richie had said that Ayn Rand's books were more philosophy than novels, anyhow.

Grace said, "I guess they're okay as stories, but the heroes are completely immoral."

He could still remember the attitude he struck. A sardonic smile and "but of course."

He had always liked Grace. Once he got Dinah to Mountain Dome, he hoped Grace would visit too. He would ask her if she remembered that afternoon when she made a tea party for him.

But that had been the day Grace told him Dinah wasn't going with Wolf anymore. That she was going with Dylan. Dylan, the wraith, beneath contempt, he had thought, but knew even then that there was something to it, those eyes, some quality Dylan had, a music that seemed to cling to him. "Why?" he said to Grace, exposing himself as completely as he ever had: "Why doesn't she love *me*?"

That afternoon Grace had infuriatingly been the mature and rational one. "You haven't been around much, Richie," she said. "I mean, you can't expect her to love you if you're never around. And besides, Dylan is an artist. He turns everything into beauty. I would love him if she didn't."

In the safe room, he fumbled for the broad flat switch on the lamp. Impossible to miss even for clumsy hands. The greenish light brought him back to the total safety of the inner chamber. The faint hum of the ventilation system.

Grimly he thought how there was nothing beautiful about Dylan now.

The last thing he had said to Grace that day was, "Tell Dinah I'll wait."

He went out of the sealed inner chamber, into the outer section of the safe room. He never slept in the big bedroom upstairs anymore. Upstairs was too exposed. Not that anyone was going to attack him— who? Enrique and Maria or the putative cousins from Mexico? Poke and Bobby Mack who were perfectly content in their man-cave bunk-house? Just the same, he checked the panel of security camera screens: no one in the hall outside, no one in the living area. Enrique's house, the bunkhouse. The television was running at Poke and Bobby's, and someone asleep on the couch, Poke's nephew, he thought. He checked the greenhouses, which had only faint night-lights. He ought to close them down, get rid of the Mexicans, too many people up here.

He went out in the hall barefoot, with his cane, although his balance was unusually good tonight. He went up the shallow stairs to the great room with its enormous wall of windows, the silvery forms of furniture.

Much of the house had been dug into the mountainside and the rest built of perfectly fitted fieldstone: solar collectors on the roof, a wind turbine next to the barns, gasoline and natural-gas generators for backup, state-of-the-art pellet stoves. Everything carefully planned, as close to self-sustaining as possible. Tomorrow he'd check Dinah's cottage once more, make sure that Enrique and Maria had stocked the shelves and refrigerator properly. He had sent one of the hired operatives to follow her in the grocery store and note the brands of cereal she bought, but it had always been the store brand, saving money.

He paused to gaze out the windows at the gorge, where night was never completely dark. Then he went back to the elevator in its niche, took it to the second floor, to his office suite and bedroom. He sat at his desk and checked the monitors up there too.

Then Richie put on his earphones and pushed the play button. He winced because the first thing up was Lou Gehrig's farewell speech, the scratchy recording from the long-ago microphone: A tough break, but a lot to live for. Richie switched to music: "We Built This City." But Gehrig's voice stayed in his mind. Thanking everyone, his wife, his teammates, his goddamn mother-in-law—what a stupid pathetic straight arrow.

And if you can't stay permanently, he will say to Dinah, if there is something missing, would you visit on weekends? He switched back to the farewell speech, and this time listened all the way through.

CHAPTER 23

Aleda thought she was the last one awake at Aunt Grace's house. She heard pieces of a conversation in the next room where her mother and Ray were. Then Benjie cried, and in the distance, someone coughed, maybe Uncle David. She had heard him come in from the hospital. Earlier, Margaret had whispered to her that he and Aunt Grace were having a fight, and she thought it was possible they were going to get a divorce. Margaret said she didn't necessarily think divorce was a bad thing, that people *should* get a divorce if they didn't love each other anymore, did Aleda agree? Aleda said that she personally would only marry when she was sure it was someone she'd never divorce, but that didn't mean other people shouldn't do it.

Margaret said, I thought you'd be against it.

She should have told Margaret that everyone has disagreements, even her mother and Ray. If it got serious with them, Dinah would shut up, at least for a while, because she believed in the woman submitting to the man.

Aleda kept wondering what a fight between husband and wife would be like if you weren't a Christian and couldn't end it with prayer. She had always loved Aunt Grace, and she was fascinated by Uncle David, who she knew was an atheist. How could he look at a flower and not believe there was a God?

She wondered how smart you had to be to become a doctor.

If I married Travis, she thought—growing enormous in the dark, as if the house couldn't hold her or the dark hills or thick clouds above them—if I married Travis, we would always think of one another first, and if there were conflicts, we would speak softly to each other until we understood. And of course pray.

She heard bathroom sounds. Who was that? You didn't need four bathrooms, of course, but wouldn't it be wonderful to be able to go into one of them, the one with an onyx-black toilet was her favorite, and just lock the door and no one could ever knock and say, Aleda Aleda hurry up I have to go.

Finally, there was just a small creak from the stairs, and her own sigh, and her own open eyes.

This happened to her every once in a while. She didn't think it was insomnia, it wasn't a bad feeling, just a wakeful excitement, a sense she would never need to sleep again. She felt at ease and totally aware. She thought it must be what God felt like, aware of creation all around Him, all the animal noises and wind in the treetops and people's pasts and futures.

As she lay there, she circled around Travis. Travis *who she was going to see tomorrow.*

She prayed that he might be part of God's plan for her life.

In the darkest far corner of Margaret's room, she imagined him folded in the shadows, his beard, the twitch of his bright smile. He kept his distance at first, but when she closed her eyes, he hovered near her, and enclosed her, more powerful than touching, and she felt an enormous wanting just below her navel.

Travis, Travis, Travis.

She laid her right hand on the fat part over the bone, and her thighs tightened, and she pressed and rolled her hand until waves of sensation passed through her.

Travis, Travis.

When they were together, she would tell him how she yearned for him, but also that abstinence was the sacrifice that made sex better in the end.

In the morning, Aleda and her mother and Ray and baby Benjie drove off under a high gray sky with no rain and no sunshine either. There was a discussion about who would sit in the van's middle seat with Benjie, and they decided it should be Aleda first. She didn't care. She had a bag of used paperback classics, and her mind full of Travis. Benjie wanted to play, though, so she gave him her hand to chew.

They were barely out of the driveway when Dinah said, "I don't feel right leaving those kids."

Aleda said, "They aren't babies anymore, Mom."

Ray said, "We can still go back and get them."

"No," said Dinah. "I'm just saying, I feel funny about it." Another mile, the sign for the interstate, and Dinah said, "Jacob looked so little."

Ray said, "We do everything we can, Dinah, we raise them and we pray for them and at some point we have to trust them to Jesus. Your sister may not be a Christian, but she'll take good care of them."

Aleda said, "Why isn't Aunt Grace a Christian anyhow?"

Dinah said, "Grace is as much a Christian as 99 percent of the people."

"Well, Dinie," said Ray. "She's missing one important thing which is belief in the saving grace of our Lord and Savior Jesus Christ."

Dinah grunted, and then after a little space sighed. "I know they'll be fine, but I never left Jacob before."

"You leave him all the time, Mom—with me, with Ray, you even leave him with Sarah and Zack."

"At home," said Dinah. "I never left him alone and not at home."

"Let's go back," said Ray. "I don't want you worrying the whole day."

Aleda froze. Don't go back, go forward!

Dinah said, "I'm just feeling low. Give me some time."

"We could sing," said Raymond. He liked to lead hymn singing as he drove, but no one responded.

After a while, on the interstate heading east, Dinah said, "We're going to have to get everyone cell phones if we're going to run off in all directions."

Ray said, "If this works out, there are going to be a lot of good things that this family will have that we have denied ourselves before. Jesus just may command us to have some good things."

Aleda liked that. She was pretty sure she had been commanded to Travis. Called to something good. Called like the boy Samuel in the night, called like what happened to Ray when he heard from Jesus. But she could hear in her mind Dinah saying, A call! You call *that* a call? I call it hormones.

Aleda responded in her imagination: What if hormones are the way God calls us?

Not long after they started south on Route 219, Benjie got fussy, and they had to pull off so Dinah could nurse him. The hills were still brown and gray at the higher elevations, a little bit of some deep pink bush, early trees coming out but just in the low places along creeks. Benjie wasn't really hungry, just bored. Dinah got in the back this time and Aleda in front with Ray.

They stayed on 219 through Tucker County into Randolph. Ray hummed down in his throat as he drove, and Aleda fooled around in her bag, looking at the books, she'd read them all before: Jane Austen and the Brontës.

Ray said, "Which one are you going to read now?"

"I may just look at the scenery."

"West Virginia," said Ray. "Most beautiful place on earth. Look at that redbud coming out. Thank you Jesus!"

"You never talk about West Virginia," she said. "I guess I thought you didn't care about it."

He said, "I left West Virginia following a wrongful road, and I've been finding my way, and I'm thinking that coming home is part of the plan for me. Isn't that right, Dinah?"

"We'll see," said Dinah.

Ray said, "Come on, Aleda, don't you want to be a mountaineer girl?"

Tentatively, just touching on something exciting, she said, "Mountaineers is what they call their football team, isn't it?"

"The West Virginia University Mountaineers." And he gave a little whoop, not loud, but very enthusiastic.

"If we lived here," said Aleda, making sure Dinah could hear, "I might go to West Virginia University after high school."

"That would be fine," said Ray.

She thought she heard Dinah snort, and she knew Dinah was thinking keg parties and date rape, but she was pretty sure she'd never actually stop her from going to college. She did some numbers in her head. Travis still hadn't finished his freshman year. If she got into high school and did summer school, she might be able to finish in three years and go to college while he was still there. Did they have special dormitories for married students?

They didn't say a lot, not Ray or Aleda or Dinah. They stopped several times, to nurse the baby, for Ray to make an adjustment under the hood. Aleda and Dinah switched seats again. They went to a state park and sat at a picnic table and ate jelly-on-corn-bread sandwiches, which Ray had specifically asked for. Back in the car, Aleda pretended to read, but mostly imagined taking care of Travis and going to college at the same time.

They were getting higher in the mountains, passing crossroad towns with names like Accident and Elkwater. They stopped for gas at a convenience store, and Ray bought a bag of butterscotch candies. Ray talked about how the roads used to have Mail Pouch ads painted on the side of barns. "Not that we went driving all that much," said Ray, "but sometimes of a Sunday. Daddy and us boys used to go to the stock car races sometimes, too."

Aleda said, "Is stock cars like NASCAR?"

"It came first, just people racing their old jalopies, and it got bigger and bigger. We used to go over into Harrison County for the races. Hot dogs and cars, what more could a bunch of boys want?"

Dinah said, "What do you suppose they do for hospitals out here?"

"People come over from Washington, DC, to ski," Ray said, "so you know they have to have a place to fix 'em up."

Aleda closed her eyes and pretended to be asleep like Benjie. Dinah lowered her voice, probably hoping Aleda really was asleep. "I keep thinking this job has something to do with those people you knew who tried to bomb the FBI fingerprint center."

"Now, Diney, this don't have nothing to do with that. This is window-shopping."

Dinah grunted. "Well, I hope you pray long and hard before you buy."

Then their voices got softer still, the way that always made Aleda a little embarrassed as if they were kissing too long in front of her.

He said, "I know you're troubled in your heart about this, Dinah."

She said, "I've set it aside for now."

It can't be bad, thought Aleda. Travis is good.

CHAPTER 24

The higher they drove up the unmarked road, the deeper the ruts. Dinah saw an abandoned barn and an abandoned house, and then the hills started closing in around them.

She said, "How sure are we this is the right road? What if we break an axle and then find out it was the wrong road?"

"Have faith, wife," said Ray.

She thought: I love him as much as a woman can love her husband, and I believe he hears things from God, but there's no guarantee he always hears it right. And then, as if in response to Ray's faith, the road smoothed—too smooth, Dinah thought, for this kind of desolated place.

They climbed still higher and came out of the trees into a more open area. The road widened. Aleda, in the back with Benjie, had begun to lean her face forward, between the front seats, to watch what was coming.

"What are we looking for now?" Dinah asked. She had the envelope with the instructions in Ray's big round writing. "You didn't write down anything else after that last turn."

"I don't know," said Ray. "Poke said once we got this far, just keep driving."

"What if we run out of gas? Keep driving how long?"

"Trust," said Ray.

"Yeah, Mom," said Aleda. "Have a little trust."

Benjie started to whimper.

Ray said, "Do you want to stop and nurse?"

"No." She didn't think she could stand waiting. "I'll do it while you drive, just go very slow."

Aleda passed Benjie up, and he fussed louder, and Dinah was pretty sure he needed a diaper change too. She tucked him under her seat belt as best she could. He kept pounding one fist on her breast, then lifting his head and looking around.

"Hey Benjie," said Ray. "How's my little linebacker? We keep going, Dinie, we'll have our own football team."

They passed through another band of woods and then they were on a swell of hill without much of a view. Low grass and wide flat boulders, thin pines off to one side, the road still rising slowly and smoothly toward the sky as if they were at the top of a globe.

Aleda pointed off to the right. "Is that a patch of snow?"

"Might could be," said Ray. "We're high up in God's country." Again, as if cued by Ray's words, the sun came out, and he laughed with pleasure. It was beautiful up here, all right. But live here? With kids?

The road turned to a finer grade of crushed stone, and just ahead, a fence of taut wire and posts, and an open gate.

"Private property," said Ray.

Dinah suddenly felt a flood of certainty. This was too far away. Isaac had mostly outgrown his asthma, but they could develop new diseases, have attacks of appendicitis. We can't live this far away from everything, she thought, and it made her calm to be so sure. Better live in the house Grace had bought with the drug money. Or, if Ray really wanted this job, they could live back down the mountain, in one of the little communities with names, Slaty Fork or the other one. But not up here. Ray could come up here once or twice a week if he had to. We're survivors, she thought, not survivalists.

A quarter mile beyond the first fence, there was another fence and a black truck with a cap over the truck bed, windows tinted, and three men leaning their backs against it, sunglasses, arms crossed over their chests.

"That's Poke," said Ray. "With the ponytail. And the skinny short one is Bobby Mack. I haven't seen him in a *long* time. The boy with the beard is Poke's nephew, who came with him the day you were at the library with the kids, Dinah."

"Travis," said Aleda, and Dinah glanced at her sidelong. Aleda was wearing her favorite gored denim skirt that fit snugly over her butt. And a yellow cardigan sweater pulled tight by her breasts.

Of course, thought Dinah, things falling into place. She'd met a boy.

Ray came to a stop and rolled down the driver-side window. The men approached. Dinah was furious. Of course, of course. A boy.

The ponytail and big belly, the skinny one with teeth missing on two sides. The boy healthy and handsome and much too old for Aleda. Flat stomach, wide shoulders. Shiny white grin in a black beard. Travis. She needed to tell Aleda that kind of man would get a belly someday, just like the other one.

Aleda was smiling at her hands in her lap, her golden cheeks splashed with pink. Like a ripe peach. The men ambled. They had writing on their clothes. The old ones were wearing black windbreakers with the red insignia that said Mountain Dome with the *m* in the shape of mountains. Same as on the truck. The young one was wearing a blue West Virginia University Mountaineer sweatshirt with gold letters.

"Well, well," said Ray, reaching through the open window to shake hands. "Here we are, Poke. And Bobby Mack. Long time no see. This here's my wife, Dinah, and our big girl, Aleda. And the baby."

Sounding like a hillbilly, she noticed, as soon as he got close to a couple of good old boys.

"Hey Ray," said Bobby Mack, staying back and nodding, but Poke pressed his face in at the open window, taking his time. At least he took off his shades, reached a big paw over Ray to shake with Dinah. Scratchy palms. More bad teeth. No dentist up here, of course.

"Pleased to meet you, missus," said Poke. "Glad you saw your way clear to visiting us. Everybody's been looking forward to this day for quite a while." Still half in the van, he cut his eyes at Aleda in the back seat. "Hello young lady. And, Ray, that baby looks just like you."

"Bald you mean?" said Ray.

Benjie had gone perfectly still, his baby senses picking up strangers.

Poke tossed a thumb back over his shoulder. "That's my nephew Travis, Mrs. Savage. He's headed for the NFL. I'd ruther he be the next Dale Earnhardt, Jr. myself, but he don't ask me."

Poke pulled back, and Travis leaned down to the window, and he didn't take his sunglasses off. She assumed he was looking at Aleda. "Good afternoon, Mrs. Savage," he said. As big as life, expecting her to like him because he could say a polite greeting.

"Well," said Poke, "The boss wants us to get you parked and show you around, and then he'll say howdy. He's not feeling all that well today, I don't know if Ray told you, Missus Savage, but the boss has a chronic condition."

She kept her mouth shut.

"Sounds good," said Ray. "How far now to Mountain Dome?"

"This *is* Mountain Dome," said Bobby Mack with an idiotic explosion of laughter. "You been on Mountain Dome the last three miles!"

Following the black truck, they went through more sets of gates. At each set of gates, Travis got out to undo the locks. And each time, he grinned at Aleda as their van passed through and then he locked the gates again and grinned at her again before he climbed back in the truck.

Ray said, "Bobby Mack's from down in the southern part of the state somewhere, but the Rileys, Poke's family, they're from Cooper County too. More Rileys in Cooper County than Savages. Poke was like me, drifting around, wrong place at the wrong time, open to sin. Look at this road now. This kind of crushed rock is what they use for airplane runways."

The fourth gate was heavier and taller, attached to a house made of stone and blocks with a slanted roof.

Dinah said, "It looks like they're expecting an invasion. How did they know when to be out there waiting for us anyhow? Do they have cameras in the trees?"

"Yes," said Aleda, speaking for the first time since they'd met Travis. "I saw a box up a tree back there. I thought it was a birdhouse at first, but I think it was cameras."

"Why didn't you tell me about meeting this boy, Aleda?"

Ray answered for Aleda. "Why, Dinah, you knew when they came by the house."

"I knew somebody came. I didn't know about the NASCAR hillbilly."

Aleda said, "You should say mountaineer not hillbilly."

"Naw," said Ray. "Hillbilly's not an insult. Not to me, anyhow. I'm a hillbilly and proud of it."

"And besides," said Aleda, "he's a college student. He played football at West Virginia University. He took off a semester."

Dinah turned around again. "Dropped out?"

"He's going back," said Aleda.

Dinah kissed the baby's head. Why couldn't your children stay like this? Not really, she thought, I don't mean really, but she had tried so hard to keep them innocent. She didn't let them watch television or go to school. But here was Aleda all jacked up with excitement the first good-looking boy she sees. Did sex seep in around badly caulked windows? No, of course not, it was there already, in the genes and genitals. In every breath they took, sex and adventure.

Still it seemed so sad to her, after how hard she had tried, and then Aleda falls for the first strapping young man with a black beard and a white smile who knocks on the door.

Ray pointed out barns and garages and greenhouses. Then slightly below them, neat paths and stone buildings with solar-panel roofs. One last gate, then they pulled into a paved parking area. There were other vehicles there, a black Chevy Tahoe and another truck. Two little golf carts, everything black with the red logo.

Travis hopped out and opened Dinah's door. "Welcome to Mountain Dome, Mrs. Savage." Smiling like he was expecting someone to pet his beard.

Benjie was going to need diapers and a real nursing. "Aleda," she called, before Travis could help *her* out, "get me that diaper bag. Benjie's soaking wet."

"If y'all want to freshen up," said Poke, "we got everything you need inside."

"I'll do it out here," said Dinah. "Aleda, you hold Benjie." That got Aleda's hands busy. Dinah laid out a cloth on the seat and got a diaper. The men all hovered around, and she gave Aleda the wet diaper. That would keep Travis away from her.

She glanced at the house as she put on Benjie's fresh diaper. Broad and low, made of stone and brick and wood. A set of tall, carved double doors. Some dense, expensive wood.

Poke said, "Bobby Mack, you take that over to the trash for the young lady."

Aleda handed it over, Benjie kicked his fat legs in the air, twisted to the side, wanting to see.

Poke said, "Wait till you see everything we have ready for you."

Travis opened the big doors for them, and they all stepped through a tiled entryway into an enormous space with fireplaces on either end and a wall of glass directly ahead overlooking a great gulf in the mountains. Leather couches facing the fireplaces and more facing the windows. They were all momentarily stunned by the view, the brightness of it in the echoing great room.

There was a voice from their left. "Welcome to Mountain Dome, Reverend Savage."

"Well, well, here's the boss," said Poke. "Here's Doc."

"Good to meet you," said Ray, stepping toward the man, but Poke moved just a hair, a hint at blocking, as if Ray weren't supposed to touch the boss.

Poke said, "And this here's Mrs. Savage, and her girl."

"Aleda," said Travis.

Dinah didn't like the looks of the boss. She couldn't see him very well in the dim light. He had apparently come through a door near the left fireplace. He was wearing sunglasses, indoors, and a large floppy hat, like a movie star incognito or maybe he had a skin condition.

The boss had an odd voice, soft and hoarse, like something was caught in his throat. "I appreciate your coming all the way up here, Reverend Savage, bringing your wife and family. I'm in the middle of something right now, but Poke will show you around and give you some refreshments, and I'll meet with you a little later."

"Pleased to meet you," said Raymond, awkward, she could see, because his natural way was to grip a shoulder, shake a hand.

"Sure buddy, Doc," said Poke.

And the boss, *Doc*, with his sunglasses and floppy hat, turned and walked through a door back into the shadows.

Dinah was on full alert now, noticing every sound, the tiniest gesture. He wasn't very tall, and he waddled, as if he had once been fat. Something suspicious about him, what could be so pressing he couldn't stay and talk a minute?

Poke took them toward the other fireplace where there was another door. "Now that's a sign the Boss is really interested in you, Ray, some-times you don't see him for days. He's got himself a special room down the hall and he locks himself in there like he was expecting the end of the world. Right this way, ladies and gents," said Poke. "We got a bite laid out for you to eat, and there's facilities for the travelers. Welcome to Mountain Dome, which has everything a modern city does only with fresher air and fewer people to bother you."

It was a conference room with a long table and platters of sand-wiches, bowls of potato chips, cokes in ice, cookies, fruit, a pot of coffee on the sideboard. More views.

"Ray," Dinah said, "You hold Benjie. Aleda and I need to go to the bathroom."

"Right through that door," said Poke. "We got a two-holer for the ladies."

"I don't have to go," Aleda said, but Dinah hustled her down the little hall.

Inside, Dinah said, "I have to pee and I have to talk to you. So stay here." She peed, then came out and, as she washed her hands, watched Aleda's face in the mirror.

"What?" said Aleda, who was using a hand-cream dispenser and Kleenexes. "You brought me in here to tell me something."

Dinah said, "Exactly how well do you know that black-bearded person?"

"I met him that one time when they came to the house and talked to Ray."

"And you like him?"

She smoothed damp hands over her puffy hair, pressing it down. "He seems nice."

Dinah washed her hands a second time. The hand towels were thick, the walls were pink tile, and everything glowed. "You didn't mention him."

The chin went up. "Am I required to tell you everything?"

"Yes."

"You think I'm like this out-of-control person. What have I ever done bad? You think I'm a drug addict and a nymphomaniac!"

"You have no experience."

"How would I? You keep me from people my own age."

Dinah wanted to close her eyes and gather her thoughts, but Aleda was meeting her eyes in the mirror, so she said, "I know you want to meet other young people. I want you to meet young people too. I want you to be in a place where you can socialize with good Christian young people."

Aleda said, "I've done nothing wrong. A boy came to the house, just by chance, and I talked to him, and I liked talking to him. Now I get to talk to him again. That's all. It's not much to ask. To be able to talk to people my age who I happen to meet."

"He's too old for you."

Aleda shook her head and stalked out.

Dinah stayed at the sink for a while. She sometimes worried that Aleda had inherited Dylan's wildness, but she also reminded her of herself at that age. Worse than Dylan, really.

She felt danger all around. From the bearded boy, from this perfect pink bathroom with the thickest hand towels she'd ever touched. Isolated on top of a mountain. The boss in the shades and floppy hat.

She closed her eyes and tried to pray, but her eyes popped right open, and she looked at herself in the mirror. She looked like a rabbit not knowing which way to turn.

Dear Lord in Heaven, prayed Dinah. I don't like this place. Please just let this happen fast. Let me get Ray and Aleda and Benjie out of here.

CHAPTER 25

Richie had planned that first meeting so he would be in the shadows. He had seen pictures, so he wasn't surprised that she was older and heavier. She hadn't recognized him, but she had looked hostile. He had fled to the safe room. It's okay, he thought. Nothing lost. Good to run a test. She had no idea who he was, but she was suspicious of the whole setup. That was good too. Once she committed herself to coming, she would have worked through the suspicions. Let her see the little house, then he'd speak to her again. Reveal himself. He had been planning this for months, but now he was afraid she'd ask the wrong questions.

He breathed ten deep breaths then turned to the monitors.

They were all in the conference room now, voices muddled. Dinah and the girl went to the bathroom. He should have put a camera on the sinks, he thought, or at least a microphone. In the conference room, Bobby Mack was stuffing his face, how someone that skinny could eat so much. The kid Travis too. Poke was eating and talking at the same time, the husband dandling the baby. The baby kept twisting to look after the women. Richie turned up the sound. Poke was talking about how the boss likes his privacy. Organic salad all year round for his health. Poke was not supposed to be commenting on Richie's health.

Then Poke talked about security—that wasn't supposed to be part of it either. It was all supposed to be positive.

"Hell," said Poke, "you ought to see the place the boss has for real emergencies. He could survive an atom bomb."

Dammit, thought Richie. Poke was going to hear from him about that. At least Dinah was out of the room for that.

He made himself concentrate on the husband, Raymond Savage. He needed to prepare to deal with him. The trick in negotiations is to know what you want, then figure out what your opponent wants and make him think he's getting it. Indeed, give it to him, if you can. He had read *The Art of War* and Machiavelli. It was all about how to succeed with the tools you have.

The husband seemed relaxed, baby in one arm, a sandwich in his free hand. Smiling good-naturedly at the others, not saying a lot. He held the baby like a football and jiggled it. The baby seemed to like it. The husband *wants to come*, he thought, and immediately felt better.

The girl came back, but not Dinah. Travis looked happy as a clam, went right to her. They ate sandwiches together.

Dinah came back and called the girl away from the boy. This was interesting. She called her over near the door, seemed to ask her to do something, and then the girl left. Travis started to go after her, Dinah stopped him. Richie switched cameras, followed the girl, into the great room, then outside. She was getting something from the van.

Back to the conference room camera. Travis looking unhappy, Bobby Mack scarfing down another sandwich. But Dinah and the baby were gone. He scanned with the other camera, couldn't find her at first, had a flash of panic, but found her in the great room, at the big window. She was showing the baby the view. Then she sat down, opened her dress. He switched camera views so he could look down on her nursing the baby. He had not expected the feeling it gave him. He tried to track it, the feeling. Not sexual, but not asexual either. When she was a teenager she used to show her breasts to people when she'd been smoking weed. Slow and dreamy. They'd all been high so much of the time. Richie on the periphery, away at school so much. A fat teenager who talked too much. He never had a chance with her.

She lowered her face over the baby's head, her cheeks smoothed out. How she looked at that baby. He filled with an enormous sadness, something like a sob forming.

The infant made a fist and kneaded at her breast. She made a little pucker-mouth at it. Her familiar broad mouth. Then she gazed out at the gorge, and the ridges and hawks.

It's yours, he thought. It's for you. Anything you want.

CHAPTER 26

Aleda's mother was watching her every move. It was infuriating. Travis was only ten feet away, but infinitely far, surrounded by space. She didn't even dare look at him for fear her mother would notice. And then a miracle happened. Travis said, in a voice that seemed to be meant to be heard by everyone. "Hey Aleda," he said, "how about if you and me walk over to the little house instead of driving?"

Everyone stopped for a beat. Ray smiled genially, but Dinah squawked, "I need Aleda to ride with the baby!"

Aleda gathered herself up for battle, perhaps hopeless, but she intended to go down fighting. "The baby is asleep, Mom. I could use a walk after being in the car all day."

Travis said, "It's just over that little rise, Mrs. Savage. It's a quarter mile at most. We'll probably beat the cars."

Poke said, "The boy's right, it's just about as fast to walk over as drive the truck. Let the young folks use up some energy."

"No," said Dinah.

Then came the second miracle: Ray said, "Oh, let them walk, Dinie."

Her mother's cheeks turned red as fast as if someone had slapped her, and she looked like she was ready to slap back. She locked eyes with Aleda, and Aleda held very still. Dinah said, "I don't want you getting lost."

Aleda didn't think she had ever heard her mother say anything so stupid, but Travis kept his cool. He was very serious and reassuring. "Yes, ma'am! Absolutely. We'll walk right up that little gravel path, and then right down the other side, it goes directly into the driveway."

Now that she had so unexpectedly won, Aleda felt a strange embarrassment. She turned away, and without waiting for Travis, started up the path. She heard the vehicles starting, and then Travis said, "Wait up, girl. We don't *really* want to get there before them, do we?"

She waited. No, of course not. She wanted time with him. She wasn't sure what was supposed to fill the time, but she certainly wanted it. They walked slowly, keeping about a foot of air between them. He said, "Your mother is one strict lady."

He was a head taller, and Aleda was the tallest in her family except for Ray. Her left shoulder tingled with awareness of Travis. She glanced left and saw a side view of his grin.

She said, "You have good teeth."

"I had braces."

Aleda said, "Not my family. My teeth are pretty much okay, I have one crooked incisor, and my brother Zack too, but my sister Sarah, her adult teeth came in crooked, but we didn't have the money for braces. Raymond was all like, Let's do it, the Lord will provide, but Mom said Sarah's teeth were fine for eating. Sarah never complains, but she keeps her mouth closed when she smiles." Travis didn't respond, and Aleda was afraid she was boring him. She said, "She's always strict, my mother, but I couldn't believe she didn't want me to walk with you. She's like this sheepdog herding me all the time." Even if she was boring him, it felt so good to say whatever she felt like saying.

They passed some plastic covered hoop houses with shadowy people inside.

Travis said, "That's where they grow the grow organic stuff. They have a big hydroponic system. Poke says it started out just to eat, but now they've got a business going, supplying some restaurants."

"What restaurants?"

"Over near the ski slopes. I think maybe they supply a place in DC too. The one in charge of all that is Enrique, he's the cook and in charge of the gardens, and I think the business end too. Uncle Poke stays out of that end of it."

She nodded. They were already at the top of the hill and she could see the van and the big black Tahoe making a turn. There wasn't much time.

"What exactly do you do here?"

"Oh, I do the muscle work, if there's any needed. It's pretty easy. We drive the boss into town to go to the bank, he pays everyone cash. I'm doing some of his digital stuff too, the internet and his recording studio."

"Are you going to be at the radio station when Ray tries out?"

He nodded. "It isn't exactly a radio station. We're setting it up to live-stream programs, if we have any programs."

"So you're smart," she said, eager to tell Dinah.

Travis shrugged and smiled.

At the top were three boulders, and beyond them, the path downhill, then the road and a little driveway.

She stopped and turned to face him. "How long do we have? I mean alone together."

Travis laughed. "I thought you were shy."

"We're socially inept, my whole family. We hardly ever see people outside the family. So I don't know how to behave with people."

She had her face turned up to him and she was hoping for an embrace, even though she knew it was too soon. But when would she have another chance? He leaned over, and she closed her eyes, but the kiss came on top of her head, just a little affectionate kiss, like for a baby.

She reached up and grabbed his face, her fingers in his beard and pulled him down, lips to lips, a surprisingly muscular wrestling of lips. The smell of lotion and clean sweat.

She expected to be enfolded, but he took a step back and whistled. "Not shy at all," he said.

Then he stepped forward again, and this time, he *did* enfold her and lifted her off her feet with the strength of the kiss. He put her down too quickly, but that was because the cars were coming back into sight. "We better keep walking," said Travis.

"Now I can at least say I've been kissed. That was my first time."

Travis only said, "First time's a charm."

This was when the third miracle happened. Aleda got a call, or something like it. She hadn't really believed anyone got them except Ray. Aleda's call wasn't words, but a sense of outlines darkened and masses solidified: the boulders, some silver rolls of cloud overhead. Herself. Herself suddenly solid with her body and her knowledge.

She said, "I need to get away from my mother. I can't stay anymore with her watching me every second and telling me exactly what to do. I want to stay up here."

With you, she meant.

He cleared his throat and looked from side to side. "Well, if you all move up here, we can see each other every day. I mean, that's why I'm up here, because I was fighting with my mother all the time. I'm supposed to be learning how to be a man from my uncle. Not that he's the greatest role model."

She said, "Do you think Ray is going to get the job?"

"Poke says he's the only candidate. I mean, I have no idea what Doc Lock, that's what we call the boss, has in mind. Maybe he's lonesome. Maybe he wants to get religion. Your dad's a preacher, isn't he?"

"Stepfather," she said.

They started walking, not too fast.

"If he doesn't get the job, I could come back myself."

"You mean run away?"

"You could come and get me."

"They'd throw me in jail!"

"We could get married. I'm not the one who's supposed to say that, but I don't have many chances."

He made a noise, something between a laugh and a snort. "I'm going back to college in the fall. I'm on leave from the football team. I can go back. I've always liked sports better than studying."

"I could go with you. You can only be an athlete for a little while. You need to prepare for the future. To be a—teacher or a lawyer or a doctor or businessman."

"You sound like my mother."

"I'm sorry."

"That's okay. I suppose you're right, she's right. I haven't made up my mind yet."

"Will you come and get me?"

He grinned. "I'll come and *see* you."

She wasn't satisfied. She had had a call, but apparently Travis hadn't.

The vehicles had turned down the lane now, and Aleda and Travis were almost to the end of the path. They weren't going to beat the cars, but they were in plain view, so her mother could relax.

Travis said, "Was that really your first kiss?"

"Yes."

"If I'd known, I would have worked it up a little more."

"I liked it a lot. I wanted to have something to think about when I'm locked up again."

He laughed. "You'll see, you'll be moving up here. We'll see each other every day."

Dinah was shading her eyes and watching them.

"My mother wants to put a barbed-wire fence around me."

"If I had a daughter," said Travis "I'd want to protect her too."

"You wouldn't stop her from going to school, would you? And never letting her have experiences with people her own age?"

"I'm just saying, all parents try to protect their children."

"My mother was wild when she was a teenager, before she found Jesus and married Ray, so she assumes that I want to be wild too. She thinks if I walk up the hill with you in plain sight of fifty people we'll just go ahead and commit fornication."

Travis pursed his lips. "Well . . ."

"We kissed! We didn't fornicate! That's for marriage. I mean, it isn't fornication if you're married. I don't even know if you've been saved. And just because I want to get away doesn't mean I would go against everything I've been taught."

He laughed, a nice melodious laugh like Ray singing a hymn. She didn't care if he laughed, because he liked her anyhow. Travis said, "You're not what I expected." She yearned to know what he had expected, but he picked up speed again.

She waited for a moment and looked around one last time.

It was like the magic island in *The Tempest*. She was Miranda. O brave new world that has someone like Travis in it. She allowed that Dinah was at least partly right, that her body, Aleda's own familiar body, wanted to fornicate.

"Come on," Travis said, coming back for her. "Let's run."

It was absolutely the perfect thing to do, Aleda thought. They held hands, and she used her other hand to hold her skirt away from her ankles, and they ran down the path holding hands like innocent children.

CHAPTER 27

Grace was alone with the children. Dinah and Ray's three middle ones stood in a row, already fully dressed, and apparently waiting for their marching orders. Grace's kids weren't dressed yet.

The little one, Jacob, had a blanket and a teddy bear and enormous round blue eyes and a round little belly pressing out his overalls. Zack was strikingly handsome, sharp jawed and dark, blue-and-white-checked shirt rolled at the wrists with a stylish flair. He was the rebel, Grace thought. Sarah had light coloring and a high forehead, and she was wearing a long green-and-blue print skirt.

"Well!" said Grace. "How about French toast for breakfast?"

Jacob took the blanket out of his mouth. "Don't mind if do."

"We ate already, Aunt Grace," said Sarah.

Ruth said, "They only ate a little bit of toast and jelly. And I didn't have anything."

Grace said, "Then I'll make French toast. Ruth, get out the milk and eggs."

Sarah said, "We're not supposed to give you any trouble."

"You're my niece and nephews! Besides, Margaret and Ruth have to eat." She was feeling awake and strong. She was good with children. She *liked* children. She assigned chores and started the butter sizzling in the pan. Jacob stood near her looking up. "Is this our new house?"

"Oh boy," said Zack. "Sometimes, Jakey. This is Ruth and Margaret's house!"

Sarah frowned "Isaac!"

"Zack," he said, squaring his chin.

Not a squabble at the level of what Ruth and Margaret could do, but a squabble, and it made Grace confident. "This isn't your house, Jacob," Grace said, "but you can stay here anytime you want."

He said, "I like to stay with Mommy."

Ruth knelt down and opened her arms to Jacob in an elaborate show of affection. "Oh Jakey, your mommy and daddy will be back tomorrow or maybe even tonight!"

He let her hug him, then started chewing his blanket. "Ma?" he said.

"Don't be a baby," whispered Zack.

Two pans sizzling, smell of browning butter, vanilla, a hint of cinnamon because Ruth didn't like nutmeg.

Margaret finally seemed to wake up and helped Jacob up on a stool. She said, "Dad left his sandwich."

Grace wished David could see her right now, competent, in charge. He seemed to be moving on, maybe forgiving her, but she wished he could see her competence too. He wasn't really talking to her yet. "I'll take it to him when I take you all to school."

Sarah said, "You're a good cook, Aunt Grace."

"I've always cooked. When Dinah and I were little, we did all our own cooking."

"Where was your mother?" asked Zack.

"She was sick a lot."

Jacob said, "Ma's not sick, she went for houses."

"That was *their* mother," said Sarah. "We have two grandmothers. Daddy's mother is our other grandmother and we're going to see her tomorrow."

Jacob was looking toward the door again. Grace offered him the first slice of hot French toast.

Abruptly, Margaret seemed to come awake. She said, "Sarah and Zack ought to come and see what public school is like. I could take Sarah as my guest, and Zack could go with Ruth."

Sarah's eyes expanded and she seemed to be holding her breath.

Ruth said, "They both should go with me. We're the same age."

"Actually, they're between us," said Margaret. "You're younger. And I'm just saying, I'd take her as a guest, for her to see what middle school looks like. I would have taken Aleda, but she's not here. And Ruthie, think about it, it makes sense for one of them to go as my guest and one as yours. Sarah looks older than her age than Zack. No offense, Zack."

Zack and Sarah weren't taking offense. They were gazing expectantly at Grace.

"Well," said Grace, "We didn't clear it with Dinah—"

Zack said, a little too smoothly, "She likes us to have new experiences."

"We'd have to check with the teachers, and Jacob—" Jacob didn't look thrilled with how this was going. "Jacob and I could have some fun on our own. We could have lunch at McDonald's."

Sarah said, "Jakey loves McDonald's, don't you, Jakey?"

He nodded.

Ruth said, "But what about Sarah's clothes? I mean, she looks cute, but it's *Little House on the Prairie* cute, it's not the way middle schoolers dress. Kids in my class have studied diversity, so I think she'd be better off—her and Zack both—with me."

Margaret said, "On the contrary, Ruthie. Middle school kids are more mature."

Ruth frowned. "Okay, but if they're here more days, we can switch off. No offense, Zack."

Zack grinned hugely. "None taken," he said in a fake deep voice.

Margaret said, "Sarah, I'll lend you my denim jacket, that will go with your outfit, but it's got a little bit of cool factor too."

It was a gray day splashed with yellow—forsythia and the first daffodils in people's yards. Grace put David's sandwich in her bag, still not sure she'd have enough courage to go to his office. The children filled the Subaru, every seat belt taken, which Grace found oddly satisfying. Ruth told the Savages which buildings they were passing: there was Uncle David's office, the hospital down there, the schools centered around the football field. One building had the high school and board of ed offices, the other was K through eight, the two wings meeting at the office and multipurpose room.

Mrs. Oliverio, the principal for all eight grades, was in the front office when they arrived, neat and slim with short silvery hair and a gray tweed pantsuit. Grace introduced the children, and Mrs. Oliverio shook everyone's hand, including Jacob's, then personally phoned Margaret's team leader and Ruth's classroom teacher to get approval for the visitors. It was nothing Grace hadn't expected, but it felt good, a sign that she belonged here. That she was getting out of her hole.

Margaret and Sarah went right, Ruth and Zack went left, joining curious crowds of kids. There was a dangerous moment as Jacob made little tugging movements against Grace's hand as if he would follow one and then the other, but Mrs. Oliverio had a sharp eye and a big glass jar of lollipops, or, rather, as you said in West Virginia, suckers. She invited Jacob to choose one, and after a long deliberation, he chose red and said, "Thank you kindly."

Mrs. Oliverio never cracked a smile. "You're very welcome, young man." She watched Jacob unwrap his sucker, and said, "I think this may be the last year I get to keep candy in the office. Too much obesity and sugar highs. We're going to have to stop having cupcakes for birthdays and holidays. You know I'm totally into health and technology, but I'm going to miss the sucker jar." She looked up briskly. "And speaking of technology, Grace, I heard you were running for the board of education."

It was so long ago. Grace said, "I thought about it, but a lot of things got put on the back burner when we moved."

"We could really use you on the board. We are so close to getting the whole school wired, high-speed internet in every room. Not that I'm politicking. I'm an employee of the board, so of course I don't take sides."

"Ha," said the secretary.

Mrs. Oliverio said, "It's just that, Grace, you're a parent and a teacher too."

"Former teacher."

"We need people who understand education on the board. Not one of present board members still has a child in school."

Grace said, and the speaking seemed to make it true, "I haven't totally decided against it."

"You'd better decide fast. The deadline is Monday, and you'll need signatures on the petition."

She had the strangest sequence of feelings. There had been the terror, there had been the cottage. There had been the abyss between her and David. There had been Dinah.

And now Mrs. Oliverio's bright eyes. Mrs. Oliverio said, "You could go over to the board office and get a petition and bring it back over here, and I'll sign it and the secretaries—that's not politicking, that's just democracy."

If I ran for the board, Grace thought, if I got elected, the term is for three years, and by then Margaret would be in high school and Ruthie would be in middle school, and I could go back to teaching.

She shrugged and smiled. "We'll see."

As she and Jacob walked out, he asked, "How long is school?"

"They have lunch, and then there's some more school. But when they finish, there's still lots of time to play."

"And watch TV?"

They were beside the car, but her hand didn't go to her purse for the key. "Jacob, do you want to see the high school? Let's just go over to the high school and the board of education office before we leave, okay?"

Jacob said, "Then McDonald's?" Jacob, it appeared, was pretty focused on food.

"Yes," she said. "McDonald's, for lunch. And how would you like to see Uncle David's doctor office?" It was forming in her mind. She would get a new petition. She'd get signatures. She'd go by David's office and drop off the sandwich, and he would be the first, one of the first, to know. And Fredda's office. Fredda had promised weeks ago to help with the signatures. Fredda owed her something after telling David about the cottage.

"We'll visit some people, and by that time we'll be ready for lunch. How does that sound?"

"I appreciate that a very lot," said Jacob.

CHAPTER 28

Dinah watched them coming down the lane *holding hands*. The boy was at least five years older than Aleda, and Ray just chatting away with his good old buddy Poke Riley about the wonders of Mountain Dome.

"Look at it, Dinah," Ray said, and she glanced away from Aleda and the boy. The house was all curves. It had shutters, evergreen bushes, bedding flowers blooming too early. It was like the gingerbread house from "Hansel and Gretel."

Poke said, "Wait till you see the kitchen, Mrs. Savage. Subzero and all the fixins. And the boss said make sure the missus knows it's all included."

"You know what?" said Dinah. "I don't like being called the missus."

"Honey, honey," said Ray.

They were hovering around her, Ray and Poke and the little rat-faced one too, as if her outburst required attention. "Benjie's asleep," she said. "I'll stay out here with him."

"You need to see the house, Dinah," Ray murmured.

Poke said, "Here come the kids."

Aleda's cheeks were pink. "Mom! It's a hobbit house!"

Poke said, "There's a little garden out back too. We turned it over and composted it last week. Ready to go. The boss didn't want anything planted till we found out what you liked in the way of vegetables. And if you're really into gardening, you can have your own hoop house too. Well, come on, let's go in and look around."

Dinah was angry, but she was also bothered by the way it sounded as if the decision had been made, as if everyone had already decided they were moving up here. She said, "Someone has to stay at the car with Benjie."

"I'll stay," said Travis. He planted himself against the side of the van. "I like little kids."

"Thank you, son," said Ray.

Dinah felt trapped, but at least it separated him from Aleda for a while. "The second he looks like he's waking," she said, "come and get me. Don't pick him up yourself, he's not used to strangers."

"Yes ma'am."

The interior of the cottage had mission-style furniture with big orange and tan pillows. A log burning in the fireplace. Yes, she thought, it is the witch's cottage.

Poke said, "The boss said to tell you, the furnishings—he can get other stuff. If you like a different style. Colonial or Danish modern. Whatever."

She tried to catch Ray's eye, to see if he got it, that it was too perfect.

Aleda ran from one thing to another exclaiming, Look at this, look at that. Then she disappeared toward the back of the house and popped back. "Come here, Mom, look at the kitchen!"

Dinah's throat had tightened up. She was having trouble breathing. "Ray," she said, "I'm going for a walk."

"Right now? Are you okay?"

"Mom! Come and see the kitchen!"

"I'm going for a walk."

Ray followed her out the door. "What are you doing, Dinah?"

"I need some air. I don't like this place, Ray. I am not favorably disposed. Just leave me alone for a while, and I'll meet you all back at the main house. You finish your tour. But listen for Benjie."

Poke came out too. "The boss wants you to see the house."

"He's not my boss. Am I allowed to walk around by myself? Or am I being detained?"

Poke backed away with his hands up. "Whoa. Go ahead, do what you want."

She could tell Ray was thinking about following her, so she said, "I'm fine, Ray. I'll meet you back there in twenty minutes. I'll go right over the hill the way Aleda came."

Travis was still leaning against the van. She said, "I'm going for a walk. If the baby wakes, call Ray or Aleda. If you touch my baby, I will kill you. Do you understand?"

Travis raised his hands, palms out, just like Uncle Poke.

As she started up the hill, her chest felt cold without the baby, but at the same time, she really was soothed by the high sky and ridges, the reddish-tipped deciduous trees on the hillsides, the fuchsia-colored bush called redbud. The path went up past boulders, then downhill next to the greenhouses where three short men were standing and watching her. She waved, and one of them waved back.

It's marijuana, she thought. They're growing marijuana in the greenhouses and they're looking for a front—a Christian radio program run by Raymond, a cover for what they're really doing? Ray wouldn't fall for it, not once he realized they wanted to use him. He'd be too smart for them. And if Ray wasn't smart enough, then Jesus would step in and tell Ray to get away. She hoped.

There was an intersecting path from the main house, and down the path came the black golf cart driven by the man in the floppy hat and big sunglasses. The boss.

She placed herself in his way. The cart braked. He was wearing one of the black windbreakers with the red Mountain Dome logo. His cheeks seemed to have a lot of vertical folds, and she again thought he was someone who had lost weight recently.

He said in a peevish high voice, "You were supposed to be at the cottage."

She said, "I guess I didn't get my agenda." There was something familiar in his voice that she couldn't place.

"I wanted you to see things in a certain order."

"You know what? You're not my boss. I don't work for you. Raymond doesn't work for you either, and frankly, I hope he never does."

"That house is state of the art!" It was the excited querulousness that seemed familiar. "It has solar heat and woodstoves plus a pellet system. There are Egyptian cotton sheets and a full laundry and a KitchenAid mixer! And a garden and a separate herb garden!"

And just like that, she knew.

"Oh my god," she said. "Richie Lock."

He shut up and held perfectly still. Richie in Stop.

"It's been *years*, Richie!"

"Sixteen."

"Oh my God. *Richie!* Why didn't you *say* so? The last time we saw you, you were high as a kite on I don't know what." For a moment, everything fell away, and she was filled with wonder at seeing. "What have you been *doing*, Richie?"

"The last time I saw you, you were still with Dylan and you were pregnant."

"Yes, Aleda wasn't born yet. I was breaking up with Dylan." The horrors fell away as if everything were explained by crazy Richie. "Why the big mystery? What are you *doing*?"

"I came to pick you up and take you back to the house."

Something stopped her, not his wrinkled cheeks or his big hat and sunglasses, but the rest of it. There had been a fraction of a second when she wanted to hug him, to remember the carriage house, talk about when they were little kids. But the impulse passed, and the suspicion came back.

He said, "Please get in the cart, and we'll go up to the house and talk."

"Explain first. Why do you want to hire Raymond? Why him instead of some other preacher?"

He gave a little self-satisfied smile. "You didn't have a clue it was me, did you?"

"No I didn't. I'm not good at games. If you're growing weed in the greenhouses, I really don't care. I don't think it's a good thing, I've been born again and I look at a lot differently, but it's not like I would report you to the authorities."

"I've given up illicit drugs, even as business. Well, I grow a little for medicinal purposes. The hoop houses are organic vegetables. We sell to locavore restaurants."

"But why so isolated?"

"I'll explain at the house." His hands shivered as if he might be cold.

"Let me see your face first."

He pulled off the hat and laid it in his lap. His hairline had receded so far you had to say he was balding. It was turning gray, too, and his skin had a grayish cast. She noticed a metal cane next to the gear shift.

"Take off the shades."

He took them off and blinked, and now he looked like Richie—a Richie who had been through a lot. A Richie older than his chronological age. She climbed in the cart and set herself at an angle so she could watch him. He made a K-turn, and they puttered up the hill.

"You better be able to explain all this, Richie."

"I will."

Another silence, then she said, "Are you doing okay?"

He jerked his chin out at the property. "I'm doing very well."

"I don't mean how much money do you make. How are *you*?"

He said, "My dad left an inheritance, you knew that, but my mother spent a lot of it before she died."

"I didn't know Sharon died. I'm sorry." Sharon who slept with their father, among many other boyfriends, but was always kind to Dinah and Grace. "She used to give us clothes."

He shrugged. "She drank herself to death. I've invested, it's all investments now." They passed through a gate in the stone fence to the parking lot in front of the main house. He turned off the cart and stared ahead. He said, "You haven't given me a thought in all these years, have you?"

"Not true. When I first became a Christian, I prayed for our whole gang. You, Wolf, Dylan, everyone."

His mouth made a bitter twist. "*Our Gang*. We used to watch those old movies on TV, didn't we? Which one was I? The dog with the spot over its eye?"

"Richie, I've had a big change. You knew me as a confused, misguided kid. Jesus came to save us and that's the only thing that makes sense of it all. I don't know how people live without knowing that."

"They live, and then they die," he said. "Just like you."

"So why start a Christian radio station?"

"Who said it was a Christian radio station? Who said it was a radio station? I'm just playing with some ideas." His left knee began to jerk up and down. "I'm looking for new projects. I've been sick, but I'm recovering."

That at least explained the gray skin tone. "Recovering from what?" She guessed an addiction of some kind, but he kept responding to something other than what she said.

"Why did you choose to have Dylan's baby?"

"It's none of your business, actually, but I didn't choose, I was sloppy. But I don't regret it, because it's what finally woke me up. I had to get straight; I had to see my way clear. What are you recovering from?"

"I'm doing very well. Eating right, exercise. I have a helicopter pad. Doctors come up here if I need them. Everything is under control. I thought I'd give your husband an opportunity."

"Oh bullshit, Richie. This place—it's a survivalist setup. What is it? Is it the Mountain Militia?"

A laugh like a bark. "You think this is political? Do you know anything about the Mountain Militia? I hope not because it's an insult to my intelligence to connect me to that. Poke and Bobby Mack, that's my entire connection to the Mountain Militia. Your husband was part of it, too, or didn't you know?"

"Yes, I knew." Thank you Jesus, no surprises there.

"And he needs a job, yes? He's been out of work for three months?"

Three months, exactly, she thought, and drew a little farther away. "He's picked up some part-time things. How do you know everything about us?"

"I collect information. A lot of it is business related, for my investments. I've been successful in financial investments, but I invest in people too."

"Did you have private investigators?"

He looked out at the mountainside. "Yes."

"How about other people? How about Dylan? Do you know if Dylan is alive? Aleda keeps asking."

"Dylan is in San Francisco."

"He's living in San Francisco?"

"Two months ago he was. He's HIV positive and lives on the street in San Francisco He's a burnt-out piece-of-shit."

It went deep into her. Unexpectedly. "I'll pray for him. He never got in touch, not a phone call, not a postcard."

Richie's voice had become shrill again. "I know what happened to all of your little man-harem. Wolf works in a motorcycle shop outside of Buffalo."

"What about Eric and James?"

He shrugged. "They went to college, Eric is an assistant principal, James sells something. I forget. They weren't really part of it. What I never understood was why you picked Dylan. He was a protojunkie before he ever took a drug."

"We were all protojunkies."

"He sleeps on a piece of cardboard on a traffic island in the middle of Market Street in San Francisco. Why didn't you choose me?"

"Do *you* have HIV?"

"No, I don't have HIV. I told you I'm recovering. I have to take care of myself, that's all. I keep my health by paying attention to everything." The Tahoe and the van were coming into the parking area. Richie went into Go again: "The cottage has solar panels on the south side where you can't see them. I'll build a school for your kids. We'll bring in teachers. We'll hire a full-time nurse in case anyone gets sick. A doctor!"

"Why didn't you just come and see us and say, I have a job your husband might be interested in?"

"You'll have everything you need. I've thought of everything and if you think of more, just tell me."

Ray was unfastening Benjie from the car seat. Benjie was crying.

She got out of the golf cart and reached for the baby who started yelling louder once he could see her. She was glad to get away from Richie. He always had overdone it, that was Richie, but something felt worse here. She pressed the baby against her chest and the normal world came back into focus and color. She jiggled him and told him he could nurse in just half a minute.

What Richie was doing, she had no idea, but with the baby in her arms she didn't care. "Ray, come over here, I want you to meet someone. This is Richie Lock. He's the boss, and he's someone Gracie and I grew up with. His mother rented the carriage house to us."

"Is that so?" said Ray, extending a hand.

"Yes, get him to explain how he found us." Let Ray worry for a while about what it all meant. Benjie needed to nurse. Also, she noticed Travis touching Aleda again, helping her out of the big black Tahoe. She had ridden with him, in the Mountain Dome vehicle.

Poke said, "So Mrs. Savage got a ride with the boss. That worked out just fine, after all, didn't it? The boss has been wanting to talk to Mrs. Savage for a long time."

"Aleda," she said, "come over here, I want you to meet Richie Lock. He was our friend, Aunt Grace's and mine, when we were kids."

Richie got out of the cart using his cane and went to Aleda.

"Well, well," said Ray. "That's some coincidence—"

"No it's not," said Dinah.

Richie said, "Let's go over to the studio. I want you to see our setup. Then we can all sit down and discuss the details."

Dinah said, "I need to nurse Benjie."

It was just behind the house, they said. A couple of hundred yards. They would wait for her, but she said no, go. Aleda offered to stay with her and she said no, she'd go in the house and then walk over. Ray insisted that she keep the keys to the van and drive over. "Fine," said Dinah, feeling that she'd agree to anything if she could just be alone with her baby, with the realest thing in the world.

The others went in the Tahoe, Richie driving, looking too small for the big SUV. He had his hat and shades back on.

She was barely able to open the door to the main house, it was so heavy, Benjie twisting and whining. Inside, it all seemed oversized, overdone, but the fact it was Richie Lock showing off made sense of it. Ceiling too high, windows too enormous. She sat on the couch facing the view and sank down. Benjie grabbed at the front of her dress.

"Are you hungry or just needing comfort?" she asked him.

"Lih?" he said.

"Yes, Aleda went down the hill with her boyfriend. Aleda is having a big hormone surge." She needed to think about all of it at once: Did Richie really know about Dylan? Was he just boasting? Should she tell Aleda? Which parts to say to Ray?

Benjie sucked, and well-being flooded her shoulders and neck, spread through her. It was just Richie, she thought. A grown-up Richie being crazy in a grown-up way. She laid her head back on the couch and closed her eyes and named her babies: Aleda, Sarah, Isaac, Amos, Rebecca, Samuel, Jacob, Benjamin.

Why was everyone offering them a house? Grace and now Richie. Grace's offer was less crazy. People in Cooper County would help Ray get a job. Let Aleda try the high school if she wanted to. The kids must be less worldly in West Virginia. They'd join a church, get Aleda a teen group. She passed into a suspension, a miniature nap. Opened her eyes after just a minute or two refreshed and sharpened. Benjie had slowed down, was grunting rhythmically. She kissed his head, breathed in his fragrance, resettled his weight.

And saw a tiny movement out of the corner of her right eye: high above her where the ceiling met the wall. She thought for a second that it was an insect or a reflection, but when she turned her head, she saw the device, turning, scanning, stopping then turning back. She shifted positions so she could see the rest of the great room. Each corner had a camera.

Well, she thought, Richie had said his business was information. But that didn't mean she had to be on his closed-circuit TV network. She got up and buttoned her dress. "I hope you're full, Benjie, because the buffet is closing."

She shifted him to her hip and went into to the room where they had had lunch, found two more cameras. In the bathroom where she'd gone with Aleda, she didn't find any, but wondered if they were hidden behind the mirrors or in the ceiling somehow. Were there cameras in the cottage where she and Raymond were supposed to live with the kids? In the bedrooms?

She had been feeling sorry for Richie, wanting to give him a chance, certainly not planning to move up here, but touched by the past. It all slid away now. She didn't have to deal with Richie. She had to take care of her children. She was going to take them all back to Grace, get everyone together under one roof again. She wanted Aleda and Benjie and Ray and herself in the van driving away. She would crash through Richie Lock's gates if she had to.

CHAPTER 29

David had a queasy stomach and a dull headache. Was it dehydration? Hangover? It had been a long time since he'd had a hangover. He had to redo a blood pressure. He had to ask a question twice. He had an urge to say, You know sometimes the doctor doesn't feel well either. He would turn forty this year, and he had been having moments of wondering, Is this all? His anger at Grace was fading into a kind of sadness. He sometimes thought it would be a relief to hand it all over to an imaginary supernatural friend the way Raymond Savage did.

The last patient before lunch was a walk-in with chest pain, smiling and saying, Oh it's nothing, Doc, while his wife said, It's a heart attack, isn't it? Tell him he's having a heart attack. This one was easy: go to the emergency room immediately. David called ahead, but told the wife to drive, it would be faster than waiting for an ambulance. The man said he could drive himself. David said he had to be driven. He sent Merlee out with them to make sure the wife got behind the wheel. When they were gone, he stared at the chart, just to be sure. He didn't trust himself today. The emergency room was obvious. There was no downside to sending him.

Merlee knocked and stepped in, not closing the door behind her. "They're off," she said. "Men are stubborn about cars."

He thanked her. She was frowning and looking over the tops of her glasses at him. Did she expect a lunge? As if he would ever, ever do such a thing. Again. He wanted to make a promise, apologize, but he didn't have the words.

She said, "Grace is here. With your nephew. Who happens to be my nephew too, by the way. Through my ex."

"I guess I'm becoming a real Cooper County local if you and I have the same nephew."

She gave a half laugh. "Grace brought her petition to run for the board of education. She's been over at Fredda's, and Fredda's her campaign manager, and we all signed it out front already, but I wanted to make sure you did too. Gracie said not to bother you, but I told her you'd want to sign." Merlee frowned at his frown. "Everyone is thrilled to death about this, Doctor. That Grace is going to run against Caliph Savage and his cronies. That man, who is also my relative by marriage, thinks he owns the county. Grace will be just the person to stir things up. And don't say you don't think she can handle it, because it's just what the doctor ordered, so to speak, Doctor. Oh, and she has your lunch. You left your lunch at home."

He didn't even remember forgetting it. He got up, but Merlee blocked the door. "You'll sign, won't you?"

He said, "I knew she was thinking about it, but I thought she gave it up. With all this. Her moods have been erratic."

"*Her* moods?" said Merlee.

He felt the back of his neck heat up. "Merlee, I'm sorry. I said I was sorry. I was way out of line. I was under a lot of stress that day—"

"Yesterday."

"Yesterday. I'm terribly sorry. I'll always be sorry."

She said, "Yes, and today you're over it. Today you're fine."

No I'm not, he thought, I'm sick. He wanted Merlee to say, Oh you poor baby. He wanted Merlee to press his face against her chest. Figuratively.

She said, "You're just mad at her, Doctor. I'm not saying Gracie doesn't have issues. But mainly you're pissed as hell, pardon my French. I'd be mad too, in your place, but she did something for her sister, which you can argue if it was right or wrong or crazy or whatever, but sooner or later, you're going to get over it, aren't you? And as far as her being able to do this—well, of course she can. People will help her. I have faith in Grace."

Faith in Grace. He was being manipulated, by Merlee and Grace, in collusion.

Merlee went through the door to the waiting room. "Look who's here, Doctor! It's our nephew Jacob. Both of us have him for a nephew! And his Aunt Grace is running for board of education! Jacob, you're a lucky boy to have so many aunts and uncles!"

Grace said, "I didn't want to disturb you."

He squatted by the boy. "How are you, Jacob?"

"We ate McDonald's."

David took off his stethoscope, held it between him and Jacob. "Would you like to try it on?"

Jacob nodded, and let David put it in his ears. He pressed it to the little boy's own heart.

Grace said, "Sarah and Zack went to school with Margaret and Ruth. I've decided to get the signatures and go ahead and run for board of ed."

He wanted to say, And didn't consult me. Again.

Merlee jumped in. "We need her. Everybody's asking her to run. Everybody's signed but you, Doctor."

Once, when they first had concerns about the low average test scores and outdated labs in the Kingfield schools, they had talked about boarding school for Margaret. But Grace had said, no, we're here. We'll make it better.

And he had said, Yes, you have to fight for what you care about.

He got up, left the stethoscope with Jacob. He took the clipboard. His eyes didn't focus. He said, trying to keep it low, between him and Grace, but of course the whole staff was listening, "I assumed you'd decided not to do it."

He thought it was the first time he had spoken to her directly since he found out about the house.

"I put off deciding," said Grace, "till almost too late."

Merlee kept talking. "Someone has to stand up to the dinosaurs, not naming any names although I already did. Do you need a pen?"

"No," he said, "I have a pen." He always had a pen. Grace had ordered pens with the office number and emergency number to give out to patients. It seemed important for all these women to see that he had his own pen. When he had signed, he handed the petition back to Grace.

She said, "I doubt I have much chance of winning."

"Oh, you're going to win," said Merlee. "We'll see to it."

He finally looked in her face. Just a glance, her pie-wedge face with the sharp chin, lifted high today. A faint whiff of her fragrant, familiar skin. He felt a sexual stir. It infuriated him, that she could do that to him. She had his sandwich in her hand and extended it to him. It looked a little squashed, but he took it.

CHAPTER 30

Richie was hyperventilating. He stood outside the safe room with his hands shaking too hard to punch in the combination. He couldn't get it open. She had been with him two hours, and now she was gone. He focused on the trembling. Emotional, not organic, he told himself. He breathed deeply. Something went wrong. Look at it rationally, figure out what went wrong. Fix it. There had been a moment when she had been glad to see him, he was sure of it. She had said, Oh my god it's Richie. He had not realized how much he wanted to be seen by someone who knew him. They had talked about old times.

He rested his head on the steel door and breathed in again. Soon, he would be able to put in the code.

They had been in the studio, Travis doing sound levels, showing off to the girl. Suddenly there was a horn blowing outside. And there she was in their ugly junker of a van announcing that she was leaving. Telling the girl to get in the car, telling her husband she was going, with him or without him.

And the husband so hungry to make his damn recording that he didn't go.

Poke had said they'd drive him back later. Richie, frozen, paralyzed, could only nod. He had control of his legs then, and believed she was only threatening, that she wouldn't really leave without her husband.

The husband had said, "Honey I really want to do this."

And she had said, "Fine, they'll bring you back when you're finished."

She didn't give him a second chance. The rest of them stood there watching the van spit gravel, speed up the driveway.

Bobby Mack asked if he was supposed to open the gates.

"Of course, dipshit," said Poke. "And you better hurry."

Richie left the studio before the recording was finished, went up to the house, and waited in the main office till they brought him up, her husband. Richie offered him the job, and then he, the oaf, the husband, said probably not, but he'd have to talk to his wife about it, and could they possibly take him back now.

Richie told Poke to have Enrique feed him, then drive him back.

Up till then, Richie had been frozen, but then he started to shake. He sat a long time in the upstairs office, but the shaking got worse, so he took the elevator down, came to the safe room.

But couldn't get his fingers to open it.

It isn't over, he thought, and his fingers finally punched, but got the wrong number.

It's never over! Never give up!

The husband would convince her. Richie had suggested a short-term contract, just for the summer. We'll try each other out, he said. Why hadn't he thought of that sooner? It would have been so much less threatening to Dinah.

"That would be just fine," said the husband, and then he had one more question. "But exactly who would we be broadcasting to?"

Poke inserted himself again. "Well, hell, Ray. Everyone. The whole damn world, good buddy."

Richie tried the combination again. He heard voices. He wanted desperately to be inside the safe room. His fingers finally found the right numbers, the door clicked and he shouldered it open, leaned on the doorjamb to gather his strength and balance, and that was when Poke called from the entrance to the great room, "Hey Boss! I gotta talk to you, Boss."

He hoped Poke had not been watching with his shrewd little eyes. Poke sometimes made little comments: Having trouble walking today, Boss?

Richie propped himself against the doorframe, holding the door open, and waited as Poke ambled down the hall.

"You okay, Boss? Sorry it didn't go quite the way you planned with the little lady, but ol' Ray'll talk to her. That was good, to say just for the summer, a tryout. That was a good move."

I don't need your approval, thought Richie.

Poke placed himself directly opposite Richie and the safe room. He crossed his arms and rested them on his belly, leaned back against the wall. One of the things that irritated Richie most about Poke was his lazy style. His pretense of being relaxed in all situations.

"That was some preaching, wasn't it, boss? I never heard that kind of preaching since once I was visiting down in Boone County, and the preacher down there was so drunk he ended up taking a dive into the audience like a mosh pit, you know what I mean?"

"I'll take your word for it." Something didn't feel right. "I thought you'd left. Why don't you get on the road?"

"Well, Boss, that's what I came to tell you. You're going to go in and take a rest, Boss? In your private room?"

"Why hasn't Savage gone?"

"Oh he *did* go, Boss, he's on his way. That's what I came to tell you."

"Bobby Mack drove?"

"Here's what happened," said Poke. "We come up with Plan B."

"Plan B? What was Plan A? What are you talking about?"

"Plan A was your plan, Boss. I know you didn't lay it out for me, but I *extrapolated*, if you know what I mean. Plan A was your whole deal with the radio station and the job for Ray and the special cottage for the little lady. That was Plan A. Her leaving Ray here, well, that fried Plan A's bacon, and then I came up with Plan B."

Richie's left calf started to twitch. "Plan B," he said, as quietly as he could.

"Plan B, Boss, well, Plan B is to stir up the pot and see what happens. Stir up the pot with Travis and the girl. I had Travis drive him back."

"Travis!"

"Ye-yuh. Just Travis. Now hear me out Boss, don't go getting your blood pressure in an uproar. Just hear me out. I got to thinking, well, hell, Travis is so hot on the little girl, why not send him down there with Ray.

Who knows what will happen. Maybe they'll get down there and Travis and the girl—well, let nature take its course, you know? You see what I mean? She may convince her mama—who knows what can happen when a couple of good-looking young folks like that get up beside each other. Not that I would *suggest* anything to Travis, no instructions or anything like that. It takes more finesse than that with young people. Like I say, nothing may come of it. It's just stirring up the pot."

"Plan B is stirring up the pot," said Richie, feeling a heavy coldness in his belly. Poke had improvised a scheme of his own. Poke was way out of line. "Let me get this straight. Plan B is that you let that boy take one of my vehicles and drive it four hours—"

"Three and a half."

"—to take Savage home when I told you to take him yourself? What the hell were you thinking, Poke?"

"Now, Boss, Doc, calm down, I told you. Stirring up the pot. And Travis is the best driver we got, you know that. All those trips we took, carrying messages, checking up on things, Travis always drove. He's the next Dale Earnhardt, Jr., I'm telling you, and Ray was hot to get home, saying he should have gone with Mrs. Savage, and Travis offered, and, Doc, that was the beauty of it. Plan B came gushing up and all I had to do was let it happen."

The problem was, what was wrong with Plan B—but Richie couldn't say this because it would open something he didn't want named between him and Poke—the trouble was that Poke hadn't asked permission. That Poke was making his own plans, however well- or ill-conceived.

But of course Poke knew that, and was grinning like the cat that ate the canary. "I would have consulted you, of course, Boss, but we all thought you was taking a nap."

Richie stared at Poke's blotchy skin, the vein-swollen nose. Poke was going to die of a heart attack or a stroke before Richie. That would be a great pleasure, to send flowers to Poke's funeral.

Poke said, "A man gets these ideas, you know, the best-laid plans that man proposes and God disposes. A man's mind is just active, Doc, thinking up stuff. Maybe Travis and the girl will hit it off so good that, I don't know, they want to get married and move up here and then your little lady will be visiting all the time, even if she doesn't move up here."

"That's the stupidest thing I've ever heard," said Richie.

Poke stopped grinning for a moment, then picked it up again. "I understand you need the little lady, Boss. One of these days, who knows, Bobby and I may have to move on. I don't mean we have present intentions, but we'd like to know you were, you know, taken care of."

His calves had gone beyond twitching to shuddering. He said, "I don't like this, you know that, don't you?"

"Yessir, I know," said Poke, but smiling as if a compliment had been paid. "So I think the best thing would be for you to just take it easy, go in there with your valuables and lock the door and recover yourself, have a good rest."

Valuables? thought Richie. What was that about? Poke didn't know what he kept in the safe. And, in fact, there was a lot of extra cash in there now. He had been accumulating cash with a vague sense that he needed it to convince Raymond Savage, to buy things for the cottage for Dinah.

He waved the hand that wasn't holding him upright at Poke. "Go. Leave me alone. It's done. But if you ever do anything like this again without consulting me—I swear I'll fire your ass."

"Yessir, Boss! Absolutely. But, hell, Boss, they haven't gone far down the road. We can still get 'em on the cell phones. We'll bring 'em right back. You're the boss, Boss! I'll give him a call right now—you know nobody's doing anything without your say so. You know that!"

No, thought Richard, actually I do not know that anymore. He said, "Let them go, but tell me when you hear from Travis. I want to know exactly what's going on."

"You got it, Boss. You know it. Abso-fucking-lutely. Only, what if you're taking a rest, having one of your naps?"

"Wake me."

"You got it, boss," said Poke, grinning and saluting, and beginning to back away.

Richie pulled himself inside and closed the door, dropped himself into the rolling office chair and let the shuddering take over.

CHAPTER 31

They hadn't heard yet from Dinah and Ray, and David had gone to the hospital to see a patient with a heart attack. Grace liked being the only adult with the children for dinner.

Everyone was full of the day's events: Margaret said Sarah knew more grammar than a seventh grader.

Sarah smiled and ducked her chin. "I didn't know the math."

Margaret made the dismissive hand chop David used sometimes. "She even got the apostrophes right with plurals. I mean, *that* is impressive."

Zack told about the lizard terrarium in Ruthie's fourth-grade classroom. Jacob announced twice that he ate at McDonald's. For dessert, Grace put out yesterday's brownies plus ice cream, and they made their own ice-cream sandwiches. Afterward, she let them watch *Dancing with the Stars*.

The sky was still light enough that you could see the silhouette of the hill. Feeling happy, she loaded the dishwasher. Just as she started it, through its rumble, she heard a tapping at the sliding glass door to the deck. It was Dinah and Aleda and the baby. The kids heard too and came running in, and there was happy tumult, Ruth and Zack struggling over who got to open the slider, Jacob jumping up and down, fingers of cool air, the baby waking and wailing, and everyone telling the same stories at the same time.

Dinah sat down to nurse Benjie, and Aleda explained that they'd tried the front door, but the bell either hadn't been heard or wasn't working, so Ruth and Zack and Sarah ran off for doorbell testing, and Grace reheated dinner. Before Grace could ask questions, Ruth and Zack and Sarah said the doorbell was stuck, but now it was working, they had fixed it, and then it was back to the lizards and apostrophes and McDonald's.

Finally, Sarah said, "What about the new house? Where's Dad?"

Grace hadn't even noticed he was missing.

Aleda made a sour mouth. "Mom left him on that mountain."

Dinah said, "They're bringing him back tonight or tomorrow."

"She won't tell why she didn't wait for him."

"I didn't like it," Dinah said. "It was a bad place."

"Plus," said Aleda, "she had a fight with her friend."

Dinah said, too quickly, "Ray needed to figure it out for himself."

Grace asked, "What friend?"

But Dinah said that Benjie needed changing, and the kids wanted to help, and then Dinah and Aleda had to eat, but the kids took Aleda and her food into the other room to the TV, and finally it was just Grace and Dinah and the baby in the kitchen. Grace offered more coffee, and Dinah shook her head and rocked Benjie a little as he nursed again.

Grace just waited, and finally Dinah said, "It was Ray's big tryout. They were taping his sermon. I just left."

"What did you say about a friend?"

Dinah kept her face down. "It was like this fortress up there. Gates and security, and then they showed us a little cottage. Only it wasn't really little, it was like it was built for us, bedrooms for each kid. A garden turned over and ready to be planted with whatever vegetables we wanted."

"But that sounds wonderful. Except for being so far away."

"It was bait. A trap." She looked around, rolling her eyes as if there might be a trap here in Grace's house too. "I would have waited for Ray, though, except for who had done it. This whole trap, our hearts' desire, a ministry for Ray, a house for me. Think of the most unlikely person showing up from the past and being the boss of a survivalist enclave on a mountaintop."

Grace said, "Dylan?"

Dinah snorted. "Okay, that would be even more unlikely. But you're getting warm. Richie Lock."

Grace was stunned. She had a sharp memory of Richie playing Han Solo and flying his Millennium Falcon spaceship around the garden. "Our Richie?"

"Yes, but not mine anymore. It's his compound, up on top of a mountain."

"Richie became a survivalist?"

"I'm not sure what he is, but the people he has working for him are the same people that were part of the insane nonsense that got Ray in trouble before I met him. That plan to blow up the FBI headquarters ten years ago? Do you remember? And Richie says he wasn't part of it either, but he hired some of the people, and he wants us to come up on his mountain and live with him."

"But why?"

"You know what? I don't know why. Richie is crazy, and Ray is blinded by how much he wants his own ministry. And there are cameras all over the place, and he hired detectives to spy on us. He knows about you and David, he knew where we lived, how many kids, what Ray has always wanted. He has been spying on us all for years!"

Carefully, Grace said, "Richie always had a crush on you."

"Phooey! Bullshit. And even if it was true once, look at me! I'm old and fat with a baby hanging on my tit and four more to take care of. What does he want with me?"

"Didn't you ask him?"

Dinah thrust her jaw forward. "If your hand touches a hot stove, it pulls back before it burns."

Grace imagined Richie playing Han Solo again. "Maybe he just wanted to help. To save everyone, like he used to."

Dinah shook her head so violently that Benjie popped off her breast.

"So does Ray know?"

"That it was Richie? I introduced them. But all he knows is that we used to know him. Maybe I shouldn't have left, but honestly, Gracie, it was like I couldn't help myself. I felt like I had no choice. I was nursing Benjie and looked up and there were cameras on me. Oh, and did I mention that there's a boy up there, the nephew of one of the ex-cons, and it turns out he and Aleda already met when they came down off the mountain to invite Ray. No one told me about it, not Ray and not Aleda."

Grace wondered if this had been the real final straw for Dinah, but she kept her mouth shut.

And then Dinah did a frightening thing. Dinah, who Grace had always depended on—whose very presence stabilized Grace, laid her face on the table as if she couldn't hold her head up. It squashed the baby, and he started to fuss. Dinah sat back up slowly. She said, "It's like I don't know how to keep my children safe anymore."

Grace knew. "Stay in Kingfield. The cottage is for you. It's your money."

"Drug money."

"Ray can get a job, let Aleda meet boys here. Join a church. Let Ray start his own! That's what I mean, Dinah! You don't really want to be isolated, so you might as well come here. You have to be somewhere."

Dinah seemed to be listening, and Grace felt something pouring back into her. She hadn't trusted herself as she went around getting those board of ed signatures earlier in the day. That had felt like other people making her do things.

But she felt this was all her own. She said, "Let me play big sister for a while."

CHAPTER 32

Everyone was asleep except Dinah, who lay on the bed with the baby, and he was asleep too. She had heard Aleda and Margaret talking for a long time, then David came in. She prayed for their marriage. She stayed awake as long as possible, expecting Ray to call, but he didn't. Then she fell asleep and after a while jerked awake. He'll come tomorrow, then, she thought. Tomorrow they'd go see his mother. They'd meet his brothers and his sister. There was a Savage family graveyard to visit.

She didn't think he was in danger. If she'd believed there was danger, she would never have left him, would she? She was disturbed by her own actions, worried about Ray.

Sometimes Ray recounted the story of the old man in prison who had brought him to Jesus. An old lifer, Ray called him. The old lifer had said, Are you still in trouble, boy? And Ray had answered, Not anymore praise Jesus. I'm going to lead other people out of trouble. And this old fellow said, Wrong, boy, you'll never be safe from trouble. Stay with Jesus, and pray, but there'll always be trouble.

She hoped Ray thought of the old man when they tempted him to come and covert people through the latest technology. She had once been fond of Richie, but he was not doing God's work. If I hadn't met Raymond, she thought, if I hadn't come to Jesus, if I had stayed in Richie's world. She would not have had Sarah and Isaac and Jacob and Benjie or the lost angels. She would have had Aleda, but not the others.

All we really need is Jesus, she thought, but as usual, without Raymond next to her, she wasn't feeling Jesus's presence.

Once Ray had asked David if he thought human nature was good.

No, said David, human beings are good and bad.

Dinah agreed with David about that, but of course she believed it meant that Jesus could reach everyone, even bad people.

It was 1:30 a.m. and she was roiling with thoughts. She thought of Dylan without a roof over his head. He had been so gentle, the Jesus-touched part of him. She shouldn't have left Raymond up there. The baby whimpered, not really awake, but she nursed him and nuzzled him. His breath so sweet.

He fell asleep, and she finally drifted down too, a long soft way down.

Distantly she was aware of changes in the ambient sounds, the refrigerator cutting off, a dull distant pop. Then a column of light split her sleep, the door opened. Ray was there, took the baby from her and put him in his carrier.

Her voice was thick. "Ray, you finally came back."

He sat on the side of the bed to take his shoes off. "I'm back, Dinie," he said, and finished undressing, crawled in beside her, the twin beds pulled together for them, and he encircled her as she had encircled Benjie. He said, "Dinah, are you awake? What happened up there today, Dinah?"

"What time is it?"

"3:15."

"I'm glad you came back tonight." That's enough now, she thought. Let's just be safe now. We'll talk about it tomorrow.

He said, "They aren't bad people. They did what they said. They brought me back. They had the boy Travis drive me back."

That brought her to full wakefulness. "You didn't bring him inside, did you?"

"I invited him, but he wouldn't stay. He came in and went to the toilet and then he left. He's not a bad boy. We had a deep talk during the drive. We stopped and had dinner and talked a long time. That's why I'm so late. He fouled up his first year at college, but he's going back. I think I may have been able to help him on his way."

"He'd say anything to get close to Aleda."

Ray laughed softly. "Oh, Dinah, relax."

"You're sure he's gone?"

"I gave him a coke and a bag of crackers for the trip back, and he left. He said he'd pull over and take a nap if he needed to."

It made her nervous, that the bearded boy had been in the house and she never knew. Ray put his arm around her, pulled her close. He said, "Tell me what happened today."

"I don't know if I can explain. Richie Lock, he was our friend, Ray, when Grace and I were little, but then when we were teenagers, he was part of all the bad things. I hadn't seen him in years. But, Ray, he's been spying on us. He came up with all of that, the house, the job, to attract us up there."

Ray was silent for a second. "I don't understand."

"I don't either! I just didn't want to be around it."

"Well, I turned him down. I said I'd think about it, but if he didn't hear back, it was no. The more I thought about it, the less right it seemed."

"I knew you'd see it that way."

"Travis said some things too that I didn't like. He doesn't think they're doing anything illegal, exactly, but he doesn't trust Poke. His own uncle. I told him to follow his instincts and go home to his mother. Go back, make it right with his mother, and go back to college."

"What about your sermon for the radio?"

"They taped it. It's supposed to be more like a podcast. I think the whole idea of a church over the airwaves was just a passing fancy."

"Or a way to get us up there."

"They gave me a copy of it. I wish you would have waited, though. You didn't believe I could turn down temptation, did you?"

She fumbled for his hand, pulled his arm over her belly. "I do. I do believe, Ray. Seeing Richie just spooked me. He had cameras watching me nurse Benjie. I just went crazy." She stopped, almost felt herself falling asleep, but wanted to give it all to Ray, dragged herself back. "He spied on Dylan, too. Dylan is still alive and homeless out on the West Coast."

"We'll pray for Dylan."

"Don't say anything to Aleda, okay?" She kept talking. "I sold pills and other stuff for Richie. And Richie's mother and our father had an affair off and on for years. They drank together. I think Richie wanted somehow to get that back, when we were kids. But you turned him down, so it's over, let's forget it."

He was quiet, and she almost fell asleep again, but then, without speaking again, he reached for her, and everything was as it should be for a little while.

Around dawn Benjie started to whimper again, and Dinah crawled down over the foot of the bed so as not to disturb Ray. She sat on the floor to nurse Benjie, but he didn't want to eat very long, he wanted to play, so she wrapped him up in one blanket and wrapped another one around her own shoulders and went downstairs. She walked him from room to room, showing him the fish tank, looking out at the hill getting light. Whispering in Benjie's ear, blowing on his neck, making him give deep baby chuckles. They looked in the family room where Isaac, Sarah, Ruth, and Jacob were lumps in their sleeping bags. She counted them. Aleda was upstairs with Margaret. Grace and David upstairs. Ray. Everyone here under one roof.

She continued her circuit. David and Grace had researched this town, and it was a good enough place for them. She could still homeschool the kids if she wanted to. Margaret said Sarah was ahead of even the older kids in English. Her kids were smart, they would do just fine in any school. She thought maybe she was too tired to keep them all close all the time. Let Jesus take a turn keeping them safe.

She went back through the kitchen to the dining room with its big window overlooking the driveway. It was just the moment of earliest light, when everything was visible but flat. She looked down on the roof of the van, David's car, then turned back to the table.

She hadn't noticed till now, but one of Jacob's teds was sitting in the middle of the table, upright, anchoring a sheet of construction paper. From this side, with the window behind her, she could see writing on it, in crayon, hasty, loopy handwriting that she only recognized slowly as Aleda's.

The note said, "I'm going with Travis. I'll tell you later, A."

It seemed to take a long time for the message to reach inside her brain, but once it did, a long yell burst out of her and she woke everyone in the house.

CHAPTER 33

Grace tried for the first forty-five minutes to convince Dinah, who was driving, that the world had not ended. That Aleda running off with a boy wasn't so terrible or rare. Dinah kept her mouth shut and her lips tight and drove a little faster, and of course Grace thought in her heart that it was a pretty big crisis, especially for Dinah.

They had called the state police, and the state police had politely refused to put out an all-points bulletin for forty-eight hours. The girl wasn't really missing, they said. Going for a ride with a boy she knew within state lines was not missing. Dinah had screamed into the phone that the boy was completely unknown, and his uncle was an ex-con.

The police said there was only an issue if they crossed state lines.

Ray and David both had been ready to go look for them. Ray, of course, felt responsible, but he thought they were probably in some parking lot kissing, or maybe they fell asleep. Ray apparently liked the boy. Dinah said she knew they had gone back to Mountain Dome, and *she* was going to get Aleda, not the men, and she was taking the baby and Grace. She had been absolutely firm about what she wanted. The twins would go to school again with Ruth and Margaret. David would take care of his patients. Ray would stay at the house with the phones and Jacob.

Grace said, "Dinah, we'll find her. My guess is they didn't really run away anyhow, it's what Ray said. They're probably still around Kingfield, and we'll find out we've driven all that way for nothing."

"Not for nothing," said Dinah. "Richie has to explain." They had already tried the only phone number they had, which was Poke's, and Poke wasn't answering.

Grace wondered why Dinah hadn't made Richie explain yesterday, when she was face to face with him. But Dinah wasn't being reasonable. She was calm—white faced and stiff, but not reasonable.

Grace said, "You keep her on too tight a leash, Dinah. She wants to have an adventure."

Dinah made a noise that fizzed out between her compressed lips. In the back seat, the baby gurgled and seemed to be watching the ceiling.

Grace stopped trying to convince Dinah and looked out the window, remembering all the road trips in her life: the drive across the United States with Dinah and Daddy, stopping to see the sights, whatever got a big sign: caverns and statues carved of coal. The Mississippi River. Cactus and the Grand Canyon. She and David had taken road trips when they were planning their lives. Small cities on rivers (but David was concerned about floodplains), and in the mountains. The first time they saw Kingfield.

They had been driving nearly an hour when Dinah said, "Richie told me Sharon died."

"What happened to her?"

"He said it was alcoholism."

"That's so sad. She was always nice to us."

"I suppose. I mean, yes, she was nice, but she and Daddy encouraged all the worst in each other."

"We thought she was glamorous."

"You were little. You didn't see as much as I did." Grace waited, hoping Dinah would go on. Then Dinah said, "Richie didn't just spy on us and your family, you know. He spied on the kids too. He knows where everyone is, Wolf and Dylan."

"Where?"

"Where what?"

"Where are Wolf and Dylan?"

Dinah shrugged. "Wolf's in upstate New York somewhere working in a motorcycle shop. And Dylan—Dylan is HIV positive."

"No!"

Dinah, still tight in the face, gave a tiny shrug. "Are you really surprised? He says he's living on the street in San Francisco. But, listen, Grace, don't say anything to Aleda, she doesn't know, and I'm not sure I want her to."

"You have to tell her eventually."

"I suppose. When she asks. When she's back. *If* she gets back."

"Oh Dinah, you know she's coming back! This is her big rebellion after always doing what you wanted. And even if she has sex—well, it's not like you were ever into virginity yourself."

"She could get herself raped or killed. These are bad people, Grace. Richie Lock is insane and the boy's uncle is a creep, and she doesn't know anything about the world."

Grace almost said, but managed to hold back, Whose fault is that?

The baby started to whine, and Dinah said, "I'll have to stop. You drive, Grace."

"After you nurse him?"

"No, I want to keep moving. I'll strap him and me into the seat, we can't waste time."

Grace didn't like it, but she was like the others today, going where Dinah told her. As she drove, she reangled the rearview mirror: Dinah had her eyes shut with the strap firmly over her arm, pressing the baby to her. His fist was up in the air waving.

The road had shrunk to an old-fashioned two lanes with sheer wooded hillsides and signs warning about fallen rock. There were occasionally fields, sometimes with crooked creeks running through them, and always mountains beyond. The mountainsides mostly covered with bluish evergreens with throbbing splashes of oxblood red.

Grace liked this all, in spite of worrying about Aleda. For weeks, maybe months, her mind had been trotting in anxious little circles: how could she live in the new house? Would David ever forgive her? Was it really possible to run for elected office? How could she convince Dinah to live in the cottage?

All of that gray underbrush that had been irritating and trammeling her seemed to fall away as she drove. She realized, looking at the road, that she wasn't sure what she was wearing. Yesterday's jeans, but which sweater? She couldn't remember, and made a point of not looking down to see. To hold the strangeness.

They had all, she thought, been thrown around by the tidal wave of Dinah's anguish.

After a while, Dinah put the baby back in his seat. "I'm calling Ray," she said. They passed a little crossroads settlement, a gas-station convenience store, a church, some houses across the creek. "There's no signal," Dinah said. "I can't get a signal."

Grace started to say, Well, we're down in a valley, but then she remembered: "Didn't Ray say there was a whole area down here that doesn't get signals?"

"Shit. I forgot. Government radio telescopes."

"Do you want me to go back to that gas station and look for a pay phone?"

"No! I don't want to waste time." Dinah was silent for a second. "They have service up on the mountain," she said. "Just keep driving."

The road was rising.

Grace thought it hadn't worked, what Dinah had tried to do. The world Dinah made for her kids was too narrow. And then: but that's why I have to run for board of education. I want a larger life. To do something for all the children.

CHAPTER 34

Richie lay awake in the inner chamber of the safe room. He could hear the whir of the air-filtration system. The door to the outer chamber was open for light from the monitors. It was ten after six a.m., and he had slept in his clothes again, but his hands felt like they might be steady today.

Dinah had run away.

He got up and scanned the monitors. The bunkhouse looked quiet. He couldn't see the beds in the bunkhouses though, or the parking lot over there, so he wasn't sure if Travis had come back.

He thought he would call Grace, ask her advice. Grace had always been willing to listen, but he needed to know first if the boy was back. Last night he had phoned Poke near midnight, and Poke told him no word yet from Travis. Then twenty minutes later, Poke called back to say there was a situation, that some of the Mexicans had run off.

"Deal with it," Richie had answered. "Talk to Enrique."

Thinking about it now, he wondered what that had really been about. No one ever called Richie about Enrique's cousins who were always coming and going. Poke had said he just didn't want to make any decisions without Richie's say-so.

That stuck in his mind now. Something in the way Poke said it. Why call about that so late at night and then back off so easily? And what had happened to Travis? Why didn't he answer his phone? He had probably come in late. Or stayed in Kingfield—that was Poke's idea, that Travis would want to stay near the girl. It was an excuse to call Grace, if he wasn't back yet, to find out where his employee and his SUV were.

He switched to the kitchen camera and could see Enrique having coffee. Also smoking. He wasn't supposed to do it in the kitchen, but some things you let slip, that was part of how you maintained control. You were always trying to figure it out, what to let ride, when to come down hard.

Using his cane, Richie went out into the corridor. There were two sets of stairs to the second floor, one near the kitchen one near the great room. Nearer than either set of stairs was a setback for the elevator. He didn't want anyone to hear the elevator, though, so he took the stairs. Climbing made him a little breathless, but his balance wasn't bad.

Upstairs, he showered, ran the electric razor over his face, stopping between activities to check the upstairs monitors. Find out about Travis, and if he hadn't come, call Grace. Fresh boxers and chinos, a long-sleeve L.L. Bean polo shirt with the Mountain Dome logo. Socks and sneakers last, pause to check his ankles for edema. Fine today. Toenails needed clipping. He looked closely at his feet, his legs, his hands, less and less muscle tone. He spent too much time conserving energy, he needed to get the physical therapist in more often.

He had imagined Dinah might help with that. He had imagined her square hands on his calves, working the muscles. She had been so vivid yesterday, almost more than he could bear. Heavier and with crinkles at the corners of her eyes, but there had been that moment when she smiled, her eyes disappeared, the exact same smile as when she was seventeen. Her solidity and her smile, as warm and impersonal as the sun.

He checked the monitors again as he pulled on his everyday watch, the Victorinox. It was ten till seven. Through the monitors he saw a crow bopping its head up and down out at the perimeter fence. Men beginning to move around in the greenhouses. Maria vacuuming the conference room. He looked out the window into the pale morning. The truck was in the parking area, early for Poke.

He flipped to the kitchen, and found Poke with a mug of coffee, talking to someone off camera, presumably Enrique. Richie turned on the intercom. "Caribbean," Poke said, with the emphasis on *bean*, "Is that close to Mexico? They speak Spanish, don't they? Are there any of those places they speak English?"

Slightly muffled, off camera, Enrique said, "Belize."

"Hell, I never heard of that one," said Poke. "Is that near Mexico?"

Enrique brought a plate to the table, and Poke sat down. Richie waited till Poke's mouth was full, then said into the mike, "Poke!"

Poke jumped, looked at the outer door, the inner door, then finally at the camera. "Hey! Boss!" he shouted. "How you doing today, Boss? Feeling better about the little lady?"

Richie's jaw tightened. "Is the boy back?"

Enrique came back into view. "You want coffee, Boss?"

"Not yet. Is he back?"

Poke shook his head. "Naw. He didn't call either, and he didn't answer his phone. I figure he stayed with them in Kingfield."

That worked for Richie, his excuse to call Grace. "What about the people who ran off last night."

Enrique made a noise and turned away.

Poke said, "False alarm, Boss. You want me to come over to the safe room and help get you up and moving?"

"I'm fine." He liked it that Poke didn't know where he was. "So you never heard from Travis?"

"Not yet." Poke resumed eating. "We never heard anything. I think it's a good sign, Boss."

"Try calling him again," said Richie, having a new idea. "Maybe I'll call him. What's his number?"

Poke's eyes flickered from side to side. "I left my phone in the truck, Boss, and I don't memorize phone numbers." Then he grinned slyly. "Hell, Boss, you know I don't have the brain to memorize numbers. I'll go out and get the phone."

Something felt wrong. "Eat your breakfast first."

Poke said, "Seriously, Boss, you ought to come out of that safe room and have some huevos rancheros."

Richie was hungry. You'd think after all his plans fell apart he'd collapse too, but no, he wanted breakfast. He said, "Enrique, can you hear me? I'd like a tray. Coffee, fresh squeezed OJ, huevos rancheros with extra salsa. I'll have it upstairs."

"You got it," said Enrique, off camera.

Poke tipped his head and grinned, wiped up his eggs with toast. Poke liked American bread, not Maria's tortillas.

Richie turned off the microphone and watched Poke pop the bread in his mouth and get up to leave. He switched monitors, followed Poke out, and now Bobby Mack was there too, leaning on the truck. When had he come? Why wasn't he eating breakfast? Had he been in the truck? They talked, they glanced up at the second floor. Where Richie was.

He had a prickle on the back of his neck and a tremor in his right thigh, and started for the safe room. He didn't think they knew where he was, but he had a sense that things weren't right. He took the elevator this time, was aware of its stately, solid motion, too slow. As he came out of the elevator alcove, Poke was coming from the kitchen. Richie pretended not to notice. Poke called out, but Richie didn't wait, punched in the code, got inside, closed the door. Then watched the camera make a slow scan of the entire corridor. Poke was knocking at the safe room door.

"Doc?" he said. "Hey Boss? What's up? You said you were upstairs."

This is crazy, Richie thought. Am I hiding from him? He flicked on the speakers. "Where's breakfast, Poke?" he said.

Poke looked up at the camera, nose first as usual. "I thought you wanted it upstairs."

"I changed my mind."

"Whatever you say, Boss," said Poke, backing away from the camera. Richie watched him down the hall, then switched to the kitchen camera.

More leg tremors. He had thought it was going to be a good day. There was a twist in his thighs, as if his hips were limping. He stood in the center of the room, leaning on the rolling Aeron chair. Should he go out and have breakfast in the kitchen with Enrique?

His eye was caught by the bed in the inner room. He had had happy dreams last night, wish-fulfillment dreams. Dinah had been there wearing nothing but the pearl necklace that never made it out of the safe.

Once again he used the monitors to locate everyone. Bobby Mack was still outside, lounging on the SUV. Poke in the kitchen jawing with Enrique again.

He had the idea Poke knew very well where his nephew was and for some reason wasn't telling. He went through all the cameras one more time. Bunkhouse empty, Maria putting the vacuum away. Bobby Mack lounging on the truck. Poke and Enrique.

He shouted into the kitchen intercom, "Poke! What about that phone number?"

This time Poke didn't jump. "Dang! I forgot it, Boss! Only your eggs is ready. I better bring it to you, first, right? Or do you want Enrique to bring the tray?"

If he requested Enrique, he would look afraid. It was only his vague uneasiness. It's because I failed, he thought. I've had a failure of confidence. "You bring the tray," he said. "Leave it outside the door."

That was wrong, he thought, that was weak. He added, and knew it didn't work even as he said it, "I have to go to the can." As if anyone would ever choose the chemical toilet in the safe room over the other bathrooms.

"Okay," said Poke. "At your service, Boss."

Enrique put extra tortillas in a cloth napkin and a bowl of extra salsa.

It was all taking so long.

Poke with the tray, out of range of the kitchen camera, then Poke on the hall monitor. Giving the camera a wink. He set it down in front of the door, and said, louder and slower than necessary, "Here it is, Boss, I'll just leave it here. I'll be back in a little while. We'll talk it over when you're ready."

What did that mean? If he didn't want to show fear, he'd have to bring in the tray. The camera over the safe-room door made its scan of the hall slowly. Poke was gone, the hall was clear.

Richie pulled the door open, glanced out, side to side, then cautiously bent over, careful of his balance, encouraged by the whiff of salsa and warm tortilla. Just low enough to pick up the tray, two handed. Began to back in.

He saw movement out the corner of his eye, from the elevator setback. Poke moving fast. Richie fell back against the door, but it opened too slowly and Poke was already there, dirty nails on the door-frame, scabbed knuckles holding the door open.

Breathing eggs and coffee in Richie's face.

"Hey Doc," said Poke. "We have to talk." He nudged the tray with his belly and backed Richie into the safe room. "I'll tell you all about everything while you eat," Poke said. No joke, no grin. "Put your tray down."

Richie's first reaction was not to do anything Poke told him to. He had a flash of throwing the tray in Poke's face, of *fighting* him, but he set the tray precisely in the center of the small table to the right of the computer.

"Okay, now sit down," said Poke.

Richie pulled the chair between him and Poke, but didn't sit.

Poke grinned. "Then stand, Doc, I don't care. I'm not going to hurt you. Believe me, I don't intend to hurt anyone."

Richie's gun was a snubbie, big bullets and a two-and-a-half-inch barrel. But it was in the bedside table in the inner chamber.

Poke looked over the monitors, the pictures on the corkboard. "We always used to think it was fancier than this. We used to think there'd be a gold-plated shitter. You feeling okay today, Doc? You're looking a little peaked. I don't want you getting shaky on me."

As if in response, Richie's right leg started to jitter. The door to the inner chamber was directly behind him, the rolling chair between him and Poke.

Poke was watching his leg, which had picked up momentum, bucking and shying. "Looks like she's rarin' to go, Doc," he said. "Don't you want to sit down and take a load off?"

"What do you want?" asked Richie, and he could feel the tightening of his vocal cords, hear the shrillness. If he could get his voice deep again, maybe the leg would hold still.

"Well, Doc," said Poke, shaking his head, still watching Richie's leg. "Well, here's the thing. I know you always thought I was stupid, me and Bobby Mack both, and to tell you the truth, you're not so far wrong about Bobby. But me, I've been studying you, Doc, these several years, watching. I noticed how you plan ahead. You *strategize*. I admire you, Boss, you have all your ducks in a row. I modeled myself on you, and now I'm moving my ducks. You follow?"

Richie thought that if he pushed the chair at Poke, if he moved fast enough, he could get into the inner chamber.

Poke said, "I modeled myself after you. You take into account what's possible—for example, you have to take into account your *special condition*, the doctors and shaky legs and whatnot. I have to take into account what I'm starting with, which is a lack of resources. I said to myself, I may never have my own Mountain Dome, but with a little resources, I could retire on an island, maybe own a little bar somewhere. I've been making plans, Boss."

Richie thought he could offer a raise. Offer Poke a little more than Bobby Mack.

"But see, you started with something, didn't you, Doc? You didn't start from nothing. Me, my family had nothing. Families like mine, all through the years, things would come in, to the county, the town, but somehow none of it came to the Rileys. I swear you could take everything we ever owned, and you couldn't buy that truck out there. So the way I see it, a man needs a stake. A nest egg."

"Are you asking for a loan? A raise?"

"No, Doc, too late for that. And by the way, I'm not asking. I'm telling." Now Poke started touching things, the desk, the monitors. He glanced behind Richie at the inner chamber. "You love this little burrow, don't you Doc? Well, you've still got it. Nobody's taking old Mountain Dome away from you, no sir." He touched the landline phone, the corkboard with the photos of Dinah. "You have a regular church of the little lady here, don't you?"

For the seconds his back was to him, Richie moved himself and the chair a few inches closer to the inner chamber. His leg had calmed down. There would be a moment, he had to choose the right moment.

"Well, maybe she'll come after all," said Poke. "And listen, not that we aren't grateful, you've been okay to us. So, anyhow, Doc, I'm activating Plan C."

"Plan C," said Richie, and he couldn't help the sneer in his voice.

Poke heard it too. "Yeah, you never heard of Plan C because Plan C is all mine. And it ain't really about you, or not hardly. The short version is, we're resigning, Bobby and I, and forming a new business. The business is called Poke Riley Enterprises, and you're going to be our big investor. We'll start with severance pay."

Richie could feel the contempt rising high enough to choke him. The idiots. The stupid idiots. Did they think he wasn't going to send the state police after him? Did they think even if they killed him they'd get away? He used the anger to stand very straight. "What severance pay?"

"God almighty you think I'm stupid. You just never did give me any credit for having a IQ, did you, Doc? You just give orders in your prissy little voice, and hand us a big fat stack of twenties every two weeks, and think that takes care of everything. Well, what I want now is not the twenties, but the fifties and the hundreds and whatever you have in that safe. Part of the plan is take just enough. Not so much we have to set up some damn offshore account or something. We just want your cash and your negotiables, and then we're going to go somewhere nice and warm where they speak English."

Richie mimicked what he had heard in the kitchen. "Belize?" said Richie. "Is that close to Mexico?"

Poke blinked. "Fuck you," he said, and he struck. A fast roundhouse with a fist, Richie's vision blocked by it, then lights seemed to whiten and flash, and he staggered and nearly fell. Then it hurt, his damaged cheekbones and eye. He clung to the chair, then the lights normalized, and throbbing spread through his cheek and neck.

Poke shook his head. "I didn't want to do that."

Richie's ear was ringing and his nose running, no, it was blood.

Poke was breathing heavily. "Well, at least now you see, you ain't top dog anymore, Doc, and you would do well not to *antagonize* the people who are."

My error, Richie thought, pulling deep inside himself. Don't provoke him.

"To tell the truth, Plan C was supposed to happen after you made your arrangements with Raymond and the little lady. I never meant to leave you in the lurch, I was going to do this after you had everything settled. I was going to send Travis home and make sure Ray and the little lady were onboard, and then, right before they actually moved up here, I was going to take off with my nest egg. Sorry I got physical there, Doc."

"How much do you want? I'll cut you a check."

"A check," Poke grinned. "Sure, Doc. You write me a check for a million dollars. No, what I want is, I want you to open the safe right now and I want the cash. I know the payroll is in there, and I know it's always cash, and I know you have some extra because we took you to the bank, didn't we? And the negotiables."

Richie kept himself a far distant inside himself. He told himself he was only pretending to cooperate. He still had a play. In spite of the blood he would shove the rolling chair at Poke and use the momentum to propel himself back into the inner chamber. He would seal himself in there and use the satellite phone to call the state police. He could see it as clearly as if it had already happened.

Poke was saying, "Stocks and bonds, anything we can turn into cash. The fancy French watches too."

Richie said, "There's nothing financial in the safe. That's all with the lawyers."

"I'll take what's there. Cash and watches is fine. Now give me the combination."

It gave Richie satisfaction to say, "I don't lock the safe. Like you said, all that's in there is some cash and watches."

Poke's eyes flicked toward the safe. He didn't believe Richie.

Richie said, "It's always open," and took another tiny scoot backward.

Poke said, "What happens if I stick my face in the safe? Does it spray me with colored ink?"

"No, because there's nothing important in there."

"Nothing important," said Poke. "Cash is just shit to you, ain't it, Doc? Ain't I right?"

Poke sidled toward the safe, caught at the door with the toe of his boot. It swung open smoothly. Poke blinked. "Look at that," he said. "Stacks of money. The whole fucking payroll."

Richie said, "There's a pearl necklace I was going to give it to Dinah."

"Sweet," said Poke, his attention on the open safe. To see better, of course, he had to lean or squat. "I need a sack," he said. "Or a briefcase. Whatever."

When Poke dipped behind the safe door, Richie pushed the chair with all his strength, at Poke, and just as he'd envisioned, the momentum sent him backward, only his balance was bad, and he landed on his butt.

Poke howled, and Richie scuttled backward, got his shoulders inside, reached for the door switch, but felt Poke's hands on his legs. Richie kicked, hit the switch, the door started to close, but Richie was being dragged out. He grabbed the walls, tried to pull himself back. It would have been so simple if he'd been strong, if he'd moved sooner, if he'd been lucky. But he was dragged on his back into the main chamber, the door to safety closing behind him. Poke dropped his weight hard on Richie's legs and pulled out his phone. Richie tried to kick, and Poke gave a powerful punch to his thigh. "Get in here," he said into the phone, "and bring the damn cord and the bungee cords too."

Richie's legs were being pulled up onto the office chair, his back painfully arched, his arms waving like the limbs of an upside-down beetle.

When Bobby Mack pounded on the door, Poke dragged Richie and the chair closer to open it. Richie tried to yell for Enrique, but Poke pulled him away, shouted, "Shut the damn door!"

They kicked Richie's ribs now, and he was coughing, and they were wrapping his legs, yellow nylon. They tipped him upside down, legs on the chair, his weight on his shoulders and neck, and now they wrapped his arms, he tried to keep them free, got his left arm out of the dangle. Poke screamed at him, his gray scarred forehead close to Richie's face, and gave a hard wrench to something that made the lights whiten and darken again, and the dark turned red, and behind Richie, under his back, against the floor, the worst pain he'd ever felt.

He was swimming in and out of the dark red, weight on his neck and head. He could hear Poke snarling at Bobby Mack, things knocked over, a thud in his side, but it shifted more weight to his shoulders off the damaged thing in the back. He tried to go deep inside and far away from the pain. They were banging doors, banging him.

After a while, he couldn't keep his face above the red and black. The last thing he saw in his mind was Dinah coming to save him, and then when he came out of the blackness, her real face was the first thing he saw.

CHAPTER 35

The gates to Mountain Dome were open. Dinah had for the last hour been less angry, less fearful, sadder, convinced of impending loss. She kept having flashes of Aleda as a baby, her golden baby, receding farther away than even the angel babies.

She pulled away from that hole in herself and said to Grace, "The gates are open. It's like someone just left and didn't bother to close them."

The only vehicle in the parking area was the black golf cart.

While Grace was still setting the emergency brake, Dinah handed Benjie over the seat to her. "Check his diaper," she said, and headed for the enormous front door, but before she got to it, saw off to her left a smaller door down a couple of steps and veered that way. It was a screen door. There was some kind of brassy dance music playing inside. She rang, no one came. She knocked and peered through the screen. It was a kitchen with a long table and big stainless-steel appliances along the far wall. A door in the rear opened and a man in a cook's apron came in carrying a big bag of something like flour. He put it on the floor and clapped dust off his hands. He approached her with a frown.

She said through the screen door, "I was here yesterday. I have to talk to Richie."

He stopped a few feet back from the door and planted himself stolidly. He had a broad face and cheekbones so high they nearly hid his eyes.

She said, "Listen, my daughter ran away. I need to talk to Richie. Richie Lock. I was here yesterday." She began to wonder if he spoke English.

He said, "No one's here."

She took a breath and tried for politeness. "My daughter is missing. I'm sorry if I'm abrupt. I don't think we met when I was here yesterday. I'm Dinah Savage."

"Enrique Velasquez." He glanced toward the interior of the house. "I haven't seen Mr. Lock today."

"What about the—other employees? What about Travis?" It was coming back to her, her indignation and purpose, "Listen, I think Travis brought my daughter here last night or this morning. I need to speak to Richie!"

"Travis never came back," said Enrique, but he unfastened the screen door, and as she came in, a woman entered from the interior of the house.

Enrique said, "This is my wife. You stay with her here, and I'll go see if Mr. Lock is up."

"No," Dinah said. "I'm coming too. You have to understand, my daughter is missing. I'm calling the police if I don't find her." She had already, of course, called the police, and Enrique didn't seem particularly concerned by the threat. He didn't try to stop her from following him down a long hall. He hesitated at a door with a digital keypad, then went on to an alcove with an elevator, up to bedrooms and conference rooms on the second floor. Every bed made, everything briskly clean, windows shiny. No people. They went down to the great room, then the conference room where they'd had lunch.

"Where is he?" she asked. "Does he go out this early? What about Poke Riley and the other one?"

Enrique said, "The boss ordered breakfast early, and Poke took it to him, but I didn't see him then, and now I don't see the other ones."

She thought she detected the slightest bit of speeding up, as if Enrique were finding the absence of people strange too. He went back to the door with the keypad. He knocked and called, "Boss?"

At that moment, Maria came from the kitchen, and she had Grace with her, and Grace had Benjie who started calling "meh meh" and reaching for Dinah.

Grace handed him over.

Enrique was still hesitating over the door. Finally, he blocked their view with his back, put in the combination, and pushed the door open.

Dinah, with Benjie's weight on her hip, pushed in behind him.

Amid all the overturned furniture and spilled food and smashed computers, the windowless room smelled like dirty diapers, and the upside-down face seemed to belong to another baby, red and round. It took her a second to realize it was Richie's face, overturned like everything else.

Enrique got to him first and started lifting him, and Richie shrieked, but all Dinah knew was that something bad had happened, maybe worse than she'd guessed. She yelled, "Richie! Where's Aleda? Richie! What did you do with Aleda?"

Enrique said, "Excuse me, missus, he's hurt. We have to get him loose," and pulled out a pocketknife.

The upside-down mouth spread in a wide, full baby smile. "You came back," he said thickly, and then, when Enrique cut the ropes and he fell a few inches to the floor, he shrieked again.

Enrique said, "Sorry, sorry Boss," and Benjie started to whimper.

Richie whispered, "My arm," and Enrique and Maria lifted him up, into a chair.

"Where's Aleda?"

Grace was tugging at her, saying, "Dinah, leave him alone. He's hurt."

"I don't care. I want to know where Aleda is. Where is she, Richie?"

Richie, upright now, in the chair panting and still red.

Richie's eyes wouldn't leave Dinah alone. "It was Poke and Bobby Mack," he said. Then smiled foolishly again. "Dinah came back."

"I came back for Aleda, not for you!"

"Boss," said Enrique, "I don't like the way your arm is hanging."

Grace started picking up chairs, and Dinah smelled pee and saw that Richie's chino pants were wet and part of his shirt. It finally began to make sense to her. The Mountain Militia had victimized him too.

Richie couldn't help her, Aleda long gone, everything lost.

She said, "They kidnapped her, didn't they."

Enrique gently lifted the limp arm. "His arm is twisted bad, we have to call the emergency."

Richie whispered, "They emptied the safe. Cash, watches."

"I told you Boss. You can't trust them."

Grace pulled out her phone. "I'll call 911."

Enrique said, "The reception is better in the kitchen," so Grace left, and Enrique said to Dinah. "Listen, missus, nobody is here now but me and Maria, and the ones that work in the greenhouses, and they don't know nothing. You go to the kitchen too. We have to get some fresh clothes on him."

She didn't really want to go, but on the other hand couldn't bear the way Richie kept following her with his eyes, like the baby, trying to smile.

"Please, missus," said Enrique.

"Okay, but Richie, I swear, if you had anything to do with Aleda disappearing, even if she just ran away with that boy—"

He smiled again.

Enrique saying, "Can you stand, Boss?"

As Dinah left, Richie cried out, then again.

"Your arm is broke," she heard Enrique say.

I don't care, she thought. He deserves a broken arm. He'll heal. She found Grace pacing in front of the kitchen door and said, "I'm not sure I gave good directions, but they seemed to know this place."

"How long?"

Grace shrugged. "They said the police would probably get here first. Maybe the sheriff. I don't know how it works."

Dinah had a flash memory, from long long ago of police on a damp cold evening, the time they came for their mother, but she shoved it aside, sat down, and unfastened her dress. Benjie didn't really want to nurse and kept looking around. She said, "Grace, did you say anything about Aleda to the 911 people?"

"No, I just said Richie was hurt and there had been an assault. You keep saying she was kidnapped, Dinah, but, really, she just ran away with her boyfriend."

"He's the Mountain Militia's nephew. He was part of it."

Enrique and Maria brought in Richie in fresh sweats and a maroon robe that had been put on his right arm only and tied around his waist, leaving his left arm naked. They had loosely tied his left arm with strips of something torn, maybe a sheet, to what looked like a vacuum wand extension.

Richie seemed less silly. As they helped into a chair, he said, "Grace, you look just the same."

Grace said something polite, too warm. His bare arm was pale and hairless, didn't have good muscle tone. I don't care, Dinah thought. I don't care.

Dinah said, "I'm sorry your Mountain Militia thugs turned on you, but I'm here about Aleda. Did they take her? Was that boy Travis part of this?"

Richie said, "All I wanted was for you to come back."

"Well I didn't come back for you, Richie"

Richie nodded. "Travis never came back last night."

Grace said, "See, Dinah? We think Aleda ran away with the boy."

Enrique asked Richie if he needed anything.

"Maybe we can have a cup of coffee."

"You got it, Boss. Maria, stay beside him."

Richie swayed a little, and Maria put two hands on his good shoulder. "Dinah," he said, "Dinah. I never got to tell you yesterday—"

"I don't want to hear anything else, not from you with your cameras and spies."

Richie blinked. "Okay. I'm pretty sure Travis wasn't part of it. It's probably why Poke sent him off last night. I think Poke has been planning to rob me for a long time." He sounded okay, but he leaned closer and whispered, "I wanted you to take care of me."

She was about to scream at him, but as if coming out of her anger and frustration, there was a siren.

Grace ran out, and Dinah hugged Benjie tight and followed up the steps up to the parking lot, where there was suddenly a lot of activity, a state police car with lights and sirens and a black SUV. A state trooper with a shaved neck and a Mountie hat was at the driver's door of the SUV.

Grace said, "It's Aleda. It's the kids, Dinah."

Benjie reached and cried, "Lih! Lih lih!"

Dinah said, "Take the baby, Grace," and ran for the passenger side of the SUV. The trooper blocked her with a long gray-green arm. "Excuse me, ma'am—"

"That's my daughter in there!!"

Aleda rolled down her window. "What are you doing here, Mom?"

The Trooper said, "Who are you, ma'am?"

"You heard her! I'm her mother and she ran away!"

She was wanting to beat her fists on someone, preferably the boy, but maybe Aleda or the state trooper.

Grace was saying she called in the emergency, there was a hurt man inside.

The trooper, still blocking Dinah, said, "I didn't get a call. I had an alert for these kids."

Travis had got out of the vehicle, and the trooper barked at him to lean over the hood.

Aleda yelled "He didn't do anything wrong!" and she got out too. She was wearing a sweatshirt and pajama bottoms. Her hair needed combing. Something stopped Dinah from going to her, but Grace, carrying Benjie, went, and hugged Aleda and Aleda hugged her and hugged Benjie, and Dinah was left with her own arms clumsily empty.

The officer said, "I want everyone just to stand where they are for a minute. Stop moving around." He patted down Travis, face on the hood of the SUV, but looking toward Dinah.

Travis said, "Mrs. Savage, I swear—"

"Quiet!" said the officer, who didn't look much older than Travis.

Dinah was suddenly tired, her anger pouring down her arms and out her hands. Grace and Aleda and Benjie were hugging without her.

Enrique and Maria approached with Richie shuffling between them. Richie called, "Officer, I have to give a report. Two of my employees robbed me and—did this—"

The trooper finished his pat down of Travis. "Okay, stand up," he said. "Don't make any sudden moves." The radio in the patrol car squawked, and he looked at Richie, raised a hand to wait, then leaned into his car, trying to keep an eye on Travis too.

Travis said, "Mrs. Savage—"

"No."

"I'm not ashamed," said Aleda.

Travis said, "Mrs. Savage, last night, I was leaving, after I brought Reverend Savage to the house, and Aleda just got in with me."

Aleda said, "I wouldn't take no for an answer."

Dinah needed to do something with her hands. "Give me the baby."

Aleda had him, and turned away. She jiggled Benjie and said, "I'm not going back."

"Shh," said Grace, "You don't mean that."

Aleda said, "I may go back to Aunt Grace's, but I'm not going back to how it was." She had always had such a sunny disposition. Sarah and Isaac had been fussy, probably always hungry. But Aleda was never any trouble.

Travis said, "All we did was drive around and talk."

"And kiss," said Aleda. "We kissed a lot." Then she tossed her head. "But don't worry, Mom, it's okay, he doesn't want me." Travis groaned, but Aleda kept talking. "We got all the way here and he said he was going to call you to come and get me. Then the police started following us. Did you call the police on us?"

"What did you expect? We thought you'd been kidnapped."

"Oh please."

"Meh?" said Benjie.

"Mommy's being an idiot, Benjie," said Aleda.

The trooper said an ambulance was on the way, and now he had the report about the robbery and assault. He took a look at Richie's arm, but didn't touch it. Richie described Poke and Bobby Mack and the missing truck.

Travis, beginning to get the gist of what had happened, said, "I didn't have anything to do with it, Mr. Lock. Uncle Poke—I knew something was going on, because they always shut up when I got close, but I didn't know it would be this."

Richie was swaying, gray now instead of red. But he said to the trooper, "Travis has only been up here a few weeks."

"I had a fight with my mother," said Travis, as if anyone cared, thought Dinah.

There was another siren coming, another police car and an emergency car behind it.

Travis said, "Uncle Poke has a cabin in Webster County. If he was going to hide out, that's where he'd probably go."

Dinah, aware that she was being unreasonable, thought, what a little fink!

The trooper kept his eyes on Travis. "Where in Webster County?"

Aleda finally gave Benjie to Dinah, and Dinah immediately felt more like herself.

Aleda said, "I'm not sorry."

"You said that already."

"I didn't do anything wrong."

"You ran away!"

Travis interrupted himself giving directions to the trooper. "We just drove around, Mrs. Savage. We didn't even touch."

Aleda frowned. "Except for kissing for about an hour."

"But then we drove on!"

Dinah was feeling more and more tired. The only thing she cared about, she realized, was that Aleda was alive.

Aleda said, "I tried to bring Travis to Jesus. I wanted to marry him and we'd get an apartment and he'd go back to the university and I'd take care of him and keep his house and maybe take classes."

No wonder the bearded wonder was scared.

Grace said, "Honey, you have to finish high school first."

Everything was moving fast now, and Dinah let it happen, holding tight to Benjie. She had to call Ray. There seemed to be state troopers everywhere now, plus the people from the ambulance, who were trying to get Richie on a gurney, but Richie said, "Not yet! I have to talk to Dinah!" They had a blood-pressure cuff, but he was shrugging everyone off, his voice back to its familiar peremptory Go. "Don't touch me till I talk to her. Get off me, I have to talk to Dinah!"

She said to him, "I'm sorry I thought you were responsible for Aleda, but it was so creepy—the cameras—the witch's cottage. It was like you'd do anything. What were you thinking, Richie?"

He staggered two steps toward her, grabbed her arm for balance. His face was gray from the pain of moving. He found his balance but kept hold of her forearm, their faces uncomfortably close, him still smelling faintly of pee. He said, "I just have to tell you why I wanted you up here and then I'll go."

She nodded, and he said something low and fast. It had a proper name in it, and it took a few seconds for it to register.

"I have Lou Gehrig's disease," he said, and she felt a rush of sympathy in spite of herself. "It's what my father died of," he said.

She said, "Oh, Richie, why didn't you just pick up the phone and call me?"

"You wouldn't have come."

It was probably true, but she said, "I have no idea what we would have done, and you don't either."

They said he had to get in the ambulance. He said, "I wanted it to be business. Everything works better when money makes it clear."

Enrique touched his shoulder. "Hey Boss."

"I hired you, right, Enrique? Right?"

"Yeah, Boss, come on," and Enrique began to lead him back toward the gurney.

"I fucked up everything," Richie said to Dinah.

"Yes, you did. You really did," she said, but she and Benjie walked him to the ambulance anyhow, and when they laid him down, he kept his gray face toward her, his eyes enormous and sunken. They loaded him in, Richie still looking at her. For a second she thought he was going to ask her to ride in the emergency car with him, but Enrique climbed in. The ambulance pulled away.

She turned back to the others, the young trooper still fooling with his devices, making a report. Grace with an arm around Aleda. Travis looking young and frightened as he talked now to three troopers, turning in his uncle.

Dinah said, "I'm going to call Ray," and walked away with Benjie and sat on the low wall.

Ray answered immediately. "We found Aleda," she said. "She's okay."

He was glad but not amazed, and there was the tiniest surge of annoyance in her. He never took it seriously. No one did, except Dinah.

She told him as briefly as she could: Aleda had run off with the boy, they had driven around all night, both swore nothing happened but some kissing. Everyone converged on Mountain Dome. Richie.

"Poke and Bobby Mack robbed him?" said Raymond. "That's too bad. That's really too bad."

"Those two are so lost in darkness they'll never find their way out," she said. "And don't try to convince me otherwise. Is Jakey there?"

Raymond put Jacob on the phone, and Dinah had Benjie listen to him, and then Jacob told Dinah that he had lost one of his teds and then found it under the table, and they had eggs and toast and jelly for breakfast. Jakey always made her smile.

When Ray got back on, she said, "Richie has Lou Gehrig's disease. This whole thing was about him wanting us to move up here and be his caretakers."

There was a silence, and she suddenly realized Ray's pride was hurt. That this wasn't about him and his church of the airwaves.

She said, "I mean, the preaching was part of it too. He wanted to buy us both. He buys things. He wants to buy people. He's always been crazy, but crazy men do more harm than crazy little boys."

"We'll pray for him."

"Pray for me too."

"You have to pray for yourself, Dinah," he said.

She said, "Maybe everyone is crazy if you scratch down half an inch. Me, Richie, Aleda. Everyone but you."

He laughed. "Because I was crazy all the way through for a long time."

She closed her eyes on the people moving around. She said, "Ray, let's take Grace's house. We might as well live in Kingfield as anywhere else. There's your family. Maybe you can find a church or start your own. We'll let Aleda try the high school."

"Okay," he said amiably. "That sounds fine. People treat you good here, Dinah. Brother David gave me the key to their second car. He's a good man, even if he is in darkness. I was going to take Jakey out for lunch."

"You don't have a car seat."

"Oh yes I do. Brother David had an old one in the garage, so we're all set. Do you want me to pick up dinner?"

"No, Grace and I will get something on the way back. Grace and I and Aleda and Benjie." She felt the calm from Ray. She said, "It's so sad, Raymond. All this nonsense, and Richie just wanted to get someone to take care of him."

"We can think about it, if you want to."

"No! I'm not moving up here."

"Maybe he'll come down to us," said Raymond in his slow way that made her want to crawl through the phone deep into his arms and chest.

CHAPTER 36

Richie was sitting on the screened porch of his new house. Everyone had left, first Mrs. Sexton, his three-day-a-week housekeeper, then Dinah's daughter, Aleda, who had come after school. Now he was waiting to interview the new woman for Tuesdays and Thursdays, another Savage, everyone in this county related to damn Raymond Savage.

He had decided he would live near Dinah, wherever she was, as long as he was alive. If Dinah and her family were in Kingfield, West Virginia, then Richie would be too. If the next part of his plan worked out, they would all be here permanently.

These early fall days were warm and yellow orange. His ordinary but satisfactorily remodeled house was set on a hillside outside town with part of the basement and garage excavated out of the hill. There was no safe room, no security system. He had moved in the first of August after the hospital and a rehab ward and too many weeks in a motel. The screened porch had three views: hillside, vegetable garden, and the driveway and road.

As she left, Mrs. Sexton had asked if he didn't want to go inside where it was air-conditioned. No, he told he for the fiftieth time, he liked heat. Sexton shook her head mournfully. She interfered too much, but was a better cleaner and cook than the one who had just quit to go full-time at McDonald's. Mrs. Sexton said, "I wish my neighbor wasn't in the hospital. She'd be good to work for you."

He said, "Is there something you want to tell me about the woman I'm going to interview?"

"Sally Savage?" said Mrs. Sexton. "Oh, Sally's okay. She's honest, but you'll have to keep after her. If you want her to work."

Then Mrs. Sexton left, and Aleda showed up sullen about something. The girl was a beauty, both slim and curved, with that incredible satin skin. She occasionally helped him with his weed when his hands were shaky. He was aware this was a dangerous thing to do, that Dinah would pull her entire family if she knew, but his left arm had never really regained strength after being broken, and Aleda had been the one present the day he needed it most. It wasn't as if she smoked with him. She handed him what he asked for. They all worked for him, Dinah's family. The first time he couldn't open the coffee can, he'd called Aleda over.

When she opened the can and saw what was inside, her eyes got big. He told her it was medicinal, a painkiller.

Aleda said, "I didn't think you were supposed to have pain. With what you have."

"From the broken arm. And I have psychological pain. But I don't smoke it for pain, I smoke it to stop the shakes."

"Does Mrs. Sexton know?"

"Sexton! Are you crazy?"

"Are you an addict?"

That was what the girl was like. Interested in everything and perfectly innocent. He told her his history: how he'd started with sipping the leftovers from his parents' cocktails, not that his parents ever left much. "This is vitamins compared to some of what I've done."

She said, "Of course you shouldn't do marijuana in front of me."

"What's the difference in this and a beer?"

"You shouldn't drink beer either," she said.

He said, "Well, even though it's going to be legal very soon, I forbid you to smoke it—I really mean that. Dinah would pack up you and your brothers and sister and Ray and leave. You don't want that either."

She didn't. She liked high school, he knew. And today, she was wearing a pair of tight jeans, and she had her chin stuck out like Dinah.

She said, "Well, I suppose I have to thank you."

He'd had no idea what she was talking about.

"I went to the Goodwill store and got three pairs of jeans and six tee shirts and here's your change."

He had given her extra money last week. "Phooey. I don't want the change. Keep it. You look very good, but you don't have to wear Goodwill jeans. I'll take you to the mall and buy you jeans. I'll take all of you kids, Grace's girls, you and your sister. I can still drive that far. I'll sit in the food court and watch the obese West Virginians on their scooters while you kids shop."

She laid his money down out of his reach. "You shouldn't say that, about obesity. We're all West Virginians now."

"Oh please."

"And you give us too much money."

"Look, Aleda, let's get this straight. I'm a selfish guy, all right? I only do what I want to do. If I give you money, it's because I have more than I need, and it gives me pleasure. Don't let Dinah brainwash you. Take whatever you can get. Money is a good thing. It's the only thing keeping me alive."

She said, "There are hospitals for people who don't have money."

"But I'd kill myself before I'd go to them." He felt one of his eyes twitch. "And don't be afraid of someone else's money. My money, I had some money to start. I got it the old-fashioned way: I inherited it. That's the way 99 percent of people with wealth get it."

"So you're saying it's like just luck."

"No, I'm not saying it's *like* luck, I'm saying it *is* luck. It's good luck to inherit money. It's good luck to inherit DNA that makes you look spectacular in jeans. It was my good luck my father and mother left me a starter of money and my really, really shitty luck that my father bequeathed me ALS. Bad luck for Ray and Dinah that they don't have any money, but good luck they have friends and family like Grace and me to help them out. I'm part of their luck. And part of your luck is that I like to give you money."

She shook her head. She looked unhappy about something.

He said, "So what did Dinah think of the jeans?"

"She didn't approve, because she assumes if I change even the smallest bit, I'll do all the things my father did." She stood up straight and crossed her arms over her chest. "Also, she told me you had information. About my father."

Richie stared at her. "Dylan? What did she tell you?"

"She said if I wanted to know anything, I had to ask you. Why didn't you tell me sooner?"

It had never occurred to him that Dinah hadn't told Aleda, but on second thought, it sounded right. Dinah trying to keep her kids from the world. They were smart kids, too, as kids go. "I assumed she told you. What do you want to know?"

She took a deep breath and stopped pouting. "I want to know everything that happened to him."

"I don't know everything that happened to him."

"Is he alive?"

"He was alive about a year ago. He was living on the streets in San Francisco."

"Like a homeless person?"

"Homeless, filthy, probably HIV positive."

"Is he going to die soon?"

"I have no idea. I suppose I can get you an update. I haven't been in touch for a while with the people I use for research, but I can call them up, if you want."

She nodded. "Yes please. And I want to see him before he dies."

He was suddenly irritated. "Dylan is nothing to you, you know. He was a sperm donor when Dinah decided she wanted a baby."

"That's mean, and it's not true. They loved each other. She has dreams about him. Did you talk to him?"

"I have no desire to talk to Dylan. I hired people to find out."

"So he might be dead by now?"

"To repeat, I have nothing newer than a year ago."

Her amber eyes became huge. "At this very moment, he might be dying in a gutter. Why didn't you help him? Why did you and my mother—let that happen?"

"Aleda, I have had nothing to do with him. Talk to Dinah."

"But you had the information!"

"Yes, and I'll happily send out my sources to check again."

"Will you lend me money to go see him?"

"Now you need my money."

"I'd pay you back. It might take a long time, but I would."

"Oh Dinah would be thrilled if I paid your way out to go looking for a homeless person on the streets of San Francisco. No thanks, I'll get information for you, but that's all."

"I'll take the bus."

"Have you priced buses lately? Planes are cheaper. And don't say you'll hitchhike, because I'll go straight to Dinah."

"Then Ray will take me. Ray likes to save people. I want to bring him back and take care of him as long as he's alive."

He still wondered why they all loved Dylan. He said, "I have some pictures if you want to see them." Of course she did. He added, "It has to be a trade, though. I want you to tell Dinah what you found out, and what you think you want. Agreed?"

"She'll refuse to let me go. This is making me to promise not to go to California."

"Right. Maybe someday, not now."

He got up, staggered, barely snagged the cane for support. He didn't let her help. The broken arm, goddamn Poke, had set him back, or maybe he should say set him farther along. He went to the desk inside and from the big drawer pulled out the envelope with the pictures. He left her at the desk with them. He knew the pictures, mostly plain paper printouts, a couple of glossies. Some kind of public space with people in business clothes walking around homeless with shopping carts and sleeping bags. Medium shots, some slightly fuzzy close-ups. A report with dates and addresses.

He went back to the porch and closed his eyes. After a while, he felt her presence. She was holding the envelope against her chest.

She said, "He doesn't look *that* sick."

"I'll get updated information. I'll call later today or tomorrow. I can't do it now because someone's coming over."

She still stood there. "It looks like he doesn't have teeth."

"Do you think people living on the street get six-month checkups?"

"He has a beard like Jesus if Jesus had been a homeless person."

Richie closed his eyes again. Sometimes they made him so tired, the ones with a long future.

She said softly, "Do you think I could have one?"

"Take them all," said Richie.

235

"If it's okay, I'll just start with one."

"Suit yourself, sweetheart."

She disappeared, presumably selecting a picture to take, putting the envelope away.

Then she came back. She said, "Were you my mother's boyfriend too?"

"Not really. No, I don't think I could say I was ever her boyfriend."

"But you loved her?"

He answered her very softly, looking out at the little yellow flames of color, the last light on the hillside. "I'm going to say this once, and then I don't want you bringing it up again. I've always loved your mother. I still love her. I've had many girlfriends and three wives, but I've never loved anyone but Dinah."

Aleda was quiet for a few seconds. "Okay," she said, as if she gave him permission. "Is it okay if I leave early?"

"I can't drive you home," he said, "because I'm waiting for this woman to interview."

"That's okay, I need to think," she said.

In the event, he could have driven her home twice over, because Sally Savage was late. Richie didn't really care. One thing Cooper County had was a pool of people available for low-wage jobs.

Once a beat-up truck drove by, and he was pretty sure he saw a gesture, pointing at his house. He thought of his life here as under the radar, but of course everyone knew his business. The way it seemed to work was, they were curious and they gossiped, but at a certain point they created a profile for you, and then let you alone. He didn't mind the gossip as much as he'd thought he would. Didn't mind that Sexton reported to the whole town on his food preferences and the state of his walking. Richie was the rich man with Lou Gehrig's disease who lived up Savage Holler and ate hot salsa on everything, can you believe it.

And gave a not-insignificant boost to the local economy, thought Richie, and not just to Ray and Dinah Savage and their family. He estimated he was probably something like the fifth leading industry in the county, after the federal penitentiary and the school district, the quarry and McDonald's.

Raymond cleared brush so he had a better view and made runs to Mountain Dome for Enrique's salsa. Aleda came over after school for whatever. The boy and girl twins came on weekends and used his computers and internet to do homework and whatever else they weren't allowed to do in their own house. He paid a weekly check to Reverend Raymond and gave the kids tips.

Dinah didn't trust him, of course. She came over too, some days working in the garden, growing greens for a late fall harvest. She always had the babies with her, and he was pretty sure she didn't want to be alone with him. But that was okay: he liked to watch her in the garden, leaning over, her round rump pressing against those ridiculous skirts. Her face would become relaxed and unguarded when she talked about the vegetables. She wanted to know if they could use the porch to start tomatoes and peppers in the spring. Without consulting her, he ordered grow lights and Plexiglas panels to cover the screens. He imagined watching her tend the little seedlings. All he asked was four seasons of her backside.

The last thing to go is the ability to get an erection. Long after you lose independent locomotion and speech, your prick and your brain are fully functional. He felt tremendously sorry for himself when he thought of it. No plans, no plausible scenario for getting Dinah into bed now or later, but still he fantasized it. He didn't care if she came out of pity. He imagined her coming into his bedroom early some morning, to comfort him.

He had several ongoing fantasies. That was one, Dinah in the morning. Another was that Reverend Ray would die felling one of Richie's trees. Another was that Richie would put out a contract on him. He thought maybe one of the marijuana jockeys he used to hire when he first came to West Virginia might be willing to do it, except that he had lost confidence in his judgment of men after the fiasco with Poke. But he liked to imagine the insufferably cheerful Reverend Ray getting whacked. Not that widowhood meant Dinah would turn to Richie. He thought he had a better chance of her coming to him out of pity.

You were my first love, he would eventually find a way to tell her. You will be my last love.

Once she had said, here on this porch, as she had at Mountain Dome the day everything happened, "Richie, you should have just asked. You know I would have come."

He had had nothing to say. He didn't think she would have come to him as he was then, but she came now.

Grace visited too, not often as she was an elected official. One afternoon she said, "My sister isn't God, you know. You follow her with your eyes like she was a savior."

"I assume you don't share this insight with her," he said.

Grace said, "Of course not. I want Dinah to stay in Kingfield as much as you do."

He considered telling Grace about his plan to keep everyone here, but didn't. He liked Grace, and he liked her doctor husband, who was better at coordinating his care than the specialist he used to call in from DC. The fact is, David told Richie, there is nothing exotic about your condition. That's the bad news and the good news. Yes, thought Richie: the progress of the disease was dependable and predictable, even if people weren't. Sometimes there was a temporary plateau, but the disease didn't reverse. Not just his hands now, but sometimes his shoulders and thighs trembled and shuddered to the disharmony of his motor neurons.

Grace was wrong anyhow about Dinah being his god. Gods don't need you, except maybe for the odd ego-building sacrifice. Dinah and her family needed him, and he was going to make sure they continued to need him. He had just broached the project to Raymond. He might invest in a church, he said. Once the church was established, with donations coming in, Ray would him pay him back, of course.

Raymond's eyes had rolled toward the sky. Thank you Jesus!

Pitching it to Raymond was easy because Raymond assumed it was just one of God's mysterious ways, to provide him with an edifice for his church. Richie pretended it was an idea in passing, something spontaneous. He told Ray not to get Dinah's hopes up too soon. Let's go out and look at that piece of property I heard about, he told Ray. Then we'll talk to Dinah.

His fear was that Dinah's sensors would go into high gear again when she heard. He planned to tell her it was Pascal's wager: better to get on the good side of god, just in case there was a god, and, more to the point, a hell.

Sally Savage was now forty-five minutes late.

He watched the trees, rusty tipped, one small bush blazing red. Two Ford trucks and an old sedan passed. A school bus. Lives puttering on around him. It had taken him six months to figure out that it was safer here than probably anywhere he'd ever been. He had lived first at a motel run by what he thought must be the only Pakistani family in Appalachia. He had rented three rooms, set himself up with phone lines and computers, had meetings with the state police, the FBI, lawyers, private detectives. The physical therapist for his arm. There had been daily phone conferences with Enrique back at Mountain Dome, which was for sale now. He intended to do something for Enrique, once the sale went through. He thought Cooper County could use a good Mexican restaurant.

But he hadn't pursued Poke. Travis told the police about a hunting camp in Webster County where they found Bobby Mack but not Poke. Richie's SUV was there, but it turned out Poke had stowed a car, and he ran out on Bobby Mack who was stupid enough, when the police came, to fire on law enforcement. So Bobby Mack was going away for a long time. But they didn't get Poke.

Toward the end of August, Richie had received a postcard Enrique sent him from Mountain Dome. The postcard had fat letters wearing sombreros that spelled out Mexico but was postmarked Miami. The message had been simply "Hi Doc." Richie had passed on the information, and toyed with the idea of using his own operatives to chase down Poke, but in the end he didn't care enough. Waste of resources.

He heard a door slam, and a truck pulled away. A woman was coming up the driveway on foot. She was very skinny, tight jeans and a tee shirt. She tossed a cigarette into the bushes and paused to look at his new plantings. There were saplings with labels on them. She would be thinking he was a stupid foreigner to pay for trees on a wooded West Virginia hillside. She was not carrying a pocketbook, but she had a pair of high heels in her left hand, and she stopped to put them on. She didn't see Richie on the porch. She put her sneakers behind a shrub and walked the rest of the way in her heels, placing one foot carefully in front of the other, swinging her thin hips.

Mrs. Sexton had told him he'd have to remind Sally to do things. Like not smoke in the house. He didn't have to hire her, of course, but he thought he probably would.

She finally saw him on the porch. "Mr. Lock?" Her pale hair tied back at the nape of her neck. She was older than he was, and her tee shirt said WVU. All their shirts said WVU.

He said, "Come in through the house. The door's open."

The sound of high heels as she crossed the living room. She stopped in the doorway and looked at him, gave him a chance to look at her.

He felt a slight irritation, that combination of spike heels and WVU tee shirt, the tight jeans. Then he realized the irritation was horniness. He had expected another old tub of born-again lard like Sexton. It had been a long time since he'd had sex, on such good behavior around Dinah. He didn't really give a rat's ass if Sally Savage could clean. He wondered if she might do sex.

He said, "You're late."

"Yeah, sorry. My boy was late picking me up and then we missed the driveway."

He said, "Don't you drive?"

"I drive! My car threw a rod."

He said, "Well, you need to drive. And if you smoke, you can't do it here. My condition doesn't permit it."

She stayed in the doorway. "These days don't nobody's condition permit it. These days if you smoke, you have to get mosquito bit in summer and freeze in winter. So no problem there, I gave up smoking in anybody's house but my own a long time ago."

He wanted it all on the table immediately. "You know what I have?"

"Lou Gehrig's, right?"

"Yes. I have to sit a lot, which means my lungs are sensitive, I'm susceptible to pneumonia."

"I said I don't smoke in other people's houses."

He said, "It is a progressive disease. It's not catching."

"I'm not ignorant." She had remarkably skinny legs. Most women, even thin ones, had thighs that touched at the top, but hers didn't.

He said, "Why don't you come out and sit down where I can see you."

She chose the big wicker easy chair with jungle leaf-patterned pads. She crossed one leg over the other and twitched her spike heel a couple of times. She said, "You don't use a wheelchair."

"I use a cane."

"Well," she said, "The thing is, I've got a bad back, and I can't go lifting people in and out of wheelchairs."

Who was interviewing whom here, he wondered. "It isn't a nursing job. It's light housekeeping, two days, occasional driving. I still drive myself most of the time. Is your car going to be fixed so you can get out here on time?"

"Sure. I'll get it fixed, but my boy drives me around when I need it."

He said, "If we work something out, about the job, you can have smoking breaks."

"I can go awhile without smoking."

He tried to think of something else to ask, but was hampered by knowing he wanted to hire her.

She said, "It's nice out here. I mean the porch, but the whole setup too. Not as fancy as I'd heard, but nice. I usually work in retail, or waitress. Bars, restaurants."

He said, "You were married to a Savage? I know Raymond Savage."

"Yeah, I know. I was married to a cousin of Ray's. Twice. I couldn't live with him and I couldn't live without him, or so I thought, but I'm finally getting over that nonsense. I was a Riley myself."

If she was related to Poke, he didn't want to know about it.

She said, "I hear you've got Linda Sexton three days and you're looking for someone for two days. What happens on weekends?"

"Friends come by."

"Ray's wife and the doctor's wife." He must have frowned, because she added, "People need something to talk about. So the job is driving you around and making you a sandwich for lunch? Because if you've got Linda Sexton here three days you sure don't need a cleaner."

"She's an excellent cleaner."

She touched the tips of her left fingers to her lips, as if she were hoping there'd be a cigarette hanging there. "I always worked even when my kids were small," she said. "And in spite of what Linda probably told you, I never got fired. I'm surprised you're interviewing me anyhow, after hearing what Linda probably had to say about me. It's just that if I don't get treated right, I quit." She had a skinny chest with sharp little breasts. Premature lines in her face, chewed cuticles. She said, "I looked up Lou Gehrig's disease on the computer. It's a real nasty thing to have."

He wished they already knew each other well enough to move on to the next stage. He said, "Listen, if you want the job, I'll put you on the schedule. We'll see how it goes."

She chewed the cuticle of the finger that had gone searching for the cigarette. "Shall I do something while I'm here? Do you want me to make you a snack? Do you want a beer? My boy's not coming back for a while."

"All right. Get me a beer. Get yourself one too."

She stood, lanky without being tall, that gap where other women's thighs rubbed. "This is a test, right? You don't really want me drinking on the job."

He said, "You aren't working yet."

"I'll get you a beer, but I'm not having one. I guess I want the job. I have a reputation, you know, for saying what I think. I'm not a hypocrite. Around here, everyone's all 'Jesus loves me' on the front side and pure snake on the backside, but with Sally Savage what you see is what you get."

He said, "Can you start tomorrow?"

"I can't come till afternoon. I have to do something in the morning. Do you still want the beer?"

He did. He wanted the beer, and he decided he wanted the full time she had set aside to be interviewed.

She spent a lot of the time in the kitchen, checking it out, he supposed. Finally she came back with a rattan tray he didn't even know he owned, his beer, a glass, and a bowl of pretzels. She put the tray on the hassock between them, as if it were a tea party and he was the guest. She poured his beer down the side so it didn't foam over. She talked a little but not too much about when she worked in a bar in Pittsburgh. Pittsburgh was too big, she liked trees.

He asked about the Savages. She gave him a longish, mildly entertaining genealogy of the family. She didn't bring up the Rileys. They never mentioned salary, and he wondered later if she already knew how much he paid or if she figured she'd negotiate it later, or if it was just mountain politeness underlying the hard-boiled exterior.

When she was gone, when the beer was gilding the afternoon for him, he wondered if she might be the one he could turn to at the end. He knew it wasn't going to be Dinah. Dinah had come across his books when she was helping him move in: *Final Exit. Intractable Suffering Is*

Not Required. She had said: "I won't be helping you with any self-deliverance, Richie, if that's what you have in mind. I believe when a person dies is up to God."

"I'm not asking you."

"And you damn sure better not be thinking of involving anyone in my family especially not Aleda."

"Are you serious? Aleda's a kid." In fact, he had thought of Aleda, who he liked, and who he sincerely hoped would be a middle-aged woman by the time he needed so-called deliverance.

"Otherwise, no deal," Dinah had said, and of course he agreed to whatever Dinah wanted.

He had thought of approaching Grace, but Sally Savage would be better, if she worked out. There was an apparatus the books described, a machine you could operate with your mouth, but there were much simpler solutions if you had help, like barbiturates in applesauce.

Meanwhile, he sipped beer, looked at the trees, felt drowsy. He missed Enrique's huevos rancheros in the morning. He wondered if Sally Savage could do Mexican eggs. Get Dinah to plant tomatillos next year. Enrique said they'd grow anywhere. Cilantro.

The afternoon light slant, deepening to gold. A hawk posting high in a ribbon of sky between ridges. Is this all there is? he wondered, but for once didn't feel cheated if it was.

READING AND DISCUSSION QUESTIONS

1. Each chapter of *Their Houses* follows one of the six main characters. Whose worldview in the novel is most like yours? Whose is least? Do you think it was worth visiting the world least like yours?

2. Did any of the characters seem to represent the worldview of the author?

3. In the novel, what's the importance of the Mountain Militia and the tragicomic (and factual) attempt to blow up the FBI fingerprinting center?

4. Most of the people in this novel are trying to live lives tailored to their own needs and beliefs. Do you think this approach works for them? Does it change for any of them? Do you think most Americans are individualists? How does this play out in the public sphere in the US?

5. Grace believes her mother tried to kill her and Dinah. In fact, people with psychosis are very rarely homicidal. Do you think

Grace's memory is accurate? What effect did their mother's illness have on each sister? What about their father's alcoholism?

6. Dinah and her husband have both invented their own private versions of Christianity. What do you think of their beliefs? Why do you think they never joined a community or church to support their values?

7. The working title of this novel was *Safe Houses*, which is what the girls call their game of building homes for their toys. How do people in this story look for safety, and do they find it?

8. Raymond's mother, Mrs. Savage, doesn't have a very big part in this novel, but in some ways, she represents a previous generation and culture—one more tied to the home place than the main characters. How does *she* see her life?

9. In many ways, Aleda is the most normal and optimistic of all the characters. What do you imagine she'll be like—and what will she be doing—in fifteen years?

10. Richie gets the first and last word in this novel. Why do you suppose the author chose him for that position?

CPSIA information can be obtained
at www.ICGtesting.com
Printed in the USA
FSHW021616060519
57891FS